CW00515270

MISLAID

Also by Nell Zink

The Wallcreeper

MISLAID

Nell Zink

FOURTH ESTATE • *London*

Fourth Estate
An imprint of HarperCollins Publishers
1 London Bridge Street
London SE1 9GF
www.4thestate.co.uk

First published in Great Britain by Fourth Estate in 2015
First published in the United States by Ecco in 2015

1 3 5 7 9 10 8 6 4 2

Hardback ISBN 978-0-00-813960-5
Trade paperback ISBN 978-0-00-810055-1

Printed and bound in Great Britain by
Clays Ltd, St Ives plc

MIX
Paper from
responsible sources
FSC™ C007454

Find out more about HarperCollins and the environment at
www.harpercollins.co.uk/green

My life would be harder
without the magnificent collective
Zeitenspiegel Reportagen,
to whose members and supporters
I gratefully dedicate this book

... among the rabble—men,
 Lion ambition is chained down—
And crouches to a keeper's hand—
Not so in deserts, where the grand—
The wild—the terrible, conspire
With their own breath to fan his fire.

  —E. A. Poe, "Tamerlane"

One

Stillwater College sat on the fall line south of Petersburg. One half of the campus was elevated over the other half, and the waters above were separated from the waters below by a ledge with stone outcroppings. The waters below lay still, and the waters above flowed down. They seeped into the sandy ground before they had time to form a stream. And that's why the house had been named Stillwater. It overlooked a lake that lay motionless as if it had been dug with shovels and hand-lined with clay. But the lake had been there as long as anyone could remember. It had no visible outlet, and no docks because a piling might puncture the layer of clay. Nobody swam in the lake because of the leeches in the mud. There was no fishing because girls don't fish.

The house had been a plantation. After the War Between the States it was turned into a school for girls, and after that a teachers' college, and in the 1930s a women's college. In the 1960s it was a mecca for lesbians, with girls in shorts standing in the reeds to smoke, popping little black leeches with their fingers, risking expulsion for cigarettes and going in the lake.

The road from the main highway forked and branched like lightning. You had to know where Stillwater was to find it. Strangers drove to the town of Stillwater, parked their cars, and walked around. They thought a college ought to be impossible to miss in a town that small. But people in Stillwater didn't think you had any business going to the college if you didn't know where it was. It was a dry county, and so small anyway that most businesses didn't have signs. If you wanted even a haircut, or especially a drink, you had to know where to find it. The biggest sign in the county was for the colored snack bar out on the highway, Bunny Burger. The sign for Stillwater College was nailed to the fence by the last turnoff, where you could already see the outbuildings.

The main house faced the lake. The academic buildings and the dorms were behind the main house around a courtyard. All the girls lived on campus. From the loop road, little dirt tracks took off in all directions, leading to the faculty housing where the station wagons sat crooked in potholes under big oak trees.

The reason strangers came looking for Stillwater was a famous poet. He had a job there as an English professor, and was so well respected that other famous poets came all the way to Stillwater to read to his classes. Tommy, the smartass owner of the white snack bar in town, called them "international faggotry" and always asked them if they wanted mayonnaise with their coffee.

*

Peggy Vaillaincourt was born in 1948 near Port Royal, north of Richmond, an only child. Her parents were well-off but lived modestly, devoting their lives to the community. Her father was an Episcopal priest and the chaplain of a girls' boarding school. Her mother was his wife—a challenging full-time job. This was before psychologists and counseling, so if a girl lost her appetite or a woman felt guilty after a D&C, she would come to Mrs. Vaillaincourt, who felt important as a result. The Reverend Vaillaincourt felt important all the time, because he was descended from a family that had sheltered John Wilkes Booth.

The Vaillaincourts had a nice brick mansion on campus. Peggy went to the local white public school to avoid a conflict of interest. Her mother had gone to Bryn Mawr and regretted not sending Peggy to a better school. "Can't you imagine a college that's academically a little more intellectual?" she asked Peggy. "What about Wellesley?" But Peggy wanted to go to Stillwater.

It came about like this: Her PE teacher, Miss Miller, had said something about her gym suit, and Peggy had realized she was intended to be a man. Gym suits were blue and baggy, but as you got older, they were less baggy and sort of cut into your crotch in a way that was suggestive of something, she didn't know what. Miss Miller had stood in front of her and yanked her gym suit into position by pulling down on the legs. She placed her big hands around Peggy's waist and said something to the effect that her gym suit had never fit her right and never would.

She had felt close to Miss Miller since the day she fell down in third grade and knocked out a tooth. Miss Miller dragged her to the bathroom to wash the blood off her mouth, and the tooth went down the drain. "There goes a nickel from the tooth fairy," Peggy had said. Miss Miller dug into her pocket and produced a quarter. No other adult had ever given her so much money all at one time. The scene was stuck indelibly in the child Peggy's mind. Her allowance was nine cents—a nickel and five pennies, of which she was required to put one in the collection plate.

Realizing that her girlhood was a mistake didn't change her life immediately. She could still ride, play tennis, go camping with the scouts, fish for crappie, and shoot turtles with a BB gun. Around age fourteen, it got more complicated. She informed her best friend, Debbie, that she intended to join the army out of high school. She knew Debbie from Girl Scout camp. Debbie was from Richmond, a large and diverse city. "You're a thespian," Peggy heard her say. "Get away from me." Debbie picked up her blanket and moved to the other side of the room. Then Peggy's life changed. Debbie had taught her to French kiss and dance shoeing the mule, knowledge that was supposed to arm them for a shared conquest of debutante balls. And now this. Betrayal. Debbie never spoke to her again. Peggy told her mother.

"A thespian," her mother said, bemused. "Well, darling, everybody gets crushes." Her mother was from the generation that thought a girl's first love is always a tomboyish older girl. She gave Peggy *Cress Delahanty* to read. It was counterproductive. "You are not, absolutely not, going to join the army. Do you hear me? You are going to college. Get this out of your system. You'll laugh at yourself someday." Her mother suspected her of having a girlfriend already, and sent off for brochures about early admission to Radcliffe. She didn't believe in coeducation, but her daughter's plight called for desperate measures.

But Peggy didn't have a girlfriend. Once she accepted an invitation from Miss Miller to a barbecue at the state park. There were only women there and no other girls. She recognized the woman everybody said was the maintenance man at the elementary school. It was indirectly her fault that Peggy thought of "man" as a job title. They were playing softball and taking it really seriously, hitting the ball so hard you could get hurt. Peggy left the party to play horseshoes with kids from the Baptist church instead and get a ride home on their bus.

She began paying more attention to the thespians at school. They were fat girls and nice boys with scarves around their necks under their shirts. She auditioned for a part in *Our Town* and didn't get it. Afterward the drama club went to the drugstore for milkshakes, and the director, a senior, explained to her about lesbians. He chuckled and shook his head a lot. Everybody else laughed so loud that Peggy felt inconspicuous, despite the topic. His voice was almost a whisper. "You and your friend Miss Miller are bull dykes. You should go to dyke bars in Washington. Or Stillwater College."

"Miss Miller is not my friend!"

After that, word got back to Peggy's mother, and Miss Miller and the maintenance man were fired and moved away. Peggy insisted Miss Miller had never done anything untoward. Becoming a man and a thespian had been her idea. Her mother said, "You have chosen a very difficult life for yourself." Then they shopped for patterns, because Peggy's debut was coming up and, lesbian or no lesbian, you had to have a tea-length off-the-shoulder dress made of boiled cotton with a flower print and tulle underskirts. Cutoff overalls were fine for hunting turtles in the woods, but even Peggy wanted to be pretty for cotillion. In the end she was so pretty she stopped herself cold. She stood in front of the full-length mirror in the ladies' dressing room at the Jefferson Hotel in her slip and silk stockings and felt an almost overwhelming need to masturbate. She adjudged herself the prettiest girl she'd ever seen. "I feel pretty, oh so pretty," she sang instead, waltzing with her dress as though it were a girl. Pinocchia, granted her wish. Someone to love. Then she graduated and went off to Stillwater.

For freshman orientation she bobbed her hair and took up smoking cigarillos. She had bought some new outfits at an army surplus store. She did not question her child-hood equation of liking girls with being a man, and in black khakis and a black crew-neck sweater, she found herself rough, tough, and intimidating. She looked darling. The short cut made her curly hair form a crown of soft ringlets. She regarded her narrow hips and flat chest as boyish, but in 1965 they were chic.

Also, as much as she wanted to be a man, she was revolted by hairiness, fat bellies, belching, vulgarity, etc. Her slim father wore ascots and got manicures. His face was soft and his shirts had monogrammed cuffs. She thought black penny loafers with white socks à la Gene Kelly was the epitome of working-class butch.

The campus was a complete universe. You never had to leave. There were visiting boyfriends and girlfriends from other schools, parties and mixers, intercollegiate sports, a mess hall and a commissary, even a soda fountain. As self-contained as an army base. But no basic training. No cleaning, no cooking. The work you had to do consisted of things like ponder Edna St. Vincent Millay. If you screwed it up, they didn't criticize you. They invited you to their offices, offered you sherry, and asked you what was wrong.

I can't believe it, Peggy thought. My parents are paying for me to do this for four years. If you majored in French, you could spend your third year at the Sorbonne. But the seniors who had been away came back looking lost. New cliques had formed without them, and their French friends never visited. Peggy took Spanish instead. She decided to major in creative writing. She wanted to write plays for her fellow thespians.

Peggy's roommate was a girl from Newport News whose father was in Vietnam. This girl was used to a strict, confining regimen. She obeyed Peggy to the letter. If Peggy said "Your alarm clock goes off too early," the girl would set it an hour later. If Peggy said "I like your pjs," the girl would iron them and wear them all weekend. It didn't make her terribly interesting. Peggy was attracted to a sophomore from Winchester who was boarding her horse at a stable up in the hills. This girl routinely wore fawn jodhpurs and ankle boots, and every day for break-fast she ate ice cream, which the cook kept for her in the freezer. Because her valuable horse needed to be ridden every afternoon, she was permitted to have a car. Seniors were allowed cars, but only if they were on the honor roll with no demerits. Since among seniors demerits were considered a badge of honor, the sophomore Emily was currently the only student allowed to drive. She was majoring in art history and planned to join her father's import-export business.

Peggy stared at her and smiled until she was invited to sit in the passenger seat of her Chrysler New Yorker, parked behind the former dairy barn. Emily talked about her horse. After a while Peggy, turned toward Emily with her hands in her lap, struggling to concentrate and look fetch-ing at the same time, felt her soul rebel. She thought she had never heard—or even heard of—anything so boring in her life, outside of church. Peggy tried mentioning a class they were in together. She mentioned the town she grew up in. She mentioned a movie she had seen recently and wondered if Emily had seen it. Eventually she said, "I didn't really come out here to talk about horse shows."

That was a mistake. Emily looked at the windshield and said, "Then you're stupid, because you like me, and that's what I want to talk about."

Peggy got out of the car and walked into the trees. She heard the car door slam and saw Emily pull away around the corner of the barn. The beeches were starting to turn yellow and the Virginia creeper was already fire-engine red. Peggy consoled herself with their appearance, as she thought a more sensitive person might.

The famous poet at the college was named Lee Fleming. He was a young local man who had given his family a lot of trouble growing up. After boarding school they sent him to college far away in New York City. When they heard of his doings up there, they gave him an ultimatum: stop dragging the family name in the dirt, or be cut off without a cent.

Lee hadn't been conscious up until then that he had anything to gain by being a Fleming. That is, he hadn't realized he didn't have money of his own.

His parents were wealthy. But he had expectations and an allowance, not money. His father suggested he move to a secluded place. Queer as a three-dollar bill doesn't matter on posted property. Lee's father was a pessimist. He imagined muscle-bound teaboys doing bad things to Lee, and he didn't want passersby to hear the screaming. He offered him the house on the opposite side of Stillwater Lake from the college.

It was a wood-frame Victorian Lee's grandfather got for nothing during the Depression. It had been disassembled where it stood and rebuilt on a brick foundation facing the lake. It was supposed to be a summer place. But it was inconvenient to get to, far from any city, swarming with deerflies, and instead of a boathouse, it had a thicket of bamboo. So nobody ever used the house. It just stood there on Fleming land, taking up space. Still, when it came time to clear-cut the trees and sell them for the war effort, Mr. Fleming couldn't bring himself to do it. The house looked so nice with big maples and tulip poplars around it. The trail to the water led through suggestive shoots of old bamboo big around as juice cans.

Lee was not the man his family took him for. As a lover he was a faithful romantic, always getting his feelings hurt. But he was a top. He never could get it right. He could put on a broadcloth shirt and gray slacks and wing-tips and look as much a man as an Episcopalian ever does, but then he would place himself squarely in front of total strangers, maintaining eye contact as he spoke to them of poetry. So everybody in the county was calling him a fairy inside of a month. But he was a Fleming, and a top. He was untouchable. The local Klan wizard worked at his father's sawmill. The Pentecostal preacher lived in his father's trailer park. The worshipful master of the Prince Hall Masonic lodge drove one of his father's garbage trucks. The county seat was in a crossing called Fleming Courthouse, and the Amoco station was Fleming's American. No one openly begrudged him a house in the woods by a lake with no fishing.

Lee was serious about poetry. He thought America was where all the most important work of the 1960s was being done. He really meant it, and could explain it. John Ashbery, Howard Nemerov, and his favorite, Robert Penn Warren. Then the Beats. He had met them all in

New York, and they all had a weakness for handsome Southerners who owned counties.

At first Lee had nothing to do with the college. But then a poet friend remarked that a girls' college in the middle of nowhere sounds like something from Fellini, and he got an idea. He asked the English department to pay for a visit from Gregory Corso.

Poets came all the way from Richmond to hear him. But the girls stayed cool and distant, even through "Marriage." Corso went back to New York and told people Lee lived in a time capsule where Southern womanhood was not dead. Two publishers and a novelist transferred their daughters to Stillwater.

In short, the college helped Lee and Lee helped the college, and they signed him up to teach a poetry course. He didn't ask for a salary at first. Instead he asked the college to pay for his literary magazine, to be called *Stillwater Review*.

Three years later, the *Stillwater Review* was selling thousands of copies and keeping ten students busy reading submissions, and Lee was teaching three courses a semester: English poetry in the fall or American poetry in the spring, criticism, and a writing workshop.

He commuted to work in a canoe, rain or shine. When he pulled it up in front of his house, it plugged the gap in the bamboo like a garden gate. No student had ever been invited to the house. There were stories. John Ashbery shooting a sleeping whitetail fawn from a distance of three yards. Howard Nemerov on mescaline putting peppermint extract in spaghetti sauce. To hear one of the stories, you had to know someone from somewhere else who knew someone who had been invited—a cousin at Sarah Lawrence whose boyfriend's brother was queer. Stillwater Lake might as well have been the Berlin Wall.

Freshmen were not eligible for Lee Fleming's writing workshop. You had to take his other courses first.

Peggy thought this a ridiculous barrier. "How am I supposed to understand poetry if I've never written any myself?" she said to Lee in the third week of her first semester in his cozy office in a garret of the main building.

"How do you expect to get into my workshop if you've never written a poem?"

"Aren't you supposed to teach us?"

"You've already missed the first two meetings."

"Can I audit?"

"It's impossible to audit a workshop. You have to do the work."

"So can I enroll?"

"Name me one poet you admire."

"Anne Sexton."

Lee leaned back. "Anne Sexton? Why?"

"She doesn't sound so good, but she's got something to say. I read Hopkins or Dylan Thomas and I think, These cats sound cool all right, but do they have something to say?"

"Maybe they're saying something you don't understand."

"Then make me understand it."

"That's like saying, 'Make me live.'"

"Then make me take your workshop."

"No. You think poetry is supposed to be about you, and you don't know how to read. If you can't read Milton, you can't read Dylan Thomas. Take my course in English poetry."

"And read Milton? No, thanks."

"Then you'll never be my student."

"I'm changing my major to French."

"Don't be childish."

"Is it childish to know what you want?"

"I want you to take my course," Lee began, then stopped, realizing he had said something unusual and slightly embarrassing.

Peggy stood glaring at him, and he glared back.

She offered him a cigarillo. She sat down on the edge of his desk to light it for him, leaning over gracefully with her hands cupped around the match, a smiling seventeen-year-old girl with curly hair like springs, and he realized he had a hard-on.

"Forget the whole thing," Peggy was saying. "I can write plays without your help. I don't even need Anne Sexton's help. Screw her and Milton and the horse they rode in on."

"Sounds like a natural-born writer to me," he said. "I would very much appreciate your taking my course in English poetry."

"I was serious. I don't want in your workshop, even if it means I never see you again."

He looked around as if to indicate their surroundings—the Stillwater campus, all eight acres of it—and laughed.

Peggy didn't take his course. A week later she accepted his invitation to kneel in the front of his canoe while he pushed off from the marshy, leech-infested bank with a paddle. The first thing hc said was "This is not a date." Then he moved toward her in the darkness and pulled her hips toward his, sliding his hands down the sides of her butt, and kissed her, because to be honest with himself (as he became much later), he didn't know any other mode of behavior in the canoe. The canoe tipped from side to side and Peggy was very still and solemn. It was so exciting he couldn't figure it out. She was androgynous like the boys he liked, but she made him wonder if he liked boys or just had been meeting the wrong kind of girl. He thought about her genitalia and decided it didn't make much difference. Her body was female, female, female. Everywhere he touched, it curved away from him, fleeing. He felt between her legs, and it vanished. The abyss.

Peggy felt she was being held in the palm of God's hand. Not because he was a famous poet and the most respected teacher at her school, but because he was a man and powerful, physically. In all her fantasies she'd been the man, and had to please some pleading lover. But now a person had voluntarily dedicated himself to serving her desires. She had never expected that, ever. It violated her work ethic. She felt a wish to speak and opened her eyes, and the poet in the black mackintosh was staring down into them, rain beating down around them, and they were surrounded on every side by water. It was a good bit more sexy and romantic than she had dared to imagine anything.

Each was mystified, but for very different reasons. Peggy had thought she would die a virgin and had never given a moment's thought to birth control. And now it looked as though she might be a virgin for maybe ten more minutes. "I'm a virgin," she said.

"That can be taken care of," Lee said.

"No, I mean it," she said. "This is a big deal. You have to promise me."

"I promise you everything." He kissed her. "Everything."

He was mystified that he would say something like that to anyone—male, female, eunuch, hermaphrodite, sheep, tree. He looked her in the eyes and decided she wasn't paying attention.

He landed the canoe and carried her into the house.

Peggy was young and her patience for sexual activity was just about infinite. Her sex drive was strong, plus pent up, since she'd been looking at girls and thinking about fucking them for five solid years. And Lee was no slouch either. Between his teaching only three courses and her willingness to skip class, they found a lot of time to inhabit his conversation pit as well as the bed that hung on brass chains from the ceiling and the Bengal tiger skin.

Sometimes they talked, and sometimes he just sat and typed while she went through the bookshelves, reading Genet and Huysmans but mostly thinking about what she thought about all the time now: sex with Lee. She was feeling new feelings, emotional and physical, new pains and longings, and she couldn't make notes—there was no point; there was no way you could work them into a play, and somebody might find them and read them—but she kept careful track of them, mentally.

Being a lesbian had given her practice keeping secrets. She walked to his house through the woods even when it took her two hours. Or she waited by the road for his car. Moonless nights in Stillwater were dark as the inside of a cow. When he didn't have time to see her, she would sit on a bench overlooking the lake and stare at his bamboo.

Lee had promised Peggy everything, but he hadn't thought to include a promise that she wouldn't be kicked out of school for fraternization. Lee sleeping with a student was a scandal, and it had to be stopped. Lee was in loco parentis, but he was also indispensable. Thus Peggy was deemed to have found her calling. Girls quit coed schools to get married all the time. That's what they go there for—to get their MRS degree. Stillwater was supposed to be different, but any school could let in the wrong girl. They asked her not to come back after Christmas vacation.

It was a difficult discussion with her mother. Peggy thought she was bringing good news. Not a lesbian.

Shacking up with a famous poet. Quitting that third-rate college. Her life was back on track. Right?

Her mother shook her head with red-rimmed eyes. "I knew you would regret choosing to be a lesbian. But you are making the wrong choice, honey. I wanted you to get an education. Now you're seventeen and there's nothing I can do."

Her father said, "You're saving me a bundle, you know that? You're Lee Fleming's problem now, and I wish him luck."

"How am I Lee's problem? I'm going to transfer to another school! I applied to the New School for Social Research!"

Her father rolled his eyes. To him it was a cruel joke being played on him by his supervisor God. A social superior with an intellectual bent and a fortune in land: he had prayed many times for a husband like that for Peggy.

Peggy's mother's parting gift was a trip to the gynecologist. Peggy had never seen a gynecologist before and didn't like it. He was supposed to fit her with a diaphragm. Instead he took one look at her cervix and said, "Miss Vaillaincourt, you are fixing to have a baby and I would say it's not going to take so long that you shouldn't get married at the earliest possible opportunity." She said she didn't want a baby, and he repeated the sentence word for word with the same exact identical intonation, like a machine.

*

Lee saw it coming. She came back from Christmas vacation looking bloated. He reflected that he had fucked her nearly every day since September. He asked, "Punky, don't you ever get the curse?" She broke down and begged him for a Mexican abortion. "Why would you do that?" he said. "I'd give my child a name." She stared in horror like he was a giant spider, then clasped her fists against her abdomen and moaned like a cow. "Are you feeling sick? That's all right, it's normal."

He hadn't anticipated having a wedding at all, ever, but he felt up to the task. Fatherhood surprised him pleasantly. As a male he assumed no unpleasant duties would accrue to him. He would be responsible for teaching the child conversational skills once it reached its teens.

It was up to Peggy's parents to pay for the wedding. Peggy got as far as asking them. Her mother called her Lee's doxy and said the baby would be born deformed because Flemings marry their cousins. Her father gave her five hundred dollars and sighed.

Lee consulted his old friend Cary. They had grown up as neighbors. Cary was older and richer and fey, with a hobby of arranging flowers and a habit of getting into difficult situations with straight men. They made a date at a gay bar under a hardware store in Portsmouth.

"Urbanna is the place for a wedding," Cary said. "Rent the beach and I'll organize us some swan boats. They've got the whitest sand beach in Tidewater, and we'll jam Christ Church full of magnolias until it goes pop."

"Swan boats? What are you, drunk?"

Cary folded his arms and said, "Then get married in Battle Abbey with a reception in the yard. See if I care."

"Swan boats would drift out to the river. They have wings like sails, and no keel."

"You want the swan boats." Cary pointed at him and announced the news to the empty bar. "Fleming wants the swan boats!"

"I want an honor guard from VMI, but that doesn't mean I'm going to get it. What I need is for three hundred people to know my beautiful bride is with child, and then clear out while we go on our honeymoon, and for that I need—what do I need, man? I'm asking you. You think I do this all the time?"

"Bruton Parish Church. Then those of us of the non-marrying persuasion retire to the Williamsburg Inn for mint 'giblets,' and you drive down to Hatteras with what's-her-name."

"Peggy."

"Then you take the Peglet down to Nags Head and get her pregnant again."

"She's pregnant now. There's no double pregnant."

"Then you lay back and watch her get fatter."

"It's not fat. It's a Fleming. And we're going to Charleston."

"In January?"

"Spring break."

"She's going to be fat as a tick by March. Big old body, little arms and legs."

The door of the Cockpit flew open and four sailors came in, pushing and shoving their way down the narrow stairway. Lee immediately turned to face them and Cary tugged on his arm. "Whoa, Nelly. You're a married man."

"I got a right to a bachelor party, ain't I?"

Lee wrote a poem with swan boats in it to get them out of his system, and addressed himself to the fact that he had gotten Peggy out of his system. The easy joy and the joyful ease of sex with men, their easy-access genitalia, their uncomplicated inner lives ... He knew there were women who lived like that, even beautiful and very interesting women, but they didn't appeal to him at all. He wanted the needy staring beforehand and the tears of worshipful gratitude afterward, as though every orgasm were a reprieve from a death sentence. He just didn't want it all the time.

He had had as much sex with Peggy as a person can have, and that was enough. She was hanging around his house doing her best to keep out of his way, like she was afraid of him. She felt nauseated, existentially and otherwise. She didn't want to get on his nerves. She felt dependent. And she was. She was depending on him to do an awful lot of things, like marry her, raise her child, send her to school in New York, and finance the rest of her existence until the day she died. She had a suspicion it might not work out that way.

He, too, knew he wouldn't be sending her away to finish school. But he knew the real reason: The college paid him two thousand dollars a year, and that was the extent of his income. He didn't have a trust fund, just the prospect of inheriting from a happy-go-lucky fifty-four-year-old father who was more likely to die skiing than get sick before he turned eighty. It was no coincidence that famous authors came to visit him and not the other way around, or that he served his guests spaghetti. But quand même. The best things in life are free. A round of billiards with sailors is more beautiful than Charleston in spring-time, if they're the right sailors.

Peggy began writing a play. She got as far as the names after "DRAMATIS PERSONAE." She wanted to draw on Arthurian mythology, the Questing Beast and the Fisher King, and got stuck on Guinevere. She imagined Joan Baez, without the shrill voice and the guitar, arms out like the Virgin of Guadalupe, and there wasn't much Arthurian about it. It was Mexican. She thought a lot about Mexico in those days. The freedom down there, the eternal springtime, women scampering across desert hillsides like roadrunners. February was so cold that Stillwater Lake froze solid and her former classmates began sliding over and peeking up at the house through the gap in the bamboo. Emily actually walked up on the back porch and opened the storm door and knocked hard, five times. But without taking off her skates, and she was gone like a shot. Then it thawed and Peggy was alone again.

For a lesbian, Lee's house was cold turkey. You could go months without seeing a woman. Not that it mattered if your plan of being a pencil-thin seductress in black had unexpectedly given way to frying pancakes in a plaid bathrobe. She liked it best when there were visiting poets. They never minded if you sat near them and just listened to them talk. It was impossible to think of anything to say that might interest them, because they weren't interested in conversations with topics. They went out of their way to generate non sequiturs, occasionally playing a game they called Exquisite Corpse where you string together stories not even knowing what they're about. One of them brought along a Ouija board and let spirits write his poems. He would have let even Peggy write his poems if Lee hadn't looked at her and frowned.

At first she wondered why they were all so rich. When one of them forgot his watch or left a cashmere sweater balled up in the corner of a sofa, he would never call to ask about it. Lee explained to her that art for art's sake is an upper-class aesthetic. To create art divorced from any purpose, you can't be living a life driven by need and desire. She wanted to write plays that would blow people's minds, but he didn't want anything. His poems just were, and that's what made them so good and her plays bad.

Peggy thought about the poets' ability to fund their own publications and wasn't so sure. Lee had a friend with a printing press—not Linotype or the new offset kind, but movable type made of lead—and with it he could make anything Lee wrote look valuable. And the *Stillwater Review* could turn anything into poetry just by publishing it, even forty-one reiterations of "c*nt" arranged in the shape of the Empire State Building. "Poets were not put here to put labels on the world," he explained to her. "If that poem is about anything, it's about the act of reading. To cite it for obscenity, you'd have to say what it means, which is why I can publish it."

"I don't like it," she said. "It turns cunts into a penis."

"Cunts were made for penises. What you do with yours is your business, but those are the facts. Nothing else was ever made for penises. Never slowed me down. It's a free country." He lit up a Tareyton and blew a smoke ring that nearly crossed the room.

Peggy was inexperienced, but a feeling of unease told her things were not necessarily going to end well.

The spring was a little warmer than usual. By April you could drink and bullshit with poets around the fire all night. She had thought poets were different, but by then she knew they just bullshit like good old boys everywhere. You could take winos off the sidewalk in front of the drugstore and teach them to be poets in half an hour. They'd refuse, or maybe the ones who were closet homosexuals would say yes, but they all could have done it, and better than college girls, because college girls have inhibitions to get over. The people who talked revolution made out like if you just overcame whatever was holding you back inside, you'd be free. But you'd just be a wino in front of a drugstore, saying whatever came into your head in the most provocative way you could think of, repeating and refining it because how else were you going to kill a hundred and fifty thousand hours until your father died in a crash. The poets reminded her of barflies, in love with their own wisecracks, stiffing the bartender because they don't know what work is. But freedom isn't speaking your mind freely. Freedom is having the money to go to Mexico.

"Jesus, Peggy. You can't abort a seven-month baby. That's infanticide. You need to get your daddy down here with a shotgun, because I keep on forgetting to marry you. And I do want to marry you."

"So marry me now." Peggy had heard of alimony. She wasn't sure how much you get and if it's enough to live on, but it had to be better than being an unwed teenage mother. She was barely eighteen and wouldn't be grown up for three more years. They could have put her in a home for wayward girls.

"Dare me," Lee said.

"I double-dare you with whipped cream and a cherry on top."

He called a magistrate and arranged to be married the next afternoon for fifteen dollars.

Two

When she had the baby, she couldn't believe how beautiful he was. Rhys! She picked the name out all by herself. Labor was easy, no worse than cramps, which always made her feel like she was giving birth to a calf, then five hours in the hospital and there he was. He lay on a little cart, wrapped up in blue blankets, while she drank juice. Lee's mother picked him up and said, "Welcome to the world, little Harry!"

"What are you doing, Mrs. Fleming?" Peggy said. "Give me my baby."

"You didn't really want this baby, did you now. Not from what I hear."

"Lee!" she yelled. "Lee!"

Lee came in from the hallway. "Yes, dear? Well, would you look at that. My lord. What a sweetheart. Just look at him. Aw. Cleans up real nice."

"His name is Rhys," Peggy said. "Rhys Byrd Fleming. Do you like it?"

"But we're christening him Harry," Lee's mother said.

"Moms, drop it. This is my wife. I'm his father. This not y'all's baby. This my baby! Yes, sir! Who's my baby!" He took Rhys and kissed him on the cheek, then leaned down and kissed Peggy.

"Well, we'll be happy to help take care of him, if you need any help," Lee's mother said.

"You know what," Peggy said, "I think it's time I tried feeding him. Could we have a little time alone?"

"Yes, could you weigh anchor, darling?" Lee said.

"I'll go fix you some formula," his mother said, looking around for supplies. "Don't tell me you're going to—no. I refuse to believe it."

"It's the natural way," Peggy said. "It's good for him."

"You'll be tied to that baby like a ball and chain. You can't let him out of your sight and no one can help you with him. No self-respecting woman does that. It's like turning yourself into an animal."

"I got news for you, lady. Guess where he came from."

"Don't get all in a snit," Lee said.

"But that's exactly it," his mother said. "You don't know the chemical composition. There could be anything in there. It's unscientific."

"Science gave us the bomb and DDT," Peggy said.

"Moms," Lee said, pushing his mother toward the door, "please just let us handle this. It will be fine. It will be right as rain. Little Rhys Byrd here is a Fleming. If anybody can survive mother's milk, he can. She's just, I don't know," he said, turning to Peggy as he looked for a word, "anxious. It's her first grandchild."

"She sure acts like an expert."

"Well, she raised me. That's what makes me think anyone can do it."

There was no circumcision. Lee said circumcision was dreamed up by moralists and lotion salesmen to make hand jobs chafe, and Peggy deferred to his better judgment.

She settled in with baby Byrdie. She did all the housework. She did more laundry than had ever been done before at Lee's house, and by September you could see exactly where on the front lawn the septic system was, traced out in darker bluegrass.

She couldn't fit into the clothes she'd bought for school, so she wore Lee's polo shirts. She seldom got around to washing her hair, and it seemed to be coming uncurled. Her breasts were heavy and sore. But she felt that the thing that was terribly wrong with her would soon be all right. The thing that was wrong with her was so right about Lee and Byrdie that she figured it didn't matter. They were in perfect health and looked like they belonged in magazine advertisements for shirts and baby food, respectively. She looked like their maintenance man.

Lee had visitors who sat by the fire and bullshitted until long after Peggy fell asleep. She didn't know what they did after she went to bed, but she didn't care. She was as exhausted every night as if she'd played five hours of flag football. By the time Byrdie was eight months old, he was moving around so fast she was having to chase him. You couldn't have gates and childproofing in a house like that. There were a million things he could have killed himself on. Landings with loose rugs, big glass vases done up as lamps. Peggy spent most of her time upstairs in the playroom, keeping him cleaned and fed. She was made to bring out the baby and accept praise for her work as if she were a being of a slightly lower social class—which she was. A woman. Even if they hadn't all been gay men and thus more or less not interested in her at all, almost blind to her existence; even if they had been models of chivalry, rushing to pick up things she dropped and giving her flowers, instead of bullshitting parasites who thought they had invented crass vulgarity before inventing maudlin sentimentality as a foil (exposure to them was making Peggy at once articulate and sullen), a monosyllabic high school graduate in an oversized polo shirt with baby food on it was not going to get their attention. She couldn't pose around in pedal pushers and offer them cigarillos and sangria. She had given up smoking and drinking, and she didn't think she was obliged to wear party clothes any more than a bathing suit and goggles. Mothering was a different activity. Everything in its proper time and place. When Byrdie was three, she would put him in nursery school and drive to New York to get her degree. She was purposely vague with herself about the exact details of what kind of nursery school takes kids for a semester at a time, but she was sure it would work out.

*

By the time Byrdie was two, Peggy had begun to forget why she first came to Stillwater. She thought of it simply as "the college" where she was a faculty wife, a fine and worthy social position. Pushing him in a shopping cart through the aisles at the Safeway, she felt that the other housewives looked at her with respect. Her social position at Safeway was better than it was at home. Strangers called her "Mrs. Fleming," as though she wore a name tag.

On one occasion when she was feeling edgy and exhausted and her cartilage ached the way it sometimes did, she stopped off at the memorial park on her way home. It was the biggest public open space in the county. She drove up and down the long rows of granite grave markers set flush to the grass singing, "If you are going to San Francisco," thinking about smothering Byrdie and taking the car and just running away. Her life could start over as it was meant to start—but how was that, pray tell? As a lesbian? What about those two or three months of fixation on sleeping with Lee? Is that what lesbians do? She looked back at Byrdie asleep on the back bench seat and said, "Byrdie boy, I love you so much."

On the next occasion when she was feeling down and nasty, she drove to the state beach and sat on the sand with Byrdie for almost an hour, digging in the grit by her feet with a little piece of crab shell. She walked him along the waterline to look for fossil shark teeth. They found tin can lids and a lucky penny. The sky was clouding up. She did some shopping, drove home, parked next to a strange car, and walked right into a scene she had not expected: Lee and Emily, using the hanging bed from India.

"Fuck, Lee!" she screamed. He laughed and didn't allow himself to be distracted. The baby was still in the car—a baby, unlike milk, won't spoil in the heat—so she walked right back out of the house, got in the car, and drove to the college, thinking she didn't know what. She wanted to rat him out. It had to be against college policy, a professor making one student after marrying a different student! She drove the loop road, looking for a familiar face, and pulled up in front of her old dorm and cried.

For Peggy it was a life of work, mostly. Occasionally she got creative. She made cuttings of the lilacs and forsythia at the college, rooted them in water, and stuck them out in rows around the edge of the yard.

Sometimes Lee got invited to give readings. As he explained, he wouldn't have any time at all to devote to her at these other colleges in strange cities. Poets and professors would want to have late dinners with him, after his readings, and then they would probably stay up drinking until all hours. The compatibility with Byrdie's habits was nil. The plane tickets were only for Lee. He didn't have the money. A reading is not a business trip. It's nonstop socializing. She was his wife, not an appendage.

She went along once, to a literary festival half an hour away at VCU. It was as bleak as he said. Byrdie had no patience for up-and-coming writers. Poetry made him throw toys that clattered on the linoleum. Too big for a stroller, he couldn't be rolled captive around the business

district. She ended up watching him play in a dry fountain, longing for home.

Lee felt that vacations were a chance for her to see her
family, and that it would be ridiculous to go on expensive
trips when you live in a country place so pretty that
famous poets leave New York and Boston to spend entire
weeks there. So their first real excursion as a family took
them up to Westmoreland County, where Lee's brother,
Trip, had a place on the Potomac. For such a rich man, it
was an awfully rustic house, built as a hunting lodge when
men used to rough it. The woods were full of snags that
were still allowing huge grubs to mature and reproduce,
so that if you left the light on in the outdoor shower, you
would find things sitting on the bar of soap in the morning that looked like they were from the Precambrian.
Luna moths thudded against the screen like birds, trying
to get at the porch light. Hemlock groves towered over
wild myrtles and rhododendrons. Every sunny spot had
its snake, black or green or copperhead. It was beautiful,
creepy, threatening.

You couldn't swim in the river, because the jellyfish
were swarming, so Trip took his houseguests to Stratford
Hall, the birthplace of Robert E. Lee. First he showed
them the house in Pevsner's book on architecture and
emphasized its beauty and significance. After lunching at
the restaurant they toured the estate, Peggy's sidelong
glance catching Lee's reverential look when presented
with the cradle in which the infant Robert E. had been
laid after his birth. Lee was only eight years older than
her, but at times like that, she felt you could really tell.

The tour concluded with a visit to the kitchen, where the white tour guide took a plate of gingersnaps from a silent black woman who never raised her head. The tour guide passed them out, giving Byrdie four cookies while everyone else got one.

When the plate was empty the black woman, whose nappy hair was greased back awkwardly and who seemed somehow a cripple or a hunchback although she was neither and had a pretty, tender face, rose again from her stool in the corner and carried the empty plate into another room.

Byrdie stared. He had never seen anyone like her. She was not an adult. Or was she? She wore a uniform or costume—a calico dress. "Is the colored lady a slave?" he asked Lee.

Everybody turned to laugh at Byrdie. The memory branded itself on his brain: the gales of laughter, everyone offering him their cookies, the slave woman with her eyes on the floor.

The second time Lee rubbed Peggy's nose in an infidelity, she drove the same route she had years before, inexorably drawn to the college where her life had first jumped the tracks. It was about four years after the visit to Stratford.

By that time Byrdie had a little sister: Mireille. Lee didn't seek sex often enough for Peggy to think she needed birth control. Sex only happened when Lee was in a certain strange, dramatic mood, acting out something Peggy could not grasp.

Then there she was. Born into ambiguity and ambivalence, an incontrovertible baby. Mireille at three was a sallow blonde with downy hair so white it was almost invisible. She clung to Peggy like a baby monkey most of the time. When she said "Daddy," it didn't sound like a request for love. She said "Daddy!" as though unpleasantly surprised. Two clipped syllables that seemed to encapsulate all her mother's resentment, as if it had been passed along in utero. He would fill her bowl with applesauce and she'd say "Daddy!" and he had to add applesauce until she had more than Byrdie. Then she'd eat just the extra piled on at the end and push the rest away. Lee disliked her, but he expected her to grow on him sooner or later. She would get old enough to be more than just a reproachful bundle of petty envy that had grown on Peggy like a tumor. She might turn out to be a pretty, playful tumor that moved about under its own power. There's something appealing about a narrow-minded, scheming blonde who plays with boys like a cat, Lee thought.

One day Peggy came home from the Safeway and walked in on a wasteland. Arms full of groceries, she scanned a little forest of pottery figurines at her feet as she walked through the living room to the kitchen. There was more pottery next to the trash can. She had made these statues at the college art center and considered them emblematic of her frustration as a housewife. They were pinched pyramidal figures with tiny round heads, done in dull shades of blue. Their necks were very thin and easy to break. Most of the heads were gathered in a pie tin on the floor.

"Lee!" she yelled. There was no answer. She set the groceries down and walked out the back door. And there he was, in a net muscle shirt, getting in the canoe with a boy. Making his getaway as soon as he heard the car, right in the middle of letting some teenager help him turn her sewing room into a weight room because she didn't have time to do any sewing.

It was a betrayal of just about everything—her privacy, her pottery that was a cry for help intended to be heard by no one, her struggle to be a good mother and sew little dresses for Mireille. The intimacy she and Lee still shared. The vestiges of heterosexuality she occasionally saw in him and cosseted like rare orchids. All of it gone. The more sacrifices she made for her family, the more he took his power for granted. He got all the love in the world, and she got none at all.

She drove to the college. She had a vague notion of storming into his office and breaking something.

As she rounded the main building, she spied the grassy slope under the tulip poplars going down to Stillwater Lake, and she followed a mad impulse.

She stopped the car and said, "Byrdie, could you take Mickey and stand over there by that tree?"

He said, "Yes, ma'am," and toted his little sister and her blanket over to the tree, warning her with a gesture to stay put, came back to close the car door, and rejoined her in the shade.

The lake made Peggy angry. It ought to be bringing Lee to her, on his knees in the canoe, to offer her an explanation and an apology. But the lake was empty, because Lee was not alone and would never come to the college dressed as his true self. He was back at the house by now, sweeping up her art with no pants on.

"Don't move, Byrdie," Peggy said. "This'll just take a second." She put the car—more precisely, Lee's irreplaceable VW Thing—in second gear and drove slowly and deliberately into the water. She watched the water pour in around her feet and kept going. She revved the Thing until the wheels were in mud up past the axles, even up past the lower edge of the doors.

As the engine died she heard a sucking sound. The car was still moving forward and tilting.

Peggy felt an anxiety she had not anticipated. She had expected it to be like driving down a boat ramp. She floundered to shore, up to her knees in mud that ripped her shoes right off her feet, and turned to watch the car settle into place nose down, rear bumper in the air. Around it, a maelstrom was forming. It didn't look like it would be easy to get back out.

A security guard ran up behind her to ask if she was all right.

"Where's my kids? Byrdie, Mickey, c'mere. Come on, honey. It's all right. I love you, baby. I just didn't like that car."

"You're crazy, Mom. I'm going to tell Dad."

"Now, sweetie, ain't nobody crazier than your dad. We're all crazy!"

The campus security officer asked, "Mrs. Fleming, are you saying that was not an accident?"

"Nope. That was theater of cruelty."

The officer sighed and said, "Mrs. Fleming, you're a card," and they went together into the administrative building to call Lee. That was one advantage of being a wife. It was Lee's job to discipline her, not that campus security would have involved the police in anything short of murder.

A week later, they got the car out with a farm tractor and some oak planks. It was doable only because the water in the lake had fallen to the level of the car's submerged front axle, leaving a wide and hideous beach of glutinous brown slime. Mrs. Fleming was firmly established as a legend on campus, and Lee was ...

... livid? Was he livid? Are there words to describe how Lee was? Less privileged men sometimes fancy themselves egotistical sociopaths, but they don't know the half of it. They don't even know how it's done. In most cases they've even apologized for something at some point in their lives.

Lee had never been hot-tempered. A lesser man might strike his wife. A man who trusts in the rule of law files a formal complaint. For example, "My wife is a danger to herself and others." A hearing is conducted. Fees are paid. A judge issues an order. The order's execution makes the wife kick and scream, undermining her credibility. Seeing the force necessary to crush an annoyance he merely wanted rid of, the complainant heaves a sigh of regret.

That was Lee's reaction when faced with the desirability of having Peggy locked up for a while. As a wife and mother, she was impossible. The theatrics! Who attempts suicide in a convertible in a lake ten feet deep? She was in hell. He was in hell. Yet she refused to leave him. She couldn't leave him. She hated both their families, and she knew no one else well enough to get invited to their house. Thinking about it made him melancholic. Lee found depressive feelings unpleasant. He saw that something needed to be done. He conveyed the reality to her many times, repeating it like he thought she was slow: "I'm going to call a doctor. You're not well."

With every repetition he could see her edging toward the door. That was where she belonged: the door. The closer she got to it, the more his heart brightened with clarity. He threatened her in a low, friendly voice, pitched so as not to alarm her.

In exchange for leaving, she would have more options than she'd ever had before. She would be free.

But behind his tone of concern, Peggy detected her true choices: find somebody to take you in, or spend an indeterminate amount of time behind bars enjoying tranquilizers and electroshock. She had read enough lives of the poetesses to know all about inpatient psychiatric care. She knew he would be able to get her committed with no trouble at all. Driving a motor vehicle into a lake in front of your kids is not against the law—on private property it's not even littering—but it's madness.

Lee's feelings were more complex than he let on. When he met Peggy, he'd thought his homosexuality might be a great big cosmic typo. He told himself, Listen, it's not like sex with men was your idea. He had been an exceptionally good-looking boy. He scored his first blow job for attending a show-jumping competition. Soon his penis was buying entire weeks on skis. An unbeatable deal, and habit-forming.

At heart he knew he was normal. No more conflicted than any other married man. He was a sexual being. He couldn't give that up on account of a three-month fling with his wife ten years before. Like many a married man before him, he took the deal they had hammered out — you give me your life, in return you get my kids—and canceled both ends. He didn't want to be privy to her martyrdom, and he didn't like her influence on his kids.

Lee truly did adore his son. He would kill time in the evenings with a glass of rye whisky and romantic fantasies of dropping Byrdie off at boarding school in his own father's matte gold Mercedes while vivid orange maple leaves swirled every which way. The other boys would be squirming, their elegant mothers adjusting their little tiger-striped ties, while Byrdie in fuck-you-Nantucket red pants would swagger up the brick walkway already a man, raised by a cool single father, the coolest boy at Woodberry, with the longest skis, most outré collection of French porn, best way with horses, etc.

He could allow himself these fantasies on his small salary because his parents were not averse to Byrdie. Genetic and other contributions made by Peggy to Byrdie's makeup were beneath their notice. They weren't conspicuous, anyhow. He had Lee's face. It was only from the back, if one of them was out in the yard in the dusk, that he had trouble telling his son and his wife apart, though Byrdie was still a little smaller. Same narrow build, same style of dress, same curly brown hair. If Peggy ever cleared out she might haunt him for a while that way, but only until the resemblance faded.

Byrdie's loyalty was tested in a remake of the dog scene from *Henry Huggins*: Peggy by the open driver's-side door of the Fairlane, Mireille on her hip like a limpet, calling for Byrdie to come get in the car. And Lee on the porch saying, "Don't you get in that car!"

Byrdie said, "You're crazy, Mom," and walked back to his father.

"You're scaring Byrdie," Lee said.

"Fear is part of life for all sentient beings," Peggy said. "I'll come back for you, Byrdie. Don't be scared."

"Like hell you will," Lee said.

Mireille began to cry and Lee came down from the porch. "Come on, Mickey," he said, using the name Peggy used for her. He held out his arms. "Come to Papa. You're not going anywhere."

"Shut your trap, asshole," Peggy said. "I've heard just about enough of your bullshit."

Mireille wailed and Byrdie said, "Mom!"

"I love you, Byrdie!" Peggy called out. "Don't forget it! I love you so much!" At last she set Mireille down on the passenger seat. She did a five-point turn and drove slowly out the pale, sandy driveway while Lee, unprepared, thought hard about calling his father to say his daughter had been abducted.

Instead he challenged his son to a game of cribbage. Women will say they're leaving and go to the grocery store, or drive into Richmond for a movie. If it wasn't a minor event, it was one he needed to minimize, at least until after bedtime.

But she didn't come back, and Byrdie lay down like a dog by the door to wait for her.

Peggy's decision hadn't been spontaneous. It bore few of the hallmarks of madness. It took days to plan.

She had a tank full of gas. The trunk was full of khakis and old polo shirts, blankets, an air mattress, food, water, spray primer in black, her portable typewriter and spare ribbons, onionskin thesis paper, and many other supplies. She wasn't going to a motel, much less her parents, or even to the New School for Social Research.

Instead of heading for the highway or the interstate, she turned onto a little county road. It went to dirt with a sign, END STATE MAINTENANCE, and she kept going. "Look at that, Mickey, blue butterflies," she said. They were flying almost as fast as the car. She didn't want to raise a cloud of dust. They came out on a gravel road that was part of a forgotten battlefield monument and passed a cairn raised to the memory of the Confederate dead. "Look at that, Mickey, a pyramid," she said, curving off to the right into the trees again and following a dirt track that paralleled a river. Up ahead she saw the towers of a nuclear plant, flashing for a moment through a gap in the trees. An old crossways, with a sign as though it were still a town, two wooden stores falling down, pokeweed up to the rafters. Then a floodplain, a desert of stubble and sand. Topsoil had filled the river below, flattening it until it turned its own banks to mud flats, making the farmers poor and stealing their land until they just up and left, leaving their houses and barns behind.

She turned away from the river again. They zigzagged. Peggy was looking for something specific: an open barn, an abandoned house.

It was into such a barn that she drove the Fairlane, and into such a house that she took Mireille. A tall, drafty house, swaying with the trees around it. They stayed overnight.

When they crossed south again, headed for tobacco country, the gleaming red Fairlane was a dull dark gray.

Finding an abandoned place in southeastern Virginia wasn't going to be as easy. Without the big rivers as highways, things had developed on a smaller scale. There were no palatial plantation houses anchoring medieval market towns. The houses were small, and they generally had people living in them. The economy revolved around the tobacco cartel. It meant a man could make a living forever off his inherited right to harvest—or at least launder—a set amount of tobacco. Tobacco made the difference between staying on the land and giving up.

Wherever it wasn't tobacco, it was cotton. Sometimes corn and soybeans with hogs attached. When the soil announced it couldn't take any more and gave up the ghost, the subsidies came for doing nothing. With the result of pines. Endless tracts of pines growing on naked grit, allowed to get maybe twenty feet tall before somebody came along and harvested them with a nipper, right off the stumps, *thwap*. Deafening.

Where there were no pines, there were swamps full of game. Boom, bang, squeal. More deafening. Hound dogs starving by the roads every fall and winter, thinking every truck that passed was the hunter who'd brought them, running for its doors. Death by trust.

People generally were hard-hearted and hard of hearing and possibly not eager to understand you when you talked. They were independent people. Tobacco was not their only cash crop. Peggy and Mickey passed a billboard that in 1967 had said BUY A FLAG! FLY IT HIGH! In 1970 someone adjusted it to read BUY A BAG! FLY HIGH! No one fixed it, and in 1975 it was rotting in place. Its symbolism was timeless.

They drove flat, lonely roads until Peggy spied a solitary cabin with flaking green paint. It stood under trees in a shallow pool of water. She pulled in and honked the horn. She got out of the car and yelled, "Hey!" She kept yelling as she splashed up to the door. But the house was empty.

There was a thick layer of dust on two liquor bottles and an empty baked bean can, and a newspaper from 1951 in use as shelf paper in the pantry. There was no furniture, but the windows had glass. No footprints. Stiff toile curtains.

Wading around outside the house, she saw that previous tenants had built up the ground in the crawl space. The house stood on dry pillars. And the water wasn't seepage from below, just a big puddle from the last rain. It was the kind of land you can't build on anymore, marl where the soil doesn't "perc." The cesspool had no cover, but it was deep and black and smelled of earth. She fetched naval jelly from the car and smeared it on the joint of the pump handle. The water rushed out cold and clear. It was a deep well, drawing water from under the clay.

"We're going to put down stakes right here," she said to Mireille.

That night Mireille slept.

She was used to a house where people made noises at all hours. Her father getting drinks for guests, her brother staring at them over the banister and getting reprimanded, her mother puttering in the laundry room, opening the door to check on her, the top-heavy house creaking as the inhabitants shifted their weight. Here her mother lay down when it got dark and clasped her hard to her side. There was nothing that could move in that wind-struck shack. It had done all its settling long ago. There were floorboards that creaked, but nobody to step on them. The only sound was the rushing of pine needles on the trees filtering the dusty air. The pollen was so thick the car was dusted canary yellow the next morning. The humidity, when the temperature got up in the afternoon, was an invisible weight bearing a person to the ground. Mireille slept again.

By the second morning, she was no longer an irritable child. She peeled herself off Peggy and looked around for something to play with.

Peggy did not pay visits to her parents of her own accord, but this was a special case. In general they alternated holidays so as not to miss any relatives: Easter here, Fourth of July there, and so forth. Invariably they ate with Peggy's parents on Thanksgiving because Lee's mother didn't cook. Then everybody came to Lee's parents' for Christmas. They had maids making eggnog on rotation and a two-story tree in the front hall with a Lionel train around it, and the kids idolized them. Peggy's parents, on the other hand, thought she spoiled the kids beyond belief. Her mother had knelt on the rug next to Byrdie, holding his new NERF ball behind her back, and said, "Now, I know you're not used to hearing the word 'no,' but I don't want to play ball right now. I want us to play Go Fish with your sister. Can you do that one little thing for someone else?" Family get-togethers involving the Vaillaincourts were tense, stubborn confrontations about child-rearing practices, seething under a facade of ritualized gentility and studiously avoided by everyone.

Thus Peggy believed that while Lee might set the wheels of justice turning, he would hesitate for days before calling her parents. Yet it was summer vacation, and they would be calling Stillwater to see when she was bringing the kids to swim in the pool. She decided to drive up and preempt them.

She knew where the key was hidden, but she rang the doorbell. "My, my!" her mother said. "Aren't you tan!" She let her in, looking her up and down. "You've been playing tennis again!"

Peggy laughed. "No, Mom, I've been gardening."

"I would know if you'd been gardening," her mother said. "The back of your neck would be red and wrinkled as a turkey. No, you've been playing tennis. At your age you should be riding or playing golf. Something you can wear a hat and gloves at."

"Well, isn't this a surprise," Peggy's father said. "What brings you to our neck of the woods?"

"Let me get Mickey," she said, turning back toward the car. "I didn't know if you were home."

"Where's Byrdie?"

"School," Peggy said. "What a great kid."

"He's a little spoiled, but he's a fine boy," her father agreed.

"How's Lee?" her mother asked.

"That's what I wanted to talk to you about. Lee's not— as a matter of fact Lee and I are not getting along. We separated."

"You're not living with Lee?" Her mother drew back in dismay.

"I've got my own place. Be honest, Mom. Lee Fleming! How long was that going to work?"

Her father chortled.

"Well, is he fine with it?"

Peggy sighed. "Sure. He has a new girlfriend."

Her father guffawed.

"Are you getting a divorce?" her mother asked.

"Not so far."

"Do you have a lawyer?"

"I'm not getting a divorce, so why would I need a lawyer?"

"Lee's out there right now, deceiving you with some two-bit hustler," her mother said earnestly. "I don't remember you signing any premarital agreement. He's going to have to settle something on you. We'll force him."

"You and what army? I'm telling you, I cut out of there with no forwarding address. If I go to a judge, Lee will get custody of Mickey, too, not just Byrdie. I couldn't make Byrdie come along. He didn't want to, not with a choice between me and the Playboy of the Western World. Now name me a judge Lee's not related to. I wouldn't touch a court of law with a ten-foot pole. Screw me over, fuck you. Screw me twice—"

"Watch your language, young lady!" her father interrupted.

"Anyhow, he's broke. He won't have a cent until his mom buys the farm, and that's going to take forty years. If she dies first, his dad marries some deb and we never see a cent."

Peggy's mother took Mickey by the hand and stood in the archway to the dining room, making as though to take her someplace else to play, but not wanting to miss anything. "Let's play boats," Mickey said.

"I don't have boats. I guess you don't have boats anymore either, now that you don't live on Stillwater Lake."

"Mommy made the lake fall down. Now we play boats in the yard."

"Where are you living, honey?"

"We got a pyramid, and blue butterflies!"

"Where do you live?" Peggy's father said, addressing himself to Peggy.

"Rented house," Peggy said. "Nothing special."

"Where?"

"I'd rather not say. I don't want Lee serving me with papers."

"I'm concerned about you, honey."

"I can make my own decisions."

Her father laughed. "I noticed! Do you have a phone, where we can call you?"

"Not in the house. There's a party line at a bait shop."

"You should get a phone for safety. Just list it under a fake name."

Peggy stopped off at her dad's churchyard to let Mickey play. The church was one of the oldest in the country, nearly square, with gated pews shining pale green and the Ten Commandments in loopy gold script on alabaster tablets at the front. Austere, creaky, ancient. She picked up a bench and let it fall. The echo ricocheted off the walls and made Mickey jump. They walked around the outside, stroking the soft salmon brickwork with its tracery of lime and the dark pottery of the glazed headers. In the graveyard a solitary angel kept watch over a boxwood. Broken columns—the oldest graves. The next era, bas-relief willows and skulls. Then cast-iron crosses. Then the newest graves, granite monoliths. The names were always the same. Except for one. The cemetery had apparently been integrated. A cluster of mauve plastic roses poked up from the foot of a tiny mound. At the head was a temporary marker, a cross made of unfinished pine, already weathered, reading KAREN BROWN 1970–73.

Peggy remembered the Browns. A nice black family who lived on the school property like her parents. Not neighbors exactly, but close by. And here they had lost a child like Mickey. A child who ought to be older than Mickey, but would always be younger. How sad. She looked at her daughter, and then she did something terrible. She drove to the courthouse, to the county registrar, whom she knew, and said, "Morning, Lester!"

"Miss Peggy! How do you do?"

"Fine, thanks. It's beautiful out! My dad asked me to come down here. He's doing Leon Brown's back taxes and now the IRS says they need a birth certificate for their little daughter that died. Because of the deduction. He didn't want to ask Leon for it."

"Ain't that a shame."

"Her name was Karen."

He fired up the Xerox machine and dug around for his notary stamp, then pulled out a hanging file tabbed with a B.

In the car on the way home, Peggy glanced at Mireille repeatedly and said, "Karen. Karen? Karen. Karen."

"Who's Karen?"

She poked her in the side. "You are Karen! You can't go to school with a boy's name like Mickey! You have to have a girl's name, and your girl's name is Karen. Karen Brown. My girl's name is Meg. Meg Brown. Meg and Karen Brown."

"We're girls," Mickey said.

"You bet your sweet rear end we're girls!"

Three

Where the yard ended, the pines started. Among them were old ruined houses, just humps left of their two brick chimneys, and little burial grounds. They were popular destinations. Along with thin slabs of marble, some still standing, they had beer bottles, mattresses, and old car seats. The nearby ponds had their banks trampled down from fishing.

Every time they came back from a voyage of discovery, Peggy would examine her house carefully from the deep cover of the underbrush on the edge of the yard. But there was never any sign that anyone had dropped by. No tire tracks in the mud.

Peggy had not forgotten the intellectual and social ambitions she had started life with only a decade before. Years so weary and routine laden, they seemed like a single year that had repeated itself. She wanted to be creative and self-reliant. Her plan was to be a successful playwright. With her earnings from royalties she would one day have a comfortable home again, worthy of

Mickey and Byrdie. Though she had her doubts about whether Byrdie would visit, or even want to talk to her, and how all that would make her feel.

First she had other things to attend to. She had saved housekeeping money for years in a sock and had enough to spare to buy provisions. They were not big eaters. They would need a kerosene heater and lamps, but not until the fall. First renovations were in order. She nailed down linoleum to keep from falling through rotten places in the floor. There was a fair-sized gap in a corner of the kitchen, under a dead boiler that sat flaking rust. She discovered the hole when a possum crawled out and startled bumbling around like a fool. Luckily she had a broom and could herd it back down into the crawl space.

The lawn never needed mowing because of the standing water. The bug situation was correspondingly dire, but no worse than the Mekong Delta, as some poets called Stillwater Lake. Still, she fixed the screen doors before she covered the cesspool. That was the obvious order of priority. She acquired a camp stove to heat water. It was easy to sell Mickey on the virtues of simple foods that require no cooking or dishwashing, such as potato chips and cocktail wieners.

She set up her portable typewriter on the table. She would write under a pseudonym as did the Brontës. Anne, Emily, Charlotte, and Branwell. Also known as Acton Bell, Ellis, Currer, and—did the boy Brontë even write? Or just drink himself to death?

She couldn't remember. She had no place to look it up. She had snagged some books of plays on her way out the door: Shaw, Hart, Synge. She hadn't thought to take the one-volume *Columbia Encyclopedia*.

It didn't matter to her plan. She could still copy the basic principle. Publish under a fake name while dwelling in the lonely fastnesses of the moors. She wasn't clear on what moors were, but the Brontës made them sound every bit as damp as Tidewater. As well as freezing and tubercular, but that wasn't her problem. She would be the Brontë of warm, malarial moors, the dramatist of the Great Dismal Swamp.

After the big money started coming in, she would move to New York. From her picture window above Astor Place, Mickey and Byrdie at her side, she would laugh at Lee's creaky house, his stagnant lake, his noblesse oblige pseudo-income.

Lee had distractions, what with his work at the college and keeping track of where Byrdie was at any given time (students were lined up to babysit and passed him like a baton), but he got a judge to issue a warrant. The charges: kidnapping, reckless endangerment, vandalism, and something about the welfare of a child.

The judiciary was happy to help. The police were not so responsive. Lee called them several times a day, wondering where they were. He wanted them to take copies of Peggy's fingerprints. She hadn't stolen any money when she left. Ergo, he surmised, she would soon embark on a life of crime, endangering Mireille's safety in a criminally insane manner.

But the sheriff and all his deputies seemed to regard Peggy as a grown woman with a right to run away. And who would have expected her to abandon a little daughter? It troubled them more that she hadn't taken the son.

As they fantasized (a primary investigative tool of law enforcement) freely and at length about her motives, alone or over drinks with friends, the sheriff and his deputies consistently came to feel that getting her son away from Lee ought to have been her first priority.

After they finally came and went, Lee dragged himself around the house to eradicate all traces of her. Clothes she hadn't worn in ten years. Light reading for ladies such as the Foxfire books and *Virginia Ghosts*. Her Mirro omelet pan, open admission of her inability to make an omelet. Cher records. They all went into the trunk of a beat-up Volvo and from there into a Dumpster at a wayside. Except the Cher records, which he abandoned on the shoulder of a deeply shaded back road, to make sure no one would suspect he had anything to do with them.

"You're suffering from female trouble," Cary told Lee over lunch at the Bunny Burger. "It's time you sought professional help."

"A shrink only helps when you don't know what you want. I feel I'm in touch with my desires, thank you."

"I meant a psychic. Your aura is navy blue."

"Cary." He used the tone his daughter used to say "Daddy."

"I took a course at Edgar Cayce," Cary protested. "My ESP is very strong!"

"And when did you get the diagnosis? In the poetry workshop business, we always wait until the check clears."

"I have a heightened sensitivity to feelings. Some people only know what you're feeling when you're looking at them, but us psychics can feel it over hundreds of miles. We're tapped into the web of life."

"And what do you call people who know what you're feeling and don't give a shit?"

"That's why they call it female trouble."

"My wife is masculine as a mailed fist," Lee said, paraphrasing a necktie ad from a magazine. "Did you get it on under the pyramid yet?" The Edgar Cayce Center in Virginia Beach was famous for its rooftop pyramid, modeled on the geometric eternity machines of the Egyptians, under which lunch meat would not spoil and orgasms were exceptionally rapturous.

"You want my help finding them or not? You got anything on you now that belongs to one of them? Something related to them, a picture or something."

"Peggy gave me these gray hairs," Lee said. "And she might have bought me this shirt."

"Let me touch it."

Lee held out his arm. "And? What's she feeling?"

Cary closed his eyes and stroked Lee's cuff. "Oh, yes. It's almost there. Her emotions are coming into focus. I can read you now, baby. It's so strong. She thinks you need to lose twelve pounds."

Lee turned his dispassionate gaze on his sandwich. "With friends like you, who needs marriage?" he said, taking a large bite. He thought of Montaigne and Étienne, and felt something was missing from his life.

Lee's parents hired a private investigator, who drove to Caroline County to see whether she was at her parents' house. Just because they said she wasn't there didn't mean she wasn't there. He reported back that the Vaillaincourts' apathy made his blood run cold, as a hardened professional. Peggy's mother had referred him to her husband, as though the search were a business matter, and Mr. Vaillaincourt had told him, "She knows where to find us!" He claimed to be expecting a call any day. If it never came, well, that was Peggy's problem.

The Flemings understood the Vaillaincourts better than the detective did. A ruling class is made up entirely of hardened professionals, insofar as it does not sire sissies. Where more sentimental men might remark of their daughters' marriages, "I'm not losing a daughter, I'm gaining a son," Peggy's father had been heard to say no such thing. When two females vanish from a patriarchy, both of them attached to a homosexual, the ripples can be truly minimal.

Soon the detective, a working-class townsman, sympathized with Peggy. If a woman ran away from people like that, might she not have reasons? He didn't have to know Lee was gay to dislike him. He had other reasons to feel distaste for the Flemings, such as the way they confined him to their front hall, never asking him to come in or sit down.

With his assistance, they placed a newspaper ad featuring Peggy's senior portrait from high school. The picture showed a big-eyed, arrogant girl in an off-the-shoulder drape. Her long hair, straightened on curlers under a dryer hood for the occasion, was pinned up into a chignon. The likeness was not good. Lee had neglected, in ten years of marriage, to take a close-up picture of Peggy. All his snapshots were from a distance, his wife holding a child or underexposed in the light of a campfire.

The ad appeared many times in newspapers all over the state. MISSING PERSON, it announced, with a generous reward.

Thousands of people saw it, but no calls came in. Simple, truthful, educated people, the kind who could read and believe a newspaper, sipped their coffee and felt sorry for the parents whose daughter had run away. Not patronizing the haunts of runaways—heroin shooting galleries and red-light districts and whatnot—themselves, the upstanding citizens had no cause to examine their consciences for signs of Peggy.

Nor would they have found anything anyway. The runaway was keeping a very, very low profile.

She couldn't help herself. Life with Lee had been so drab that running away had a bounden duty to be exciting. She felt she had a right to ask that much. That was why the dramatic flight, the abandoned houses, the new identity.

She hoped he would hunt her with all his might so she could spite him and laugh. Yet she was not in a hurry to deal with stress. Her game was to be invisible. She knew Lee well, and by heading southeast, she had hidden in the folds of his own cerebral cortex. She knew he felt contempt for her. He would imagine her growing old in food service somewhere along Route 1, at Allman's or the Dixie Pig, dreaming of New York City, never getting the money together to get past DC. He would never imagine her fleeing a rural backwater for its murkier depths.

She was right on all counts.

Lee's first stop, Transient City: Fredericksburg, an hour south of Washington, DC, on Route 1. Home owner-ship rate 5 percent. The local gentry had surrendered to solvent government employees and Beltway bandits. Sold every stitch of land, skedaddled to Stafford County or points west. The city was a half-empty ghetto with foreign immigrants. The place you would fetch up if you were trying to get over the Mason-Dixon Line and failing, in Lee's opinion.

He had lunch at Woolworth's without seeing his wife. He sat down on a bench in front of a gift shop (the new suburbanites still came into town when they needed kitsch) to wait for her.

He was like a man buying the first lottery ticket of his life. He reads the notice on the back warning him that the odds against him are twelve million to one, and he concludes that he has a chance of winning.

Lee looked up and down the street, watching for slight women with brown hair. He watched for women with blond children. He watched for anyone at all. It was a quiet afternoon, paced by the rhythm of traffic lights. He stood up and walked, thinking he might ask after her, if he happened to see her kind of store. He walked the length of town and as far as the railroad tracks. Ice cream, real estate, musical instruments. Porcelain figurines and teacups. He shook his head at his own dumbness, got back in the car, and sat.

He imagined doing the same thing in Fairfax, Manassas, Reston, Falls Church—all the sprawling towns where he and Peggy knew no one. Where she was driving around in a candy-apple-red '66 Fairlane. Why was he looking for her, when he could be looking for that car?

He drove to AAA in Richmond. He acquired maps of the state that showed every gas station. He needed a map because without zoning, businesses could crop up anywhere. Almost at random, you might see a barber pole or a green sign with yellow block script announcing the Department of Motor Vehicles. A one-and-a-half-lane highway would round a blind curve and there you were— already past it—the town you were looking for with its post office, gas pump, and population of four.

He returned to northern Virginia, where gas stations grew thick on the ground. But the second day of searching brought no sign of Peggy. Neither did the third.

From being mired in lottery-style thinking, Lee drifted toward magical thinking. He no longer demanded that divine providence reveal Peggy and Mireille in an instant. He was certain if he tortured himself long enough, quizzing gas station attendants on whether they'd seen a conspicuous car containing a woman and a little girl, his persistence would be rewarded. The car was black now, and the woman was routinely addressed as "sir" because she'd given herself an inept crew cut, but he didn't know that.

His task would have been easier if he'd ever granted her a credit card beyond the one for his father's Amoco station. It had his own name on it. He discovered it in his wallet, transferred there from hers. It was her way of telling him she had gone through his wallet and taken nothing. She didn't even have a bank account. Financially, she existed as a tax deduction. A deduction Lee would go on taking whether she lived with him or not. It was only fair. She was much more expensive after she left than before.

Stillwater Lake retreated far from the bamboo grove. It stood in yellowish-gray mud streaked with reddish brown that looked to Lee like diarrhea. The shore went out for forty yards and down six feet before the first puddles appeared. The standing water was almost white, writhing solid with mosquito larvae like maggots in a corpse.

The college could not be relied upon to fix the lake. What it had lost in aesthetics, it had gained in acreage. The lakeshore was the property line. The administration planned to build a spacious campus center on land that used to be underwater. Lee's parents told him to wait a couple of years for grass to grow and he wouldn't know the difference.

But the level kept dropping. The college hired a civil engineering bureau to produce a hydrogeological report.

Stillwater Lake, the engineers said, was unnatural, built using a method commonly used to create cattle watering holes in areas without streams. But on the much, much larger scale made possible by slave labor. The Great Pyramid of puddles, concocted from a limestone depression by a forgotten megalomaniac. The lake bed was thousands of tons of clay, dug from riverbanks farther east, plastering an enormous hole.

Occasionally the lake would burp. A bubble of methane would rise from some unseen cavity and a circular wave would race toward the gloppy shores. Lee had not seen it happen because he was unable to look directly at the lake. It pained his retinas. He expected it to heave and drain completely any day now.

He could identify the culprit. He would have known her anywhere, kneecapped her with a high-powered rifle at four hundred yards. He knew everything about her. Except where she was.

The next year, Karen was four years old going on five and still blond. Nonetheless, registering her for first grade as a black six-year-old was easy as pie.

Maybe you have to be from the South to get your head around blond black people. Virginia was settled before slavery began, and it was diverse. There were tawny black people with hazel eyes. Black people with auburn hair, skin like butter, and eyes of deep blue green. Blond, blue-eyed black people resembling a recent chairman of the NAACP. The only way to tell white from colored for purposes of segregation was the one-drop rule: if one of your ancestors was black—ever in the history of the world, all the way back to Noah's son Ham—so were you.

Meg felt very clever as she handed over the birth certificate. The races of the child's parents were marked right on it: colored and colored.

When the clerk saw on the slip of paper that that Mrs. Brown was colored, she glanced up in surprise. But a close look revealed that it was true. Meg's coarse curls and knobby heel bones were dead giveaways to the connoisseur. The daughter was one of those pallid, yellow-haired black kids you sometimes see. Frog-belly white, no trace of pink, curly tendrils all around her hairline. Probably anemic and undernourished—a lot of rural black kids had worms—but very close to passing. "Was she premature?" the clerk inquired. "She's so little."

"She's small, but she can read," Meg said.

"I can spell 'astronaut,'" Karen volunteered.

"That's a third-grade word," the clerk said. "You're very smart for such a tiny little thing. You sure you don't want to have her be white?"

"We're black and proud," Meg said.

"I'm blond," Karen objected.

"There's no blond race," the clerk corrected her. "But it don't matter. All God's children attend the very same school. We like to know who's black so we can help them out with affirmative action and a free hot lunch."

*

The first day of first grade did not go as Meg had hoped. In the early afternoon, Karen descended from the raucous and chaotic school bus sniveling. White girls, she said, had called her "nigger," while black girls had called her "half-white" and sung a song, "crybaby, crybaby."

"Crybaby what?" Meg asked ominously.

"Suck yo' mommy titty."

"Did you slug them? You've got to slug kids who are mean to you. Like this." Meg demonstrated. "You take and hold their shirt collar and punch them right in the nose."

"I grab their collar and punch them in the nose," Karen repeated solemnly.

"Never call them 'nigger' back. It's a bad word. Just grab on *tight* to their shirt and hit their nose *hard*. Then let go and run away *fast*. Never hit anybody bigger than you, or anybody retarded. Only first graders."

"Okay."

"And never cry, or say mean things. Insults just aggravate them. If you want to cry, laugh. It sounds the same. They can't tell the difference."

The next day Karen came home early, in her teacher's car. Her knees were skinned and she had a split lip. The teacher wanted to see where the ethereal yet scrappy representative of the sadly nonexistent blond race, whom she had freed from beneath a heap of children shrieking racist taunts, lived and with whom.

She was impressed with the simplicity and poverty of Meg's life. There was something monastic and almost elegant in the neatly scrubbed cabin standing in four inches of water in a settlement that had been given up decades before. Meg offered her a choice between water from the pump and warm Fresca. As she drank the Fresca, she wondered silently to herself about the Lord's mysterious ways, choosing an anemic black child with arms like twigs to demonstrate the ironies of nonviolent resistance. (She assumed Karen's tactic was nonviolence, possibly because Karen pulled her punches to the extent that mosquitoes she swatted flew away stunned.) She told Meg that Karen was very special. They prayed together.

When she had gone, Meg said, "You should stop telling people you're blond. There are a lot of mean jokes about blondes. It's nothing to be proud of."

Karen became the special concern of every adult at the school. Children instinctively hated her for being different, and adults identified with her for the exact same reason. To be perfect (adorably wee and blond) yet marked for failure (black and dressed in rags)—don't we all know that feeling? The principal, who had voted for George Wallace for president, couldn't watch her bounce away across the schoolyard without musing that a petite female with a white body and a black soul might in ten or twelve years' time be a sort of dream come true, assuming she moved away to the city and pursued a career in show business, broadly defined.

He spoke about her at a teachers' conference, and it was resolved that she would be groomed for export despite her handicap. It was decided to skip her over second grade, since she knew the names of the months and all nine planets. Skipping her would catch her up to the other smart black kid and save them from creating an extra independent study group later on. Her promotion would have the added virtue of raising black enrollment in the all-white "academic" track to two and acquitting the school of lingering charges of tokenism.

Karen's sole black classmate was a boy named Temple Moody. They sat together at lunch the day they met—the first day of third grade—and every school day after that.

To look at, Temple was about as black as a person could get, as though the school were hoping to pack as much blackness as possible into each "token black" seat in each of his successive integrated classrooms. Initially he was chosen for his mannerly comportment and tidy clothes and resented only for making it impossible for his class-mates to win at Eraser Walk. The eraser nestled in his hair like an egg in a nest. He could have hopped to the black-board on one foot. The class voted never to play Eraser Walk again. One by one, his superior achievements were acknowledged with surrender. He called it "raising the white flag."

By week five of third grade, Karen had forgotten what it was like to be bullied. Temple was not about to let competing children distract her.

It was soon a done deal among the children that they would marry. There was no question of a white boy's teasing her or kissing her. No girls of either race played with her hair.

Meg bought a packet of thirty Valentines, enough for the entire class. Karen labeled and distributed them all, but she brought home only three: one from the teacher, one from Temple, and one from a Catholic girl whose exotic last name—Schmidt—regularly made the class dissolve in laughter. Birthdays were a nonstarter, since Meg couldn't have kids over to that house. Plus the date and the year were false, so it seemed like tempting fate to make a big deal out of Karen's birthday. Christmas depressed Meg, and she did her best to ignore it. Amber "Shit" Schmidt was not a big party-thrower either.

So for several years in a row, the high point of Karen's year was Temple Moody's birthday. Possibly it more than made up for the Neapolitan ice cream and Pin the Tail on the Donkey she missed by not being white. Temple's birthday involved adults and older children—approximately fifty in all—along with hard liquor, catfish, chicken, trifle, and a piñata.

He lived in a sprawling compound on a creek bank, hundreds of years old, with a four-seater outhouse and a shed full of broken farm implements from before the trees grew. The woods leading to it were dense with greenbrier through which deer had beaten paths like a hedge maze. There was only one party game: Run Wild. The adults would settle in, on and around the porch, while the children ran wild. Eventually one of Temple's older brothers would throw a rope over a high oak bough and haul up the piñata.

The Moodys regarded piñatas as a neglected Native American tradition. They assumed partial descent from

Indians. Temple's mother had a fond uncle in Reno, Nevada, at the end of the Trail of Tears, and he mailed her authentic Indian crafts every year for Christmas: Navajo sand paintings, Pomo baskets, Hopi dolls. And for Temple's birthday, a piñata.

Temple's mother had grown up in Hampton and gone to junior college, but few other Moodys had been to school past eighth grade, and many not at all. The *Brown* decision in 1954 made a lot of school systems close their doors, and people like the Moodys lost out. Most were fundamentalist Christians, but inability to read kept them from getting pedantic about it. They deduced religious doctrine from the behavior of people more devout than themselves, and it made them a very tolerant and easy-going bunch of people. But with gaps in their knowledge of the world. Such as what lay at the ends of roads they had never driven. Where Reno might be. The look of an ocean. At the same time, they knew many things that were written down nowhere. For example, that they had lived on that creek bank continuously since the days when it was an Indian town.

Blindfolded and armed with a baseball bat, Temple would stand under the oak while an older brother raised and lowered the piñata and made it sway wildly. This spectacle moved everyone present to tears of laughter. The deliberate way Temple would duel his brother, faking and feinting, drawing his bat slowly through the air, mapping space, thrusting suddenly in unanticipated directions, trying to penetrate his enemy's mind. The certainty with which he would saber down some years' piñatas, having figured out his opponent's tactics. The hopeless struggles of years when even he ended up laughing.

Third grade was a year of grandstanding. He let his weapon fall and clapped his hands together over his head. He caught the burro's leg blind, as though he could hear the creaking of rope and the rushing of wind through crepe paper.

In fourth grade he failed to hit it at all, but did so with a dervish-like display of youthful joie de vivre. Karen was very impressed both times.

Meg spent the parties sitting at a redwood picnic table with other moms, doing what they all did: eat and offer color commentary on the children's mode of running wild that year. She spoke little and employed her broadest accent. Occasionally a mother would jump up and intervene if things got too colorful, or do some shouting at the edge of the clearing if a group of children vanished in the greenbrier for too long.

Since the mothers were not all related, the gossip was not intimate. Clans not present came up for criticism for allowing first cousins to date each other, or beloved elders to retire to the woods behind a supermarket. (It was accepted practice to let your husband camp out in summer near a source of sweet wine and steaks past their sell-by date, but you had to take him back in winter.) When it started to get dark and the bugs came out in force, Meg would take Karen home. Karen would be limp from playing, as though she had been scoured inside and out, an empty husk awash in soda pop and cake crumbs.

*

Karen lacked playmates. She lacked toys. Without a TV or playmates she was unlikely to figure out about toys. She wasn't a complainer. Meg saw that Karen was humble and a stranger to envy. Fads came and went without a peep from her. She felt no more entitled to an Atari than she would have to a Lamborghini. The gift of a Tootsie Roll made her quiver. She would nibble shavings off it like a mouse.

Meg was not overprotective, but she had doubts about Karen's going into the woods alone. Turkey season seemed especially risky. Karen moved as irregularly as a bird, and she was about the height of a turkey. "This is like Red Riding Hood's riding hood," Meg explained as she unwrapped a protective cap from the Army/Navy. The cap had a dense fake fur lining and ear flaps that tied under the chin with ribbons. Karen was under orders not to take it off for even a second. She was very blond, and you don't want to flash white in the land of the whitetail. Blue eyes, red lips: the colors of a gobbler in breeding plumage. You need that safety orange. Karen put on the hat after school every day and wandered lonely as a cloud.

The Advent when she was a seven-year-old fifth grader, she found a toy she wanted.

She had walked for an hour, on the banks of shallow ponds and under thick hanging vines, through all the fields she knew and beyond, and she came out in an unfamiliar clearing. A hayfield with a barn, and tied out in front of the barn, a Welsh pony. There was a dirt road leading to the barn, both sides mown back three yards.

The work of a busy and orderly farmer, but nobody around.

The pony looked at Karen. It was a roan in its winter coat. Its eyes were brown, with long white lashes, and it had little striped feet. She picked dandelion greens and arranged them in a pile on the grass. The pony stepped forward and ate.

To Karen's mind, its acceptance of that minor consideration placed it under a contractual obligation to her. It was the middle of December, but she couldn't imagine why a pony would be alone in the woods. To her it was plainly a lost pony, destined to be hers if she could tame it the way the boy did the Arabian in her favorite bedtime story, *The Black Stallion*. (Meg didn't have the book, but she remembered the highlights.) It was tied to a piece of rebar in the ground and had a bucket of water, and the rebar moved around every couple of days, while the bucket was regularly refilled. Presumably it spent its nights in the barn, where its feed was very likely stored. But Karen was pushing eight years old and raised on poetry, so nothing in the world was clearer to her than that whoever first sat astride that pony would become its partner and master.

Still, she was a little child, not an idiot, so she regarded its substantial weight advantage, hooves, and teeth as potential risks. She was drawn to it by forces so strong she had not dreamed they existed, and repelled by caution so strong it was insurmountable. Which added up to: She hovered near it every day for an hour, staring. Over the course of a week and a half, she approached and touched it twice on the ribs, avoiding the reach of its kick and bite. She ran terrified when it turned to look at her. On Christmas Eve, it was gone.

She asked Meg in despair why a pony would disappear. Where did it go? Could mountain lions or timber rattlers have gotten it?

"It was probably some little girl's Christmas present," Meg said.

Karen had written to Santa asking for a banana split. She could find no words to express how Meg's information made her feel. She trembled, aching with longing for something sweeter than sugar: money.

Four

Meg's financial situation was delicate. Her expenses were low. She had a thousand dollars of capital left in her emergency fund. If something worse than that came up, she'd cross that bridge when she got to it. She had no rent, no utility bills, and a daughter who could survive on a noodle a day. Karen ate dutifully, not with feeling. But sooner or later she was going to get her growth spurt and start liking food. And there was the little matter of clothing. The county had a thrift shop. Like thrift shops everywhere, it specialized in the leavings of the elderly dead. People always had acquaintances who needed children's things and seldom donated them. Well-off children wore late-model hand-me-downs, but to get in on the action, Meg would have had to join a church. And although she was prepared to accept that the world was adopting stodginess as a fashion trend— that girls were putting away their mules and feather earrings and donning prim sweater sets like Lee's mother—she could not face praising Jesus in song to put

Karen in Pendleton kilts. You have to respect your boundaries.

Still, they needed clothes. Even polo shirts are born and die, in delicate pastels that show every stain. She needed an income.

Waitressing was out of the question. Waitresses are high-profile public figures. It doesn't get any more visible than that. She might as well put her byline in the paper.

Cashier likewise, along with receptionist. Too public.

All jobs in the public eye: inadmissible.

As for invisible jobs, Meg pondered what they might be. Her mother, never a women's libber, had steered her away from vocational education toward more disinterested studies in the liberal arts. Meg had met several working women in her years with Lee. She suspected that provost and sculptor, like latter-day Brontë, were not roles she could aspire to right off the bat.

Even the discreet and anonymous position of housemaid was a hard racket to break into. You need references. Someone has to tell everybody how discreet and anonymous you are. It was a conundrum. Plus, she was known around the county as black. She suspected herself of presenting a fatal attraction qua negress. Light-skinned, slim, unattached. If the men didn't come to hate her, their wives would. The men would hate her for saying no, and their wives would never believe she hadn't said yes.

She realized with some regret she had joined a race with which she'd had just about no contact at all. She had seen black people every day of her life. She wasn't afraid of them. More like the reverse. But they might as well have been those Indonesian shadow puppets made of parchment. Her parents hadn't had the option of sending her to an integrated school. If you integrated your school back then, the Commonwealth would shut it down. And although Stillwater had started admitting black girls a few years before she left, none had applied for admission—at least not that anybody knew of. Of course an applicant could be black and not know it. Possibly Stillwater had been integrated from the start. That was the standard defense of whites-only institutions: We're not the DAR. We don't check pedigrees.

Once Meg even caught herself saying "nigger." Some kid had shown up at school in a rabbit fur coat (her father was an auto mechanic notorious for payday splurges). Karen admired the coat and had been allowed to pet it. Meg shook her head. She said, "Typical nigger—rich, buying your daughter a fur coat when you can't afford to take her to the dentist!—Oh, gosh, Karen, I didn't mean to say that. I'm really sorry. Here, hit me on the arm. Make a fist."

She went on to explain at length that she had merely meant the father was not good with numbers, and that this quality had once been called shiftlessness. Such a man works hard, but he never gets ahead, because whenever he gets some money, he puts a down payment on something he can't afford, and it is soon repossessed. This unfortunate custom had given rise to the concept, etc.

"I think a fur coat is rich," Karen objected.

"Rabbit is not rich, and fur is tacky anywhere south of Vermont. Rabbit is poor tacky. Rich tacky would be fox.

A girl your age could wear dyed sheared beaver, maybe, if she lived on the shores of Lake Baikal."

Karen frowned.

Meg felt more strongly than usual that many thoughts life had taught her to articulate were not her own, while many of her thoughts went unexpressed for lack of a suitable audience.

For this and other reasons, she concluded that although she desperately needed someone to talk to, she also needed a career where you work alone and don't get roped into chatting with people on any subject whatsoever.

She looked glumly at the typewriter and poured herself a drink.

Her writing was going well enough. She told herself she was honing her craft and would soon be making money. But it was like honing a primitive stone tool, not a forged blade. Life with Lee had taught her to be laconic. She could quip. So her plays all ended on page two.

Typically they were murder mysteries with no mystery. A woman sneaks across the stage and plunges a knife into the neck of a sleeping man. He says a few choice last words and dies. She expresses her ambivalence as the police come to haul her away.

Meg's first paycheck materialized as she drove to the grocery store early one morning. She saw a cardboard box on the shoulder. She stopped, because a box like that nearly always contains kittens. Not worth money, but tell that to Karen. Karen worshipped kittens as gods.

Except this box was full of pornographic magazines from England. Dry, clean, and in excellent condition. What mysterious denizen of the county had felt called upon to make an obviously cherished collection vanish anonymously? Frightened of being observed at the wayside Dumpsters, hitting the brakes for a second or two to unload years of costly, intimate personal history ... or had his wife done it? The girls were chunky, posing in what appeared to be their own backyards, private parts concealed by fluffy fur and sometimes adorned with ribbons. They were lavish, glossy mags on heavy paper. No amateurs, no swingers, no contact information, just girls next door, apparently the first to return after the neutron bomb was dropped on Folkestone, because how else could they romp naked in middle-class gardens with low hedges and sea views?

Meg felt on some level it was the strangest thing she had ever seen: innocent porn. No wonder it had to go. A wife who discovered it could no longer feel superior to the whores in her husband's freak books. She would see that in England, for reasons unknown, a woman can simultaneously be cute as a bug's ear, a serious rose gardener, and a nymphomaniac. The false dichotomies promulgated by Tammy Wynette et al. would vanish like morning fog, leaving her alone with her self-doubt.

Or were they the possessions of an old man, trying to manipulate how he would be remembered? His heirs, trying the same thing? Was he rich, poor, addicted to *Masterpiece Theatre*, raised in the Church of England, in love with flowers, an Englishman?

There was no way of knowing. The cover price was high, suggesting a wealthy man, but pornography is a classic payday splurge for the shiftless.

The magazines didn't turn her on. One woman standing over another with a whip, absentmindedly fingering its thick, braided handle: that image, seen for a fraction of a second while leafing through a coffee-table book in the Lambda Rising Bookstore in Georgetown before she fled blushing, was burned into her memory, and she seldom had an orgasm in which it was not implicated. These girls, with their apple cheeks and dahlias, were by contrast disquietingly perverse. But they had to be worth money to someone.

She weighed her options. The county did in fact have a junk shop. It lay in the crook of an unfinished half-moon road, just off the new four-lane highway. She got twenty dollars for thirty-eight magazines, but the shop owner leered in such a way that it was clear to her she would never again sell pornography to a filthy-minded good old boy. Since that demographic sort of dominates most aspects of the pornography market, her days in the second-hand sex industry were over almost before they began.

But the scavenging bug had bitten her. Her next find was a dead raccoon. She took it straight to the bait shop and sold it to the bearded white guy behind the counter for six dollars. He said in good repair they could go as high as ten.

Roadkill in good repair: not an easy assignment, even at first light. She started swinging by the county dump several times a week.

Like Dante's *Inferno*, the dump had circles. The outer circle was where people unloaded discrete and possibly salvageable objects such as planks and furniture. In the next circle, plastic sacks hit the ground and were pushed into piles with a front loader, and somewhere back of that were the looming brown mountains of decay and the overweight turkey buzzards that couldn't fly.

It was to these mountains that items were taken directly when no one was supposed to know they were in the dump, for instance human bits and parts from funeral homes. It was also said that a certain white man who had treated people badly had driven his pickup deep into the dump to unload construction trash, and while he was still in his cab a black man at the controls of a lordly Caterpillar had unceremoniously covered him with dirt and shoved his truck, still running, into the mountains of the dump, burying him alive. Whether he was crushed or asphyxiated or fell unconscious from the fumes or rotted from the inside out due to the radioactivity of his load depended on whom you asked. The truck had never been found, nor looked for, because people were scared of the radiation.

Or so the story went. There was no question of his having vanished in the usual way. He would never run out on his family like that.

Meg first heard the story on her return visit to the junk shop with a chair from the first circle of the dump. The shop owner said he leaned toward the carbon monoxide theory as being more "mercified." Meg said she didn't believe anything about it, because the police would surely investigate the death of a white man and arrest eight or ten black people just to get started.

"Not if the sheriff wants reelection they don't," the shop owner said. "This is the New South. Niggers have impunity." Nodding sagely, he drained the day's eleventh can of Georgia Iced Tea (Busch).

Trash picking did not bring Meg much money. But enough for peanut butter and store-brand Cheerios with a brittle crunch like powdered glass, plus Karen's favorite nondessert food in the world, BLT. Mayonnaise is an irresponsible splurge when you don't have a fridge, but there are small sizes available, especially in places where people live hand to mouth and "large economy size" is regarded as a long-term investment that would tie up needed capital. The bait shop sold mayonnaise in jars barely bigger than a film canister. Polishing off a package of bacon at one sitting was no problem for Karen.

"If you are what you eat, I'm bacon," she announced blissfully one day. Meg imagined her mother hearing this, and felt grateful they were not in touch.

Someone driving by saw a man get out of a van in front of Meg's house and mentioned it at Mrs. Sutton's Restaurant. Soon it was common knowledge that she had a white boyfriend.

White in Virginia in those days was a fairly narrow category. It didn't include anyone with dark hair, such as ... such as ... such as people with dark hair, who on good days were called "Spanish." But it made room for the red

cheeks, green eyes, and thinning rat-tail braid of Lomax
Hunter, a Mattaponi Indian.

They met not long after Meg started collecting night
crawlers. Leaving Karen asleep on the backseat of the
car, she would wander around with a miner's headlamp,
staring at the ground. There weren't many places with
good lawns, just a few churches and cemeteries, but
when it worked it was a license to print money. A dozen
night crawlers was worth fifty cents at the bait shop,
and on a dark night after a rain you could pick up a
dozen in three minutes, which makes ten dollars an
hour. You have to be sneaky, because other people will
horn in on your night crawler grounds. Meg was not up
for turf battles, especially not nocturnal single combat
with strange men. When she scented competition, she
drove away. Gradually Karen was getting too old to pass
out automatically if you laid her down, and too big to
hide under a towel. Big enough to be conspicuous, so
you wouldn't want to leave her alone unconscious in
the places frequented by the drifters who gather night
crawlers. So that ultimately night crawlers were a
glorious, lucrative interlude, nothing more—the first
of many fitful, sporadic, hand-to-mouth seasons of
wealth, adequate to cement in Karen's mind an indes-
tructible association between worms and Pepperidge
Farm cakes.

Put off by the competition for worms, Meg thought it
over and decided to hunt for ginseng instead. Ginseng
grows in the woods in daylight, where a child can help
you look for it. Even sassafras will bring in money, they

say. There's all kinds of valuable stuff growing in the woods.

The bearded man who ran the bait shop said he would miss her gentle touch with the worms, as many of his suppliers grasped the worms too tightly and injured them. He put Meg in touch with a hippie who dealt in herbal medicines.

As it turned out, this hippie was not in the ginseng and sassafras business. But he said he could give her fifty cents per psilocybin mushroom.

"We got more cow patties than lawns," Meg said. "Fifty cents a shroom beats four cents a worm any day of the week."

"You got that right," Lomax replied. "Drugs is where the money's at."

Lomax was a middle-class Indian. Rather than on the Mattaponi reservation, he grew up in a tract house in Spotsylvania County. Both his college-educated parents had office jobs pushing paper in the highway department. A social outcast at work, Lomax's father had become an avid chipmunk watcher. The house's large, flat backyard was the scene of unceasing warfare among the solitary ground squirrels, except in mating season, when they pursued momentary alliances that provided for nonstop action and inaction. He had founded a chipmunk conservation group and authored its bylaws.

Stoned, even at age ten, Lomax found the chipmunks easier to take. His mother sympathized. Of her three children, Lomax was her favorite. He never caused her any trouble. No sports, no extracurricular activities, always willing to talk to her husband about his hobby.

Lomax's home life taught him to value harmony, but school told him that Indians were wild, nonconformist rebels. The Chanco story in fourth-grade Virginia history laid the groundwork, and *Billy Jack* and Wounded Knee put the icing on the cake. He dropped out and bought a Dodge van with his drug-dealing proceeds, informing his parents he was heading west to join the Ghost Dance. He got as far as Bristol, Tennessee. At seventeen he declared his financial emancipation and moved into the van in the yard with the chipmunks. He applied for SSDI (Social Security Disability Income) with a letter from a psychologist at a National Guard recruiting center.

At twenty-one, certified unemployable, Lomax could pass for a middle-aged man. He was starting to lose hair up top, and his pot belly put a strain on his shirts. His meetings with Meg always started with the same ritual greeting: "Yo, Chief!" To which he replied, "What up, Poodlehead?" She would send Karen outside to play and spread her haul of psychedelics on the table. He would sort the mushrooms into fat and soft (fifty cents apiece) and scraggly and moldy (fifty cents a dozen, a folk aphrodisiac for livestock). She would pour him a glass of Seagram's gin and they would talk.

Lomax was a talented raconteur. At their first business meeting he described visiting the Mattaponi reservation with the Order of the Arrow and what a drag that was— the chief dressed up like a Sioux in a hawk-feather wig and moose-hide bedroom slippers—until he talked a boy into eating jimson berries. The kid went out-of-body and couldn't find the piss button. They ended up at the hospital getting him catheterized. The twists and turns in Lomax's story made Meg laugh. By their sixth meeting he regarded her as an intimate friend. He made her listen to his heart, which was beating about a hundred times a minute.

"And I'm just sitting here!" he said proudly.

"And you get SSDI for being insane? Man, if my heart was fucked up, that's what I would get disability for."

"No, man, that's stupid. Because if your body's fucked up you can still work, like keypunch or a switchboard operator. But if your mind is wasted, you're certified unemployable. They won't even draft your ass."

Meg said that she had never applied for public assistance in any form, not even the free school lunch, and Lomax nodded.

"I can appreciate that. In my line of work, you like people minding their own business. One girl, she pulled a disappearing act last year, I had to hand it to her. I went down to see her and her place was trashed. Floorboards pried up. Electric sockets hanging out the wall. But I know she's all right, because she had two Chesapeake Bay retrievers. The one of them had a head on it like a bear. It could bite through your tires. The other one was the most nervous animal I ever saw. They was both laying dead in the mudroom. She could *only* have shot them herself."

"Wait a second." Meg looked at him questioningly. "She shoot her own dogs?"

"Nobody else could get close enough to those dogs to shoot them," he assured her. "She couldn't take them down to Dominica. There's a quarantine."

"She's in Dominica?"

"I don't know! She might be in Cuba or Antigua." He shrugged. "No human soul ever put the time she did into dog food. Every day she made them a pot of stew. If she had to go, it was a mercy she killed them. Sometimes you have to think about the best interests of the animal."

After Lomax drove away, Meg considered his remarks on the dogs and decided an alarm system might be in order, as well as a way of storing cash and drugs that didn't involve the bed where she slept.

She took Karen down to the shelter and let her pick. And thus it was that they acquired a six-year-old spayed cockapoo bitch named Cha Cha and eventually several sets of nesting Tupperware suitable for burial in the yard.

It was their eighth meeting before Meg knew there was a girl sitting outside in Lomax's van the entire time, and only because Karen brought it up. Karen asked whether the girl in the van could come out to play, and he promptly responded, "She's a little old for that. She's my girlfriend."

Karen objected. "I'm not old, and I have a boyfriend!"

"What's his name?"

"Temple Moody."

Lomax looked at Meg with one eyebrow raised. "He Canadian?"

"He's black like us," Karen said.

"Y'all *black?*"

"So black it'll blow your mind," Meg said. "Blackhearted as coal. Versed in the black arts."

"So you're a witch, and your boyfriend is a warlock?"

Karen snickered. "Yeah. We got a real voodoo doll made of wax and hair. That's how Temple could hypnotize ants to join his ant farm."

"Well, I'll be doggoned," Lomax said. "You're joking, right?"

Meg managed to keep a straight face, and Lomax suddenly felt insecure. He suspected that as an Indian he was supposed to know something about magic and spirits, but his grasp of the world was congruent with the grasp of his two hands. Now at least he had an explanation for Meg's interest in herbal medicines.

He went back to the van and told his intermittently dozing girlfriend about it as he drove her home to their trailer 120 miles away in the woods near Danville.

"I wish I were a witch, but I'm the wrong generation," Flea (short for Felicia) said. "Witches are born every seventh generation, and my grandmother was already a witch."

"You're saying Poodlehead and her daughter can't both be witches. But if her boyfriend was a sixth-generation warlock?"

Flea paused to think and said, "You're so smart."

"We could both be witches and not know it. Hell, I don't know what my ancestors were doing seven generations ago."

"Can you cast a magic spell?"

He sucked on the roach clip smoldering in the ashtray, cleared his throat, and sang, "Hey-a ho-yah ho-yah, hey-a ho-yah ho-yah, ohm anautcha sheila, ohm anautcha rama."

"Isn't it Shiva, not Sheila?" Flea asked.

Flea was a dropout, like Meg, with intellectual ambitions that outstripped her resources. But on a smaller scale. Like Lee, she was a sexual outlaw who had left home young. But not to go to boarding school. She had ditched sixth grade to move in with Lomax.

It was no fault of his. She had long legs. Her girlfriends were older, and she pitched her voice low. She wore makeup and tight pants and styled her hair. In a dry county, there are no bartenders to turn away jailbait for a man's protection. There was only a low stone retaining wall by a river, where everybody went to party. When they met, it was dark. The morning after, he got a surprise.

He saw himself as her protector. As long as she was with him, she wasn't hanging out at the wall, waiting for whomever. He could make an honest woman of her. He proposed marriage.

Her father said Lomax was a rat. Flea puffed on a cigarette and said he was just jealous. Her parents drank. She could repeat many things that made her seem worldly and mature. There was no privacy in her childhood home. Every conflict was open for all to see, so she knew love was wrapping paper and a battle for supremacy. Her clique of eighth graders taught her feminist pride, as they understood it: it meant knowing how to wait for a better offer. Lomax brought order and stability to her life and allowed her to be a child again. With every day she spent riding around in his van, she became more innocent and ladylike. She never had to beg or flirt. She just asked for what she wanted—a Darvon, say, or Mountain Dew and pork rinds—and he would figure out a fast way to get it. No effort was needed to catch his eye. He was always watching her, more often than he looked in the rearview mirror.

Sometimes he needed her to do difficult things, but here her experiences compared favorably to those of her friends who were thirteen and unattached and still going to the wall. Among her friends his social status was in a class by itself. They called him "the Candy Man" and envied her openly.

Even after she turned twelve, her father refused to consent to her preengagement, so they could not be married. Still she lived as an adult, her lover's all-round helpmeet. She was older than Byrdie by about six weeks. To look at, she was a leggy, wispy, lovely girl. But almost nobody ever saw her. She was under orders to stay in the van, where she killed time listening to the radio.

Sometimes watching Karen fall asleep at night, Meg suspected her of weaving romantic fairy tales to herself about her father and brother. She might well remember them, or the lake, or her paternal grandparents' house at Christmas. Every time one of Meg's stories featured a lost royal child, fairy changeling, or disenfranchised heiress (she especially liked retailing what she remembered of *Mistress Masham's Repose*), she watched Karen's face closely. There was no glimmer of recognition. But during ugly-duckling-style stories—the kind where someone underappreciated turns out to be a princess, if only by marriage after the story is basically over—Karen would sit up straighter and appear dissatisfied, setting her mouth in a horizontal line. Confronted for the first time with Cinderella, she protested her working conditions and said the midnight rule was unfair.

It disheartened Meg to think that Karen might regard her minimal roster of chores and homework as equivalent to the labors of Cinderella. In reality, it was much stranger than that. The mind of a child! Children have no hearts (cf. *Peter Pan*, another story Meg could reproduce fairly accurately), and their minds are rickety towers of surreal detritus. Of course Karen remembered Lee and Byrdie. Once there was a house, a boat; once there was a big, mean boy. There were men, wading pools in sunlight, termites, stamp hinges, and coffee-table books of illustrations by Maxfield Parrish. There was a push-button gear shift, high up on a dashboard. There were little white buttons on Lee's pink shirt where she lay in a haze of Pernod fumes while he slept it off. It was all there. But as memories. Not photographs. Not stories. There were no anecdotes, no mentions of "your brother." She had no way of connecting the dots.

Her memories were far less vivid than her dreams. Once in a dream she met her father. He lived in a red-and-gold castle on a miniature golf course. He was the monarch King Vitaman. It would have shocked Meg to know how seldom Karen thought about him. Deep down, she didn't think she needed a father. Maybe at one time she had one, past tense. But she didn't have one, present tense, and that was plain as day.

The virgin birth had suggested manifold alternatives to her. Karen received no religious instruction from Meg, but as an outcast she spoke frequently with Amber Schmidt. Schmidt told her about the Blessed Virgin Mary and said it could happen to anybody. As a girl you could never be the Second Coming, but you might be His mother.

Garbage in being garbage out, Karen had a vivid nightmare. God came to her in the form of a leatherback sea turtle like one she had seen at a beach house in Duck, North Carolina, when some poets put it in Lee's bathtub. God's penis looked like elbow macaroni. She ran across the room to her mother's bed and yowled, "Mom!" Meg seemed nonplussed, so she improvised: "I had a bad dream mean boys were chasing me on bikes!"

"Come here, darling baby," Meg said gently. She pulled Karen under the blanket. She stroked her sweaty face and tangled hair and said, "Sleep, my love. I will never let anybody hurt you." Holding her child in her arms, clueless Meg pondered the opportunity costs of childhood in a world without sidewalks. Having grown up at a school with athletic facilities, she knew how to swim, hit a tennis ball, ride a bicycle, and even— unusual for a rural Virginian—roller-skate. Her poor daughter, always having to choose between the road and the woods.

And the black box in her arms whimpered itself to sleep with longing to be a normal person who is chosen, not a special person who is discovered. To be the kind of duck who gets included by wild swans because she's unobtrusive.

Possibly she felt special enough already as a blond black midget and did not wish additional attention. A recent visit to Schmidt's house had gone poorly. She had ridden the pariah's all-white school bus to a little subdivision of mobile homes in a wheat field. They barely had time to put on a record and open up *Tiger Beat* when Schmidt's father entered with a razor strop to whip his daughter for letting a nigger in the house. When Meg picked Karen up, they were playing two-square in the road. Every car that passed had to slow down, and if the driver was a man under about twenty-four, Schmidt would make eye contact and hold her hair up off her neck. Karen was glad to leave, but she got a scolding from Meg for playing in traffic.

Lee applied himself to being a caring father by acquainting Byrdie with the finer things in life. His grandfather had a hunt near Berryville and often invited him to take part. There Lee rode a fit yet docile stallion named Idle Vice (a pun on "edelweiss"). This was, to Lee, an animal in whom no feeling person could help but take delight. Lee set Byrdie on him at the first opportunity, expecting euphoria.

Byrdie said the horse was stupid. He said the dogs were slobbery and too numerous. Fuchsia coats with cordovan boots embarrassed him. The bloody stump of the fox's tail made him sick. He refused riding lessons. He would not go cubbing. He would not go hilltopping. He would not go basseting, or even aim his .22 at a squirrel. He spent hunt days reading a book under a tree. Horses in Byrdie's mind were free to bound over obstacles, on their backs effeminate slaves to equine virility or aging little girls, but only at races where a person might bet on them.

Lee and Cary took him to a steeplechase near Warrenton. They tailgated at the finish line and waited. The day was mostly halftime shows of various kinds. Lee waxed enthusiastic about a fellow who rode an Arabian in flowing multicolored robes. He invoked Pegasus and Helicon. Cary mentioned Lawrence of Arabia.

The show rider appeared to Byrdie much like a belly dancer on a goat. He walked purposefully to the concession stand and ordered three beers. He figured if you order one beer they might think it was for you, but if you order three, they think your dad sent you so he wouldn't have to interrupt an important conversation. He sat down behind a horse trailer with his three flimsy Solo cups and sipped, struggling at first against the awful taste. Soon the tide turned. He chugged the rest and began staggering around feeling better than he'd ever felt in his short life.

He leaned against a paddock fence and stared at horses resting. Lee came up behind him and said, "I see you found the Peloponnesians."

It was an excruciatingly bad pun on "polo ponies." A demonstration game of polo was scheduled for later on, and sure enough, grooms in magenta and cyan began to come out and wrap the horses' legs and ask them to step into little rubber bell-bottoms. Byrdie turned away in disgust and lisped—being drunk and not entirely in control of his tongue—"Horses are for Bruces."

"Hortheth are for Brutheth" was very quotable, in Lee's opinion. He and Cary quoted it at every opportunity. It took on a life of its own and was heard at parties all across the state. Every time anybody said it, it was a maul driven into the space between Lee and his son, who soon expressed strong interests in other sports. Lee said he personally didn't see how letting a horse run away with you over fences was any less cool than regattas, Pebble Beach, or downhill skiing with helicopters. The festive colors and the drunkenness were the same, and hunting was more dangerous and expensive. Byrdie had nowhere to run but school. He had read enough Billy Bunter books and *Stalky & Co.* to live for the day when he could go away and be with real boys.

Lee's finances did not admit of boarding school. But his parents loved Byrdie and so did Meg's. There was general agreement that he couldn't go to the local day school, where the lacrosse coach taught math and physics as sidelines and the girls would be coached by their mothers to seduce him.

The first day of ninth grade, Lee drove Byrdie and his things to school in Orange. The campus was the way Lee remembered it—the back road in over the Rapidan, the main building perched on the bluff, the nine-hole golf course. Other things had changed. Byrdie had a black roommate, a stolid middle-class kid from northern Virginia who had no accent of any kind, as though he had been worked over by Professor Higgins. His other room-mate was the son of a fashion photographer and an iconic model. The upwardly mobile kid was obviously going to be a bore, but the neglected child of artists seemed promising. His mother helped carry in his meager belong-ings and hung around the door to the triple room sneak-ing a cigarette, reaching down to tousle her son's hair and flirting with Lee as though her life depended on it. Lee would have been happy to tousle the kid's hair himself, but he stopped himself and said, "Byrdie. Let's take a walk."

Byrdie flipped his suitcase shut and shoved it under the bed. Knowing he had landed in a triple, he had insisted on coming early to avoid the bunks. He was almost done unpacking before the black kid (bottom bunk) even showed up.

They walked over the lawn toward the chapel. "You got any tips for me? Last-minute advice?" Byrdie asked.

"Seek and ye shall find. Knock and the door shall open. That means don't be afraid to say what you want."

"I want to talk to Mom."

Lee was silent for a moment and said, "She knows I was planning to send you here. Maybe she'll come see you. You'll let me know if she does."

"Is she really okay by herself?"

Lee looked down at Byrdie, wondering whether Mireille was a taboo topic. He decided she was. "Your mother is fine. She's hard as nails."

"I'm afraid she'll come by and embarrass me."

"Here," Lee said with a sense of relief. He took out his black book, a tiny leather binder, and wrote neatly, "Can't talk now. Send letter." He tore the page out and gave it to Byrdie. "Carry this in your pocket, and if she shows up out of the blue, just give it to her."

Byrdie put it in the inside pocket of his blazer and said, "I thought you knew where she was. I thought you were waiting for me to be old enough, and maybe today's the day you were going to tell me."

"Oh, Byrdie," Lee said, shaking his head. "I wouldn't hide that from you. I wish I had something left to hide."

"Remember Antietam?"

"Sure," Lee said hesitantly. "A lot of good men died—"

"No, I mean when I drove the car." Byrdie had been allowed to guide Cary's Maserati through the narrow right-angle curves of the battlefield memorial during an otherwise forgettable excursion to the Inn at Little Washington because it had an automatic transmission. "That was the best day of my life. What I mean is, I know you're weird and everything, but the real problem is you don't care about normal stuff and you don't have any money. Dad, I'm in school now. I need decent golf clubs."

Lee sighed. "Byrdie, you're not thinking straight. Who do you know who has decent golf clubs?"

"Grandpa."

"So tell me, is he going to invest in duplicates of things he already owns?"

"No."

"But would he buy himself something better and give you his castoffs?" Lee shifted to the Tidewater-plantation-owner accent, a lilting drawl carefully cultivated in certain circles and said to be unaltered in its abject Anglophilia since 1609: "Grandfather, I was wondering, have you seen those new golf clubs, made of rare Siamese elephant parts? Coach claims they're unsportsmanlike, for the other teams, if we're the ones to have them."

Byrdie interrupted, "Yeah, yeah, I get it. But it's not going to work. It's not like he ever gave you anything!"

"I want stuff he's only giving away over his dead body. I'm Sherman and the Grand Army, and you're the little match girl. Golf clubs, what a fucking joke." Byrdie laughed, not sure why. Lee stooped down and enfolded him in his arms. "Byrdie, I love you desperately. I want you to have more than I have. Meaning more than the shit nobody else wants."

"I love you, too. But don't touch me. There's people watching."

Meg all but knew for sure that Byrdie was at Woodberry. She thought of driving there to see him, then imagined the look on his face. Would he be happy to see her? Probably not. More likely enraged. Or just distant. It had been a long time, especially for a kid.

She drafted long letters and tore them up. You don't burden a teenage boy with your guilt. Especially not when you really are at fault. She had abandoned him. He had been nine—long past the cuddly stage—but it was entirely possible that he missed her. Maybe he cried for her at night when he was sad. She suspected he was much too cool for that, and that Lee would be giving her bad press.

The same ambivalence about consequences kept her from coming clean to Karen. Hiding Karen from her father: It might not solve any problems she currently had. But once upon a time it had solved a problem, and now it prevailed by force of habit.

Hiding Lee from his daughter was different. It solved a future problem: the problem she would have if she stopped hiding him. Karen was not going to be happy. She might be happy to hear that her father was alive and well. But she would not be happy with Meg.

Here a person might ask: Was Meg self-centered or what?

Meg was self-centered.

Early life spent fighting for chances to be herself, planning the cockeyed social suicide of manhood in the army; weeks of unrequited lesbianism; willing submission to a teacher who ran circles around her socially, intellectually, emotionally; marriage to him. For comic relief, visiting poets and two introverted kids. Would any sane person expect a life like that to result in a warm, affectionate personality? Meg was a shallow smartass brimming with fierce, self-sacrificing maternal feelings, saddled with a passion to be loved that no one had seen but Lee. She knew she was ridiculous. That's why she expressed her love for Karen through irony.

And that irony of ironies, her lifelong poverty. From the poverty of a rich kid with an allowance designed to teach the virtue of thrift, to the poverty of a poet's wife feeding houseguests on a budget, to genuine poverty, to faking poverty for the DEA. Too late she noticed that bringing Karen up poor wasn't ironic. It was poverty.

Once you've lied to your child for years, it gets hard to find reasons to tell the truth. Karen's reaction to the truth would be to throw herself into Lee's arms. When he found out Meg had raised Karen black, he was likely to revisit his plan of commending her to psychiatric care.

Because people never grow accustomed to lies. They either believe them or they don't. And a big lie is never forgiven. The person who told the lie stops existing, and in his place stands a paradox: the truthful liar. The person you know for sure would lie to you, because he's done it before and confessed. You never, ever believe that person again.

The lie Meg repeated to Karen every single day was a very big lie.

Little children don't remember the past, and they believe anything you tell them. So Karen didn't know she had been done to. But Byrdie hadn't been so little when Meg left. He had been nine. Old enough to have a worldview and draw his own conclusions.

Meg was fenced in: On the one side, her lies to Karen. On the other, her crime against Byrdie.

There was only one way she could hope to be loved by any child, ever: carry on. Byrdie would never trust her. But Karen might, if she was kept from the truth.

Meg's feelings for Byrdie were fierce and self-sacrificing. Feeling that he was at Woodberry made her unbearably nervous. September 1980 was a month spent on edge.

The fierce desire to see him, the self-sacrificing willingness to avoid disrupting his life. In October she capitulated and did what any normal mother would have done: She bought a watch cap and sunglasses and stalked him on a weekday afternoon.

And she found him. He was alone on the tennis courts, practicing a two-handed backhand against a ball machine.

She sat down inside a boxwood shrubbery—it was old, with a capacious interior—to watch. Feeling the smooth curvature of something artificial under her ass, she noticed that this particular hedge was a repository of many empty liquor bottles. It was dark in the shade of the bushes with sunglasses on. She stroked the dirt to check for broken glass and sat down again. She watched Byrdie practice.

He stopped, startling her. But he didn't leave the court, or even look her way. He gathered the balls in a basket and dumped them back in the machine.

He was only fourteen, but almost as tall as Lee. He looked a lot like Lee, but with Meg's suntan and brown hair. He could not have looked any healthier. He didn't look happy, exactly, but he was working on nailing a two-handed backhand.

Meg felt her heart constrict. There was so much she wanted to say to him. Things any normal mother would say, like that a one-handed backhand is more versatile. She was flooded by overwhelming emotions, which she immediately repressed, and the upshot was small, narrow emotions, tightly squeezed.

She realized she had better get out of there before anybody saw her. She wasn't crying, but her movements were awkward, like a blind baby kitten pawing at nothing. She backed out of the bush crab-style, clinking bottles as she went, right into a groundskeeper with a rake. "Hey, you," he said.

She panicked and ran. Like the wind, like a thief caught in the act, like the prowler the groundskeeper said she was when Byrdie came up the hill to look at the bottles.

With Byrdie away at school, Lee's parents gave him money to hire a detective again. Their main motive was concern for Byrdie's peace of mind. They wanted to find Peggy before she had a chance to reenter his happy life and turn everything upside down.

The detective went to see the Vaillaincourts and poked around thoughtfully. He toured the school, trying to get a general sense of what resources Peggy had to fall back on. He walked through the churchyard and saw Karen Brown's grave. With very little legwork indeed, he found the registrar who remembered Peggy's acquiring a birth certificate for a dead black child.

He told Lee he had good news and bad news. The good news: His wife definitely had balls, and his daughter might be enrolled in school under the name Karen Brown. The bad news: Being named Brown in America is like being named Lee in China. Finding them was going to be expensive and time-consuming.

He asked how Lee wanted him to proceed, repeating that they might both be passing as black.

"Peggy's not that stupid," Lee said. "White, she's a dime a dozen. A black lady who looks like her would be the talk of the town. More likely it's the other way around. They're up north somewhere, passing for white. Peggy always wanted to move up to New York."

The detective said, "I'm going to be honest with you. I don't think I have a chance in hell of finding them, and I don't want to spend any money you don't have."

The detective went to the powder room. Lee retreated to the back porch to consider his alternatives.

They were unappetizing. His daughter was not legally his property. There's no sole custody without a divorce, and divorce was not an option. He would have had to settle something on Peggy, possibly even pay her alimony. You can keep a wife on a very short leash. Divorce is like handing it over to her as a whip.

He could use Byrdie as bait. Publish an appeal by the lonely boy desperate to see his mother. Say Byrdie was gravely ill. Run a newspaper ad offering a generous reward for any and all information leading to a dour lesbian with a blond limpet of a daughter. Hire a bounty hunter.

But Mireille might be growing up black in Farmville, or as an ethnic Pole in Baltimore. The shock of seeing her again might do him in.

It occurred to him that if he let it be known he was in the market for a wife, he could get a compliant young cook and housekeeper within weeks and a replacement child by this time next year.

On his own back porch he was always the same. Self-stalemated, dangling in the wind, exhausted. Besieged by emotions, none stronger than the self-respect he gained by doing nothing. It was a good reason to get up and offer his guest another drink.

They agreed that it was hopeless, but the detective promised to keep an eye out for her anyway. He performed a farewell service for the Fleming clan: He had a forensic artist create an updated image of the missing child. This was an expert with training in physical and cultural anthropology who worked scientifically. He knew that the lissome Mireille, entrusted to a mother like Peggy, would turn into a freckled, husky tank. Her hair would darken to a shade between dishwater and mousy.

Even Meg couldn't have seen Karen in it. And the description gave her race as white. So even if it had been a good likeness, people who knew her would have said, "Funny how that missing white girl Karen Brown almost looks like our Karen Brown!" But almost no one saw it. Snatched children on milk cartons were still years away.

Eventually it appeared in a pamphlet aimed at school administrators and teachers. Distribution was hit or miss, and it missed.

If Lee had known how Mickey was living, how would he have reacted? If he had known his daughter had but one toy, a rabbit-skin mouse Lomax bought her at Horne's?

She carried it in her hand. She would balance it on a fallen log and lie down to squint at it with one eye closed so that it loomed like a buffalo. Her spiritual kinship with Lee would have been obvious to any impartial observer, were there such a thing as an impartial observer. What is a poem, if not a toy mouse viewed from an angle that makes it appear to take over the world?

Lee was not that observer. His thoughts on his back porch surrounded him like a carpet of mice, immobilizing him via his unwillingness to cause them pain. The mice of introspection were as effective as any buffalo herd. He was strong, and the energy that kept him motionless was his own. Expending it on self-defeat exhausted him every day.

Five

At school *Byrd Fleming was accounted slightly weird but* popular, neatly straddling two pigeonholes without fitting in either. He could hang around with rich kids, slinging derogatory remarks about the middle classes with blasé aplomb, without being regarded as a wannabe. When it came to food, beverages, and drugs, he was unsurpassed, awing even the teachers with his disdain for clove cigarettes and Tokay. All the boys copied his way of making gin and tonics. The rich kids liked him because he never claimed to have done anything he hadn't done. Deep powder skiing: Sounds cool. Twelve-meter yacht: Sounds cool. Orgy in a model apartment: Sounds cool. In exchange he offered them solidly grounded, reliable secondhand knowledge of nightclubs, high culture, and sex for hire.

He finagled a single room his junior year and stayed in it senior year, because it was on the ground floor and he could get in and out without using the door. In warm weather he could often be seen and heard sitting in the window, picking out Jerry Garcia guitar solos on a Gibson Hummingbird somebody left at his dad's house. He dressed perfectly in boat mocs, oversized khakis, threadbare button-downs, and a navy blazer with OMNIA PRO DEO on the breast pocket. He shrugged when people asked what school. Said somebody left it at his dad's house. His black cashmere overcoat soft as chambray: Don't know, some faggot forgot it at my dad's house. Fleming's dad's house was widely regarded as something akin to the Xanadu where Kubla Khan decreed his stately pleasure dome.

And compared with the other kids' homes, it was. But no one had seen it. Lee and Byrdie had had a minor disagreement after Lee's first parents' weekend, freshman year. "You should tell your little friends to stop coming on to me," Lee had said.

"Dad, are you bonkers? What are you talking about?"

"The tall kid, what's-his-name. Chad. Thad?"

"Thad's a senior. He has two girlfriends, one at Madeira and one at Chatham Hall!"

"And they use him and don't put out, and he thinks he can work that magic on me. If I fucked every high school senior who wanted his poetry in the *Stillwater Review*, my dick would be worn down to a nub and it would still be useless juvenilia. You tell him that."

Byrdie drew back as though a cream puff had exploded in his hand. He closed his eyes and resolved to avoid boys who wanted to meet his father.

The first couple of times he was invited to friends' houses for the weekend, he went. He sat waiting for their moms to serve roast that was getting cold while their dads carved it, and played Monopoly with their little brothers until bedtime. Then it occurred to him that the school administration wasn't in the habit of calling parents to check whether visitors had arrived. He and a friend would sign out for the weekend, take a taxi to the Greyhound station in Orange, and check into the residence hotel where the more alcoholic members of the school's kitchen staff lived. Given a sufficient bribe, the taxi driver would continue to the ABC store, pick up two fifths of Tanqueray, and deliver it to the hotel.

With time Byrd and his friends became more adventurous, on one occasion flying in a chartered plane from Fredericksburg to Savannah to board a chartered fishing boat.

That trip was subsidized by a frustrated boy from Detroit whose parents had sent him away to boarding school as a punishment. He wasn't sure what he'd done wrong that finally clinched it. Paint his room black, probably. He'd done plenty his family would never have found out about. But paint your own room black, and you've blown your cover.

His initial idea for revenge on his parents was to charge calls to them. He would chat with friends at home for as long as he could stand it and leave the phone off the hook at both ends, so that his parents were assured a phone bill of $400 or more for every week they kept him at Woodberry. This earned him widespread resentment, since there was only one pay phone per hall. Meanwhile, he let his grades suffer, applying himself to learning only useless skills such as landing a switchblade over and over in the center of the dartboard that hung on the back of the door to his room.

Byrd Fleming opened his eyes to the possibilities. Fleming didn't have money, but he had something many boys don't know exists and many men never learn: He knew how to spend it. He convinced the boy from Detroit that the closest contact to be found anywhere between the high culture parents aspire to and the sordidness their sons crave takes place in the general vicinity of off-Broadway theaters. Obediently, the boy worked on his parents for months, raving of Brechtian virtues such as mind-numbing tedium and repetition, until they hauled him and Byrdie to New York over Thanksgiving in a Learjet. They left at the first intermission, leaving their son in the care of Byrdie with money for dinner and a taxi. The boys sat out the performance and followed a beautiful woman of around thirty-five in a tight, silky sea-green dress to a diner on the West Side Highway. They made friends with her, letting her mother them for hours, watching theater people and (they hoped) thieves and hustlers come and go. They drank coffee.

They didn't feel any older afterward. Just cooler. Not cool like an imprisoned gangster condemned to shank a dartboard five hundred times a day, but cool like rich, free young geniuses, eyes open to all that is human.

They tipped the waitress twenty dollars and hailed a cab back to the Waldorf. The next morning, they told the boy's parents exactly where they had been and what they had done. They were met with open delight. It turned out parents don't mind if you seek and cling to the dark underbelly of the naked city, as long as you do it in a well-lit, public place, high on coffee and testosterone.

The boys were turned loose the next day, Saturday, to explore the Village on their own. They had proved their trustworthiness. They came to dinner at a steak house in midtown with a bag of records and only very slightly dilated pupils. That evening they were allowed to leave yet again, to attend a folk music concert, trailed by praise for their youthful energy. They walked deep into Alphabet City, where no cab would take them, and slam-danced to a girl band playing in half-slips pulled up over their tits and no underwear, surrounded by junkies. The parents complimented each other on the positive effect of the steadying hand of Byrd Fleming.

But that was before the trip to Savannah. Who cares, it was worth it, and Byrd knew he would always be welcome at the Gothic revival castle on Lake Shore Drive, once the parents were dead.

The second pigeonhole where he didn't quite fit was that of the romantic egoist—that figure from *This Side of Paradise* or *A Portrait of the Artist as a Young Man* who takes himself seriously but doesn't yet know why. Who takes not knowing as a first symptom of seriousness and wears its ignorance accordingly—right side out. Such young men are commonly mama's boys and lazy as sin. Byrd worked hard on trig and calculus, even though he was sure they had nothing to do with him. He read William

Styron novels in secret, but for school he wrote precise prose, as dry as he could make it.

A teacher once asked him about his mother, folding his hands like a guidance counselor. There were stories. Byrd replied, "My mother was a God-fearing Christian woman like my father." It sounded like a joke. It was in fact the quintessence of how he explained her to himself. He couldn't imagine anyone staying with his father for more than five days, and she had stayed for ten years. He distinctly recalled telling her to leave and save herself, an act of supreme self-sacrifice on his part. He never missed her, not consciously.

In his more roving thoughts, not distilled to their quintessence, he believed she was a worthless cunt. Because what kind of monster leaves her little son and never even sends a postcard?

Yet he didn't remember her being any kind of monster. Just crazy and busy and embarrassing. All his friends' mothers looked like J. Press catalog models. They would lounge against their cars, waiting for their sons on Sundays, with clever clothes on, sporty garments like baseball jackets and anoraks reconceived as pale silk leisurewear. Their legs were stunning, much better than the legs of the girls who showed up at mixers, cylinders scarred by battles with field hockey sticks and all-you-can-eat doughnuts. His mother hadn't even looked like a woman. She was a boy in a rugby shirt.

And his sister? A wraith. A taboo subject, indistinct and unthinkable. None of his friends knew she had existed.

*

Lee felt played out as a poet. Utterly spent. Increasingly, he relied on methods he had once tolerated only in houseguests—cut-ups, free association, automatic writing. After he published a found poem culled from a magazine ad and learned it had been licensed from the estate of Elizabeth Bishop, he gave up and turned to criticism.

Criticism carried social rewards of its own. For one, you can rave about Boris Vian or Viktor Shklovsky in essay after essay without running the risk that either one of them is going to turn up on your doorstep wanting to swim in your already nearly nonexistent lake or taste a genuine Virginia ham biscuit, which involves going somewhere to pick out a ham, soaking it for two days, and baking it for a day after that, so that you're stuck with Boris or Viktor for four days, moping around the yard frowning at the mud and slapping mosquitoes, before you even addict him to your food.

Anyone still living who took the trouble to drive all the way to Stillwater was generally there for the duration—five days minimum—and visitors increasingly brought along magazine-inspired ideas of Southern living. Particularly if they were out as queens and took pride in reacting to every low flagstone in the front walk like a cat being asked to swim a river. They dressed in pale and delicate fabrics like men from a mythological filmic era before the invention of dirt. They expected Lee to provide them with croissants and two fresh towels every day, as if he were running a resort. They expected salad with quixotic greens like watercress and arugula and compared pasta to Treblinka. He stopped inviting them.

Solitude, however, was boring. Before long Lee got the idea of cultivating writers who were not poets. Fiction was still too close to poetry for his taste, so he focused on literary journalists. Living with the Hells Angels, digging up Neanderthals in Armenia—he didn't care as long as they wrote it up with some smidgen of formal innovation adequate to justify charging their travel expenses to the college. The writer-adventurers would speak to the girls at length in podium discussions open to the public. When the event was over they would switch sides of the podium table and keep talking. When the crowd was down to four or five of the most determined students, they would retire to the new campus center and continue talking of the girls' hopes and dreams for their art until late at night. They would drive back to his place at two in the morning in their rental cars, their balls deep blue, laden with lurid confessional manuscripts.

For a couple of years the college was willing to indulge Lee's interest in writer-adventurers by bankrolling nonfiction residencies to anchor a "journalism" track in the English department. Four semesters, four miserable men. They all ended up sleeping with the same bartender at the same roadhouse (no blue laws anymore) out on the state highway. The entertainment value for Lee was minimal, and he let "journalism" lapse.

Lee had his theories as to why writers never had any fun at the college. Theory A was that upper-middle-class girls no longer thought of older men as male. They got along so well with their relaxed, friendly dads that relaxed, friendly guys twenty-two and over immediately reminded them of Dad. Theory B was that Stillwater was still wall-to-wall dykes. Lee felt he had no way of knowing. When he was coming up, a girl in cat's-eye glasses wearing a red bra and baggy boxer shorts over fishnet stockings was—he couldn't think of a word for it—not even a slut, because why would a slut wear glasses or baggy shorts? A girl dressed that way in 1958 might have been going to a Mardi Gras party at library school, but only if it was down the hall. These girls confronted him in class every day. Its being a girls' college that rejected men like stray kidneys, there were no overeager, pawing gazes from boys to put the brakes on them. Lee's eyes never wandered below their faces. He feared his indifference egged them on.

He couldn't tell what went through their heads. Since the rise of fashion, which he dated to the day the campus got cable TV, there had been a disconnect between the way people dressed and their backgrounds and opinions. The college's Russ Meyer film festival was organized by a little-red-book-carrying Maoist. Tri-Delts in leotards picketed the campus health center to protest condoms. Girls in fair-isle sweaters and pearls would engage him in discussions of Michael Harrington. The Christian student association sponsored dances, of all things, and its most popular DJ, a Cure fan in flowing hippie skirts, founded a short-lived campus Republicans chapter, disbanded when she transferred to UC Santa Cruz to study the history of consciousness. There was no rhyme or reason to it anymore. You couldn't trust the signals. Rugby shirts, once the trademark of Stillwater's hardest-bitten bulldaggers, were now an option for anyone, any time. Still resembling gunnysacks made from signal flags, but considered sexy status symbols by girls who brought them back from road trips as souvenirs of one-night stands.

College girls on the road! One-night stands! Lee felt like an Austro-Hungarian emperor attended on his death-bed by flappers. He felt them stealing his life—literally going back in time and taking, through their incoherent lifestyles, the little he had struggled so hard to attain. They didn't look up to him as a poet. They thanked his generation for inventing the methods of appropriation ("found poetry") and spontaneity (carelessness) that consecrated their impromptus as art. They didn't know the concepts of the work, of personhood, of authorship. He had always been looking for things to bind himself to, relations and contexts. Or at least the meaningful absence of both. Now his students skittered over the surface of life like water bugs. They made casual sexual conquests, while he made traditional ham biscuits that took four days.

The Maoist Russ Meyer fan was an especial thorn in his side. She was an outspoken lesbian feminist à la Adrienne Rich (in 1984!) and self-proclaimed local chairman of the Society for Cutting Up Men (provincial eclecticism and the so-called postmodern: discuss). She was pretty with beautiful chestnut hair and could hold forth all night with her acolytes gathered around her. Soon she had the editorial staff of the *Stillwater Review* convinced you couldn't read poetry aloud if a man was in the room and, furthermore, that a man couldn't judge poetry written by a woman. It was still a women's college, with mostly women on the faculty, particularly in the humanities, so there wasn't a man for them to exclude besides Lee. She went so far as to lead a rebellion against his magazine's publishing poetry by men. With more difficulty than he dreamed possible, he bargained them down to one female issue a year.

And she wasn't even on the editorial board! She was too busy running her film festivals and writing an honor's thesis on Warren Beatty's ass in *Shampoo*. She told him Marge Piercy's poetry was more emotionally available than his and thus more radical. This girl's lesbianism didn't mean she slept with women. Quite the opposite. She believed men were necessary sex objects, while whatever drove her to manipulate girls into banding together to do her will was a higher, sacred form of libido. She regarded the token male Lee as a dull-witted, penile one-trick pony (to her, consistency was evidence of a mind standing erect), while women were polymath geniuses until proven otherwise. Lee fantasized about accidentally fucking her to death. Not as a sexual fantasy, just as a way of seeing her dead that he might be able to pass off as an accident.

He had been hammered into an unmentionable existential crisis by one of those annoying letters gay men were getting in those days. It began, "Dear Lee, you may not remember me ..."

He remembered the writer vividly: a black-haired, post-Appalachian Trollope devotee with a singsong British accent, affectations born of a desire so blatant it can only have been unconscious to be everything his parents were not. The boy would do things like stumble in the kitchen and fall against Lee, lingering pressed against him, pushing off flat-handed against Lee's legs to stand up again. He had no idea what he wanted. Lee let him fall deeply and helplessly in love, too far to say no to anything, before he made his move. The boy had serious literary ambitions, and Lee had promoted his career with every resource at his command, gotten him a scholarship to Columbia. And there his troubles began. The boy thought he was a little insignificant speck of a person who needed a strong guiding hand. Which worked fine if he was being passed around hand to hand by men who cared, but not so well running the club gauntlet in New York.

Oh, the tragedy of it, this object of great loves who regarded himself as a speck. And now the hostile takeover, the body making explicit how little of ourselves we can claim to own. Syphilis rising from deep down organs you never knew you had, diseases of all kinds seeping through the body and stopping at its limits as if projected on a screen. The tissues like autumn leaves falling from this alien tree, infecting lookers-on with ridiculous viruses and strange contagious cancers, and the beautiful boy, who thought himself unlovable, telling Lee he had no idea who had infected him with this thing. To Lee's mind, the situation flung nihilism in all directions like an exploding volcano. He burned the letter in the sink and fled straight out the door, tying his shoes and buttoning his shirt as he drove down the highway to a free clinic in North Carolina. He was less likely to see someone he knew at a free clinic than at any medical practice in the Commonwealth, and the Carolinas might as well have been the moon. Eight days later he drove back for his results: negative. But the intervening time had marked him. He had been a beautiful boy once himself. The boy he liked so much would die piteously, radiating horrors like a Three Mile Island reactor block.

He envied straight men's lives of duty and gaiety, their world bounded by pregnancy and the clap. Nothing you couldn't laugh off or submit to. A shallow place, but how to tell them gently? Best not try. They were more fun innocent.

Case in point: Byrdie, the son growing effortlessly into lifelong boyhood. Still a schoolboy, soon to be an old boy, blithely accepting accidents as privileges—for instance, his natural immunity to HIV. (Byrdie liked studious, upper-class females. They were not exactly high risk.) Byrdie was the phoenix edition of Lee, adapted to the novel environment, and Lee was a useless relic. He had positioned himself all his life as a rebel against a hegemonic order no one was interested in questioning anymore. It had lost its power to crush and all its clumsy weapons that inspired active fear. Its dominance was equal, but separate. Its monopoly was over, by design, because it had finally figured out that if you put the oppressed in charge of their own destinies they will trouble you no longer.

Thus the editorial staff informed him that they had an innovative plan to put out the next all-women's issue as a public reading in Richmond. Not entirely public. More precisely semipublic, since no men would be allowed inside and it would be by invitation only to female subscribers and women they told about it. No male would ever see, read, or be aware of the poems. Publishing poems on paper makes authors invisible, which is what men want.

Lee sat quietly for many seconds, pondering what he knew of Mao, then countered, with a hopeful air, "Mightn't presenting authors onstage encourage a cult of personality?"

"We all read together, in unison," the poetry editor explained. "It's a symbol of our solidarity. We're not invisible anymore, we're invincible." She glanced at the Maoist self-appointed editor at large, who signaled her approval with a smile.

Looking cautiously at his own hands on the table, Lee objected that institutional subscribers were paying an inflated price up front and reasonably expected four issues a year.

"If the librarians can't come to our readings, we can add an extra issue to their subscriptions," the managing editor suggested.

"So if people insist on authors and the cold, dead printed word, we hand them an extra book for free."

The irony was too heavy for her, and she said, "Yes!"

Lee spread his arms over the empty chairs to his left and right and said, "Let's just save the reading, give everybody three issues for the price of four, and tell them to fuck themselves. It would be more like performance art."

There was a silence at the oblong table studded with cups of oat straw tea. The Maoist sat leaned over her notepad, writing fast.

Lee added, "Do you all mind if I ask you all something? Because there's one thing I don't get. You think men are cold, unfeeling two-bit Caligulas and you hate them. So far so good."

"You shouldn't take it personally," the poetry editor said.

"You think if you fence men out, women will finally flower and go to seed. I'm not wild about men myself, and they definitely can't stand me. I teach poetry at a women's college, for fuck's sake. So could you please find another scapegoat for your struggle against patriarchy? I'd like to produce a magazine, if I may."

The Maoist looked up. "Lee, if you're alluding to your homosexuality, the notion that homosexuality is less patriarchal than heterosexuality has been conclusively disproven. Gay culture is based on male bonding, which reinforces patriarchal structures instead of undermining them, and it produces exaggerated forms of dominance, for example in the leather and B&D subcultures or in its celebration of pornography, prostitution, and promiscuity. I realize it's not your field, but gay liberation is turning back the clock on a hundred years of feminism."

"Christ," he said in exasperation. "Where'd you read that, *Ladies' Home Journal*? You think women don't sleep around, just because they bring a moving van on the second date? Feminism was cooked up to keep the black man and the homosexuals down. 'Hey, Mr. Charlie, why don't you hire your wife? That way you can double your money, instead of letting some faggot make enough to feed his kids!'"

The girls gasped.

Lee paused to double back and revise what he had just said, but he saw it was impossible. Returning to poetry, his rock of abstraction in the storm of reality, he proclaimed, "I built up this magazine from scratch, and I'm proud of it. It's mine, not the college's. And I can move it to another college, if that's what I have to do to publish poetry." He closed his notebook and stood up from the table. "My final offer," he said. "You publish four issues of a poetry magazine a year, in book form, or you resign."

"We resign!" the Maoist called out, but she felt a hand on her arm.

"I need this for my résumé," the girl next to her whispered.

Lee turned around. "That's exactly it. You need this for your résumé. Guess what? You're all fired. I don't need you for my résumé. I don't need to read unsolicited poems to reject them. I can get the best poets in America by asking if they've got anything for me. Suck on that." He wiped his sweaty palms on his pants and flounced out.

"He wouldn't dare fire us," a girl said anxiously.

"Maybe he has a point. It was his idea, having a magazine and all. And it's not his fault he's a man."

"It doesn't make any difference," the poetry editor pointed out. "We can put it on our résumés either way."

"He needs us to do layout and stuff envelopes," one girl said hopefully.

There was instantaneous consensus that the last speaker was right. Lee would hardly type up copy, open mail, maintain the mailing list, or do anything else except call the shots.

So there was no point in taking the mass firing seriously. They continued the editorial meeting without him as though nothing had happened, tacitly assuming four printed issues a year, one featuring black writers and one with women, both with interviews to add context.

Out on the placid, viscous lake, heading home, Lee raged bitterly ... but inwardly, not enough to rock the canoe. To be at once a disinherited black sheep and a straw man liable for the sins of patriarchy! It was too rich. In their stupidity and immaturity, the Stillwater students of recent years increasingly called to mind the fact that he had a daughter. A daughter who would already be too old to start on time at Foxcroft, should he ever find her. A daughter old enough now to come calling. But she didn't, meaning she didn't know he existed. The closer she got to the age of his students, the more he hated them. The more options bright women had, the fewer of them turned up in places like Stillwater. He gazed down at the green broth beneath his keel and thought, They ought to change the name to Pillwater. The college's primitive septic system was letting so much untreated urine into the lake that its hermaphroditic mollusk species had all turned female and died out.

Lee often thought of his children.

That is, he thought of them whenever he was alone and angry, which was often. To feel angrier, he thought of Mireille. When the adrenaline spiked uncomfortably, he would console himself with Byrdie. Of course Byrdie had the potential to become an arrogant ass because everybody worshipped him, but so far he was safe in the secondary phase of education where things still revolve around universal ethical values. No one sat him down to say, "You are the type boys imitate and girls fuck. You are the phallus spoken of by Lacan. You have power. Now abuse it." Back then they saved that stuff for MBA programs, and something kept Byrdie from picking it up on his own. Perhaps being abandoned by his mother had put a dent in his self-esteem?

Woodberry's prettiest, richest day student made a desperate play for Byrdie. But he had no interest in long-term alliances forged at teen summit meetings. His Stillwater babysitters had taught him all about being a sexy girl's favorite spoiled darling, and he wanted more. That naive faith shielded him from false coin.

He recognized her tactics at once, partly because the student body included the heir to a very large ranch and a Bostonian who would be king of France just as soon as France reintroduced the monarchy, and he'd seen girls stalk them. The girls worked slowly, studying every trace and footprint, keeping their quarry moving for months until it lay down exhausted. At which point, in Byrdie's opinion, a girl in love would have pounced. Her hands would have gone out and encircled the boy she loved, drawing him away from human society and down to a mattress. Whereas an aspiring bride-to-be would establish a public surveillance post at a distance of five feet and never budge.

The pretty day student became known as his girlfriend almost before he'd exchanged a word with her. They ate lunch together every day, or certainly at the same table. And in fact she was charming, pretty, and very smart. They were in AP calculus together. They attended basketball games and formal dances. But she didn't pounce, and Byrdie knew a woman worth fucking would make the first move in spite of herself. She would know what she wanted and coax it out of him, absolving him of all responsibility and bathing him in a flame of eternal femininity that would make sex so unlike masturbation that nobody in his right mind could ever get them mixed up.

That romantic belief in transcendent submissiveness, borrowed from Hesse's *Steppenwolf*, kept him a virgin until college.

Lee's sex life was a lot like Byrdie's, but he knew the reason. Beyond his little AIDS scare, he had gained weight. His back bothered him. Riding English hurt his knees. Riding Western gave him hemorrhoids. He couldn't have fucked a Maoist to death if he tried. He would drive up to Orange occasionally to take Byrdie out to dinner and sometimes play a few holes of golf, but mostly he was avoiding full-length mirrors. He saw Byrdie coasting through school on gentlemen's Bs, singing in the chorus, playing piano, painting in the art room, brooding over novels, getting into stylish and inconsequential trouble, sublimating frustrations into golf, being a major cunt tease to his poor innocent girlfriend, and otherwise doing everything a boy should be doing at his age, and he was satisfied in every way. The perfect child, goddamn it.

Heading to a Chrysler Museum board meeting in Norfolk, Lee stopped off at Doumar's for ice cream. It was an old-fashioned drive-in with teenage waitresses on roller skates. He was trying to cut down on drinking during the day, especially before board meetings, and ice cream made a nice substitute. Doumar's reminded him of New York. There were signs on the wall to prove the founder had invented the ice-cream cone. Something about claims of inventing the obvious—pizza by the slice, or reading poetry aloud over a recording of yourself reading poetry aloud—always reminded him of New York.

He pulled his new blue Chevette in to the right of another blue Chevette, and thought, *Quelle* coincidence, a sister ship. As he clambered out to visit the restroom, he had to be careful to avoid colliding with the tray hung on the other Chevette's passenger-side door. Heaped with heavily salted French fries, it was serving as a feeding trough to a stocky but fine-featured child with blond hair in cornrows. She lowered her mouth to the tip of the topmost French fry, guiding it inside with her tongue and a slurping sound like a robin eating a worm. The driver's seat was empty.

Husky. Blond. Cornrows. A suspicion burst in on Lee. He stooped down and said, "Karen?"

"Who are you?" the girl asked.

"I might be your daddy," he said.

"My daddy's in Leavenworth for fragging his CO," she replied.

That settled it for Lee. He recognized Peggy's sense of humor. He jerked the door open, disregarding the greasy fries that tilted onto his clean khakis, and took her by the arm. "Come along," he said. "We need to clear some things up."

"Get off of me!" she said. She raised her voice and called out, "Marcella! Marcella!"

A shiny, pyramidal white woman with fine, limp hair—also in cornrows—came around the corner from the ladies' room and said, "What are you doing? You get away from my granddaughter right now."

Lee let go and backed away. He had seized the arm of a repulsive child on gut instinct without the least stirring of sensitivity or rationality—the child looked nothing like anyone he knew—feeling momentarily manly for what? For acting out like a drama queen? He didn't even look around to check that he knew no one there. He simply closed his eyes, placing his right thumb and index finger on his eyelids, thankful it was Doumar's.

"And you'd best pay for those fries," the woman added. To the child she said, "Don't eat food off the ground."

"I'll buy her new fries," he said. He eased her door shut and reached for his wallet. "Watch your arm there. I'm so sorry. I mistook her for someone. Just sort of a confusing couple of years. Would five dollars be all right?" He extended the money toward the grandmother, inadvertently creating a suggestive still life: gold cuff link, gold watch, eel-skin wallet, five-dollar bill. The woman was nearsighted and lacked glasses. Lee's face was fuzzy to her, but the still life was not. "I'm really very, very sorry," he added. "I saw her hair and thought she might be my daughter."

"Well, she might be," the woman said. "She might well be."

"I don't think so," Lee said.

"She's a foster child. I just call her my granddaughter because my kids is growed up. You could be her father. What did you say your name was?"

"I got to go," he said. "I simply must book. I got a meeting. Excuse me."

"But you should keep in touch. Let me get you my card. I'm a hairdresser."

As she went for her purse, he lowered himself into the driver's seat and lurched into reverse. He stayed in reverse, backing all the way out to the main road, thankful he didn't have a front license plate.

Six

There were new families in the county where Meg lived, drawn by the cheapness of two-acre lots with fishponds at their lowest points and septic tanks and wells going uphill in that order. Their motive for moving to the county had a name: "white flight." And the more white people moved beyond the city limits, the more wanted to come. They had a snowball effect. Anybody with a little money to invest could make a good living building houses on spec.

You wouldn't have noticed the newcomers just driving around, especially in summer when the leaves were on the trees. But behind the bushwhacked shoulders of the roads lay new home developments, sometimes as many as ten or twelve families, screened from view by thick buffers of vines and tree snags.

The new families founded a countywide Parent Teacher Association with a political agenda. They hoped to tear down all the public schools and build new ones. The current schools were in towns, convenient to stores where the kids could dash during breaks to grab such necessities as wax lips and fast-burning ten-cent cigarettes. They were overcrowded, because integration had been achieved by closing two-thirds of them. Most white children still went to private schools ("Christian academies"), although the voucher program that once paid their tuition had been phased out years before.

Thus many a newcomer discovered that his dream home was served by a decrepit public school that was 80 percent black. He was subsidizing it with his tax dollars. Yet he couldn't get a voucher to pay for private school for his own kids. There was a lot of anger.

But there was also realism. The Supreme Court had invalidated one segregation scheme after another, no matter how well it worked. But that was partly because the movement made strategic errors. It called the voucher system "Massive Resistance to Integration" and school choice "Passive Resistance." In public relations terms, it was a fiasco. When the Supreme Court went on the warpath, imposing busing that turned white people into refugees, they surrendered. The new way forward was to be subtle enough to fool even themselves.

The PTA wanted the school board to solicit money from the federal government to open new, centrally located, fully integrated public schools and bus all the kids to them. Out in the country busing was more a convenience than a burden. It even provided employment for drivers. The new schools would have air-conditioning and no asbestos. They would be large enough to allow children to be taught in separate classes according to their abilities.

No one had thought to criticize the school facilities before. When it came to quality of education, people always talked about class size and teaching. But to the newcomers, property developers, building contractors, and subcontractors of various trades, it was plain that quality education requires modern buildings. There was a good deal of overlap among the four groups, and Meg did not find their self-interested motives entirely sympathetic. But they made their opponents sound like unregenerate Klansmen.

At the first meeting she attended, all it took was for a speaker to favor modern athletic facilities, and the Pop Warner coach countered that a varsity football program, chronically swamped with aspiring players, would foster un-Christian rivalry for starting positions. A member of the school board opined that children should play sports in familiar surroundings where they speak a common language and learn at their own pace. A third speaker explained that some people's natural talent would be complemented by other people's ability to read playbooks, so that the all-county varsity with the deep bench would be victorious in the region and possibly even the state.

Eye contact and whispers raced around the room, and Meg got the feeling she was expected to say something. She was at once a newcomer and black. It was longer than anyone could remember since a black person had voluntarily moved into the county. Quite possibly it had never happened ever before. There were no other black people at the meeting.

She raised her hand and was called on. She said, "I look forward very much to seeing my daughter in a modern middle school with an adequately staffed and funded library, the sooner the better. You know that Andrew Carnegie founded the public libraries so that working people would have the opportunity to better themselves."

It was a brilliant speech, simultaneously demanding a modern school, praising a robber baron, and exhorting her Negro brothers and sisters to self-reliance and work. After the meeting, the PTA founder made a point of embracing Meg. "An Oreo," she told her friends later. She remarked that Mrs. Brown was as well-spoken as if she had grown up watching PBS. Her collar was clean (polo shirts and hair relaxers led a difficult coexistence in those days). She was divorced or a widow, but no one saw her turning tricks or even smiling much. No one had met her boyfriend, but it was always the same van. One saw her buying not steaks with food stamps, but canned goods with cash. And her daughter (Karen spent the meeting reading the book of Bible stories that was chained to the chaise longue in the ladies' room) was, if not the most popular child among children, the idol of the suburban émigrés. The ghostlike, flaxen-haired black child was almost a matter of civic pride. They hoped she would stay in the county and marry a light-skinned, blue-eyed man to found one of those conversation-piece dynasties.

At subsequent meetings, Meg went on to sing the praises of functional plumbing, heat in the winter, and modern electrical systems that don't shock the kids every time they touch the filmstrip projector. There wasn't a trace of separatism about her. She was so delightful and approachable! A natural ambassador of the newly ascendant educated black middle class. The newcomer mothers just loved her.

Two of them had founded a feminist encounter group. They discussed for months whether they might not invite a black woman one time, meaning Meg. Then their curiosity got the better of them, and they invited her.

The group's founders had never been to any other feminist encounter group, but somewhat belatedly got the idea out of *Ms.* magazine. In between calls to action on the ERA and arousing tales of men who gave head, there appeared mentions of meetings at which women learned to speak openly about their concerns, their wishes and desires, and their bodies.

Once you go black, you'll never go back, men were wont to say, but why is that? They all knew the joke about their flat noses (that's where God braced his foot when he was stretching the first black man's penis) and had heard inexact rumors of the Hottentot Venus. Such thoughts of racial "difference," insinuated shyly at several encounter group meetings in a row, troubled the white liberal moms of the PTA but excited them as well. They planned to get answers from Meg if they could.

However, when Meg was ushered in, they happened to be talking about a course in sex magic you could take in

Virginia Beach. "I wouldn't take that course for a million dollars," a woman said. "When they say life force, they mean sperm. You have to swallow, like he's doing you this huge favor."

Meg sat down in a big armchair and said, "I think the fluids might be a yoga thing. Like you're handmaiden to the Dalai Lama, and you massage his root chakra, and he uses his penis to drink your menstrual blood like coming in reverse? Some guy told me about this one time."

The women stared at her, captivated. Their knowledge of obscure sexual practices came almost exclusively from magazines (books such as *The Joy of Sex* were short on specifics, enjoining readers to follow their hearts), on very rare occasions from women whose husbands had returned from prison demanding things that demanded explanation, and 0 percent of the time from men. "What else did he say?" her hostess asked, her tone as encouraging as she could make it.

"I'm not sure. We were pretty buzzed. He was one of those people into Wilhelm Reich and *Total Orgasm*. What was it now? I know! I asked him about tantra, and he said the post-structuralist emphasis on *jouissance* is an artifact of a modern construct, sexuality. Or maybe it was the other way around. *Jouissance* means 'orgasm' in French."

"Was he French?" She recalled that the French like black people, or might be black themselves—she wasn't sure.

"They're *all* French," Meg said. "It's like people used to just get it on, but modern science started sorting us into categories. So you get assigned this identity, like 'straight woman,' meaning woman who likes men. Except ninety-nine guys out of a hundred, if they touched you, you'd scream. And the hippies and the male chauvinists say the same thing, that sex is a form of play and you should relax. But what makes sex great is that it's exciting. Sex isn't relaxing! Relax and free your mind is what you have to do when somebody's raping you! But that's all men ever think about, getting you to relax so they can rape you and go to sleep."

She surveyed the room to see how her audience was reacting. They were aghast.

Unable to backpedal, she decided to sum up. "So, the theory is basically that they had to define sexuality as a one-way street to orgasm so they could market it as a therapy that's not predicated on attraction to a certain individual." She concluded with a "Whew!" to show she was done. There was silence. Meg put her hand on her purse and glanced at the door, thinking it was time to leave.

"I think I know what you mean," a woman ventured. "You're in love with the wrong person, so you tell yourself you have needs and your husband can satisfy you."

"It's more like what society tells you," Meg answered her. "It's a way of labeling you. You fall in love with one man, so they tell you you're into men, which is a joke. Nobody likes *men*. I mean, come on. Most of them are disgusting."

An especially cute woman leaned forward and said quietly, "My husband makes me play that I'm a whore who'd do it with anybody or anything. I think he's in love with my niece. My marriage is a joke, and his idea of a solution is to role-play that he's a motorcycle cop. In the garage. He makes me keep my seat belt on. God, I hate that fucker. I fucking hate him."

"That's exactly it!" Meg said, inexpressibly delighted, yet worried, because everyone was taking her seriously and she had said way too much. "The idea is that the concept of sexuality was invented to stop us from stepping out of line and wanting people we're not supposed to want."

"What's the guy's name? Does he have a book out?"

"I don't remember. Besides, I don't know that he's right." She rose to their disappointment by adding, "I mean, he's right about women, because women fall in love with individuals. But won't guys fuck anything that doesn't fuck them first?"

"My husband says he fell in love with me at first sight," the cute woman said. "If that's not proof, I don't know what is."

"Same with mine," Meg agreed. "Love at first sight."

"Where is he now?"

"He's deceased. He was much older." Meg shook her head and made a sad face, feeling ecstatic. Her first act on leaving the encounter group would be to find the cute woman's motorcycle-cop husband and punch him in the nose. "He was an entomologist," she added, feeling that an intellectual in the family might make her butchering of Foucault seem less out of place. "I'm finishing up his manuscript about the butterflies of southeastern Virginia. That's why I live down here."

When the feminist encounter group wound down, Meg rescued Karen from the group of kids out in the yard playing doctor and headed for the car, vaguely worried that she had blown her cover. She went over every moment in her mind. Somebody must have noticed something. Mustn't they? It was so obvious that she could not possibly be anything she said she was—black, straight, an entomologist's grieving widow. But no. No one had noticed a thing.

As she was preparing to drive away, a not-very-cute woman appeared at her window, introducing herself as Diane. Her husband was an electrical contractor, but she was nominally the owner of their business and not a housewife at all. There were government contracts for minority-owned businesses, and women were a recognized minority.

That made Meg laugh. "The majority of people are women!" she objected.

Diane replied, "Not in construction. It's a great line of work. We're cleaning up. I don't want to say how good, but we're doing all right. It's a shame I never learned a trade." She looked searchingly at Meg, eyes lingering on her V-neck, and Meg thought, Dyke.

Now, you'd think two dykes might be on the same team. But sexual deviance doesn't trump anything. It just makes a person more paranoid. The weak are always the first to turn on each other in a clinch, like Peter denying Jesus three times before the cock crowed. If ever two deviants were on the same team, it was Jesus and the rock on which he would build his church.

To Meg, an unattractive lesbian was a clear and present danger: someone whose feelings she might hurt. There weren't many of those in the county—people vulnerable to her—and maybe just one (Karen). Also, Diane was white, meaning she couldn't be trusted. There was proof: a roadhouse named Ye Olde Coon Hunting Club with a big sign. Any well-intentioned white person would do something about the Coon Hunting Club before he or she started building schools.

Diane told Meg to stop by for coffee if she was in the neighborhood, and Meg lied that she would.

Two days later, Meg heard the slurping sound of tires in the mud and peered around the window shade to see Diane emerging cautiously from her car. She went out to meet her.

Diane sought a political favor. She wanted Meg's support at a public hearing. "We want the board of supervisors to apply for a grant to build public housing," she explained. "Some people in this county live in conditions I just can't believe. Especially black people, no offense. It's not sanitary."

"My people, the black race," Meg said, offended. "We got one thing in common. And that's that we're exactly like the white race. The white people around here don't live in a housing project. Why should we live in a housing project? We never did before. We have our own driveways now. We just need better houses."

"Not if you can't pay for it," Diane said. "People living on squatters' rights have no equity. To fix up a house, you need a loan. We can't just *give* you the land. It wouldn't be fair, when the taxpayer has to pay cash. I think moving to a town is a fair trade for not seeing your kids go barefoot to the outhouse."

"I don't think of this as an aesthetic issue," Meg said.

"I didn't say it was aesthetic," Diane said. "It's pretty swampy there now, but what are we going to do? Put a housing project on good farmland that's already drained? No offense."

Just a few months later, Meg's shack was inspected and condemned as unlivable. Not remotely up to code. A contractor would be paid to tear it down. In its place she was offered AFDC (Aid to Families with Dependent Children), food stamps, and cheap rent in the housing project to be known as Centerville.

Meg and Karen moved to Centerville the summer before Karen started eighth grade. Temple Moody now lived right across the courtyard.

It was a one-story complex, built on a slab, with a minimum of nails and wood that hadn't cured. You could reach up and pull the siding right off. That looseness kept the air circulating between the siding and the tar paper, which was important in such a damp environment. The newly drained soil was still putting out huge cabbage-like foliage that covered the courtyards between the wings of the building in an almost impenetrable thicket, with pigweed six feet tall by April.

For Karen, Centerville held endless pleasant surprises: Neighbors. Playmates. TV. Telephones. Flush toilets. Long, hot showers. The paradise that is modern life.

It even had a little shopping center across the road, with a Greek restaurant (self-service, with gyros on the menu as "Mexican Taco") and a florist.

At first Meg continued to do business with Lomax at her old place, uneasy about her new lack of privacy. She had graduated over the years from collecting mushrooms to warehousing bales of pot for over a week in exchange for sums in excess of two hundred dollars.

It was risky—the bales were fair size and fragrant—but at her old house, it had worked fine. There she had no neighbors and a moat. Almost nobody ever stopped over but Lomax, and Flea kept careful watch. But there was no question of continuing in that line. You can't stash pot in an empty house. Sooner or later it's going to get ransacked. And you most certainly can't carry bales of homegrown through a federally subsidized housing project. There was no driveway in Centerville, just a busy parking lot. Who was Flea going to watch out for—everybody? Meg had to move up in the world.

Lomax had already made his career move. A childhood friend had looked him up. This was a man known as "the Seal" because he was AWOL from being a Navy SEAL. For years he took it out on the navy by running his speedboat out to the mothball fleet with a grappling hook and stealing vital parts for scrap. That was more gratifying than it was lucrative. More lucrative was a connection he made in a waterfront bar in Yorktown while eating raw clams in an informal contest that proved to all present that he was made of sterner stuff than most men. One of the losers told him there was major cash to be made by someone with the cojones to transport certain bundles to a certain parking lot in Newport News. These were to be found strapped in inner tubes on the beaches of the barrier islands of the Eastern Shore. They originated in Colombia and had been dropped from airplanes.

The Seal was game to try it, but not naive. He agreed to take the job, but privately he planned to bring the bundles only as far as Poquoson, there entrusting them to Lomax, who would drive them to Newport News.

Once a month thereafter, Lomax accepted a package and payment in advance from his dear old friend. He sat down in Crosby Forrest's seafood restaurant to wait, and Flea drove the bundle an hour, past stoplight after stoplight, past the MPs manning the gates to the naval shipyard and the air base, and heaved it into the bed of a pickup in a certain parking lot. It was that simple.

Then they got into a discussion about street value, and they got creative.

That was Meg's career opportunity.

The next shipment was two bundles. One went into the bed of the pickup as usual, and the other, smaller one went to Meg's apartment in Centerville. She didn't do much with it. Mostly it just sat there like utilities stocks, paying dividends. All she had to do was measure level tablespoonfuls into Baggies. She worked during the morning, by natural light, so matter-of-factly that passersby would have thought she was bagging sugar cookies for a bake sale. Sooner or later Lomax always dropped by to pick them up.

She was making enough money to think about the rainy day when she would blow out of there. She was of two minds about where she wanted to retire. Something about her current profession made her value the ethos of a hacienda in Mexico. But as a writer, she still aspired to make it in New York. Plus she didn't feel it would be fair to Karen to move her to Spanish-speaking schools.

She subscribed to *Writer's Market* and queried five agents about her play *The Wicked Lord*. They all said the most interesting character dies too near the start. She reacted by writing a play in two days and a night about a utopian lesbian commune defending itself from real estate interests. The villain saved his appearance for the end. The lesbians became the bacchants of Euripides, killing him in a festive manner.

It was gripping and seemed to write itself. But she knew you can't publish material like that.

She outlined a romance novel set in colonial Virginia, with a ghost, called *Blame It on Beldene*. The draft ended on page fifteen.

As a writer, she was struggling. As an accomplice to the wholesale drug trade, she was setting new benchmarks for excellence in felony crime.

The combination of relative prosperity and a mailing address (the shack had not enjoyed rural free delivery) allowed Meg to money-order books from catalogs. Karen routinely appeared with Temple in tow to beg for Newbery Medal winners. Temple would point out that with two children reading each book, it was effectively half price.

Meg had mentally adopted Temple the day she caught him outside watching her type. As he entered her bedroom she perceived his spontaneous awe of her Olivetti's all-powerful machinery, the medium through which Logos becomes the printed word—their shared ideal. He lifted it as gingerly as a rifle and admired its dark curves like a tiny Steinway. She let him type a little. He left clutching an Ezra Pound couplet as though it were a fifty-dollar bill. There was something very inspiring about Temple. He made her think literature mattered.

His parents, now her neighbors, were soon her friends. His mother, Dee, turned out to be an unflappable realist quite to Meg's taste. She had taught second grade before they closed the black schools. She had lived for thirty years in her husband's hereditary compound before rural renewal took it away. Yet she despised nostalgia in any form.

Temple's father, Ike Moody, also looked to the future. He expected a socialist revolution. His leftism was securely closeted. Even Dee didn't know the extent of it. From attending party meetings and summer camps, he had acquired an excellent grasp of dialectics as a process—enough to get him blackballed from the draft, the lumberyard, the cannery, etc.—but he always had trouble with historical details. He could sort of read. As a speller he was adrift in a no-man's-land between phonetic and dyslexic. For many years he had held a responsible position in a black-owned junkyard, selling auto parts and secondhand inspection stickers, before it was closed down for being an eyesore and an environmental hazard. Now it lay under a thick blanket of kudzu, and he and his two older sons worked nonunion construction jobs all over the state, often staying in campgrounds.

Temple was their youngest. His sister, Janice, was also still in school and had come along to Centerville. She was regarded as a strong candidate for Fall Festival Queen. She had ways and means, including hot pants that were mink in the front and suede in back. Dee would shake her head, roll her eyes, administer firm warnings, and placidly watch her fifteen-year-old daughter climb into a car with four adult men to attend a go-go concert three hours away in Washington, DC. "I was just exactly like her to a T," Dee explained. "She'll put it behind her." Meg agreed that it was probably a phase.

Dee sometimes drove Temple and Karen all the way across the James to read books in a public library. Her home library was risqué, consisting of pulp pornography for women disguised as self-help books: the horoscope of love, housekeeping with love, etc. Meg hadn't known there was such a thing. She thought women's pornography always promoted slatternly behavior, happy hookers and zipless fucks and so on. In love horoscopes, women were the stars, and their key concern in life was finding the ideal partner. The Aries man would be too rushed for the Gemini woman, but the Cancer man would slowly part her etc. and fondle her etc. Janice studied the books closely, and Meg couldn't fault Dee for letting her.

Dee's condoning of sexual freedom in children did not extend to her sons. If and when family planning is the responsibility of females, males are best kept under lock and key. She was proud to have no grandbabies yet. In her analysis of heterosexuality she resembled Lee.

As Karen's classmates approached puberty, Meg realized she hadn't thought things out very far in advance.

She thanked God for Dee and Temple. She could not imagine letting Karen play with any of the other boys, much less date them. They were very clever in their wry self-commentaries, but no good in school. Their curiosity about sex took a hands-on approach. Whereas Temple, disdaining his mother's collection, informed himself by reading the classics. The poem "In My Craft or Sullen Art" he found especially hot. At thirteen he lay abed with visions of the raging moon. Meg could tell because he refused to recite it no matter how much she teased him.

Janice felt his geekiness might be healed with judicious application of popular culture. By the time he was fifteen, she couldn't take it anymore. She took him to see *Purple Rain*. The cinema was in a black part of Suffolk. The dancing started during the opening credits, and you had to get down (that is, stand up) to see much of anything. She was pleased to see that after a quart of grape soda he was not short on moves. But she had not reckoned with the artistic and philosophical repercussions. Temple emerged from the theater electrified, ecstatic, abashed, unable to say precisely what had excited him so much. He avoided eye contact. When they got home he headed straight into the courtyard and began improvising rock songs, stomping his foot to keep time. He chanted his lyrics in a monotone falsetto while waiting for the school bus. Janice hung her head.

A council of the elders was called. It was decided that Meg would take Temple to see a showing of *My Dinner with Andre* in Norfolk. A huge risk, but Meg adored him enough to put on her sunglasses and watch cap and drive him to a city—something she had never done for Karen. Temple floated out of the theater on gossamer wings, silent, thoughtful, and more bookish than ever.

Meg was moved by the movie from beginning to end. Why hadn't the intellectuals she met ever been that nice? She remembered the role she had played in real-life dinners with real-life Andres: combination cook, waiter, and busboy. The part where Andre describes being buried alive reminded her of her whole life.

She introduced Temple to Samuel Beckett. As he and Karen stood out in the weeds, rehearsing his travesty *Waiting for Dogot* with Cha Cha, she felt so proud her heart would break. Not of Karen. Her daughter lacked stage presence. Her reedy voice reached the kitchen window without a trace of projection or resonance. To see an actress in Karen, you had to be charitable and use your imagination. It was the larger-than-life presence of Temple that moved Meg as she watched him arrange props on a cable spool, rolled two hundred yards down the shoulder from the Centerville construction site's impromptu dump, to furnish his set for *Crap's Last Tapeworm*.

Dee approved of Meg's influence. She remarked that her studious son would be the next Thurgood Marshall.

Ike said, "Not if he can't get his nose out of a book he ain't."

Dee laughed at Ike and said to Meg, "He doesn't know where I got this egghead boy, but the other boys take after him so much. I said it's time a woman had a son for a change."

Meg said she was down with that.

Temple's first great love was a white girl in the drama club whose father had a hereditary union job with the power company. "Union job" was a phrase redolent of wealth and luxury. Her expensive clothes fit perfectly. She had flunked two grades, so she was the most physically mature girl in the entire "academic" track. She did not fear Temple's dark skin. What troubled her was his prose. Being too shy to speak to her, he wrote letters. Close-written pages, front and back, torn from a spiral notebook. She felt she had a sex slave for the asking: a boy of whom she could ask absolute devotion, offering no social acknowledgment in return. No hand-holding, no publicity, no parental interference. It was an alluring prospect. But she couldn't make sense of the letters. She brought them to Karen for interpretation.

Sitting with the girl in the school's new media center, Karen read over a typical passage:

You are my Beatrice, my Odette. The passion that rules my nights, the vise grip on my trachea that cleaves my mind from the disgraced preponderance of me, wafting my spirit aloft while my body plunges into darkness with only one despairing, shameful possibility of release. Through the clenched fist of joy its tongues reach upward into my mind, the intractable flame of sorrow. All I beg is one touch of your soft hand to cool my burning eyes.

She frowned.

"Is it dirty?"

"He wants you to touch him on the eyes."

"Didn't you see where he talks about his Thomas?"

Karen looked the letter over and recognized a passage copied from *Native Son.* "Bigger Thomas is a character in a book," she explained.

She read further. The modernist literature Temple preferred was not rich in seduction scenes, or indeed in any model that might have aided him in formulating compliments. Consequently the letter was filthy. It was a pastiche of public library porn from Irving Stone to Philip Roth. It went on for nineteen pages. "He's ambivalent," Karen summed up.

Karen looked forward to their daily rendezvous very much. But as the weeks passed the girl became uneasy. She realized that Temple would never ravish her unbidden, but he might be very close to asking her to junior prom. Temple for his part suffered the tortures of the damned and compared his chosen to the Dark Lady of the sonnets. Finally she asked her mother what she should do. The answer was simple and immediate: boarding school. He never saw her again.

One afternoon Meg saw out the window that a large red tanker truck was backing through the courtyard, right over Karen's mouse town. The town for mice was something between a garden railway and the Lilliputian village in *Mistress Masham's Repose*. It was small and inconspicuous, being modeled on the county's towns of one or two stores each. It was very childish and in Meg's view due for destruction, but still the truck went right over it like it was nothing.

Meg marched outside, said "Excuse me," saw the driver's face, and marched back inside shivering. She knew that face. She even knew the name on the truck: Fleming. FLEMING'S OIL, GAS, AND PROPANE.

The driver had been a junior garbage man at the college, one of the kids who rides on the side of the truck, strong enough to heave full trash cans higher than his head. As he lowered his hose into Centerville's oil tank, Meg sat down on the kitchen floor with her back to the cabinets. There was no sign that he had recognized her.

"Mrs. Fleming?" he called out. "That you, Mrs. Fleming?" He knocked on her back door and tried the knob, but didn't come in. Cha Cha started yapping. One last time he called out, a little louder, "Mrs. Fleming! That you? I ain't going to hurt you."

Meg made herself very small and pressed into the corner under the sink. He opened the door.

"I'll be damned," he said. "I know you from Stillwater." Meg hyperventilated and hugged Cha Cha tight. "I'm pleased to see you. People was worried. Running away like that, taking y'all's kid. People thought you had ended it all."

"Just get out of my house," Meg said.

"That ain't going to help you," he said. "I'm looking right at you. I ain't going to forget I saw you."

"And can I do something for you? What do you want?"

"Oh, I don't know. Nothing, probably. I'm just surprised. I couldn't believe it. I wanted to make sure it was you. Now I'll be on my way, if you don't mind. I got deliveries to make. Good day to you." He tapped his fingernails on the counter and didn't turn toward the door.

Briefly, Meg thought of cash. Then she remembered something more likely to keep him quiet. "You like to get high?" she asked, getting to her feet and putting the dog down.

"Do I like to get high," he said. "Do I like to get high."

"I can see that you like to get high," she said. "You want to be my partner in crime? If you would step outside for a moment. You don't want to see where I keep my stash. It's personal."

"I'll be right outside here," he said.

Meg unfolded her little magnesium stepladder so she could reach the inaccessible cabinet over the fridge. From it she removed a pressure cooker containing an ungodly number—a highly illegal number—of Baggies filled with white powder, enough to get her forty years in the pen, and removed four Baggies. Then she rummaged through her hardware drawer until she found her .38. She called out, "Just a second!" Her ammo was in the next room, locked in a desk drawer. But would she have fired it?

She decided she didn't need the ammo, because she wasn't about to shoot anybody in her own kitchen.

It was a spontaneous sense: Don't shoot him in your kitchen.

It proved that at last she had become truly black inside. Her mother would have shot a strange black man in her kitchen and called the cleaning lady before she called the coroner. But Meg wasn't so sure she could get away with it. She even considered the effect on the man's family, needing his income.

She waved at him through the window to come back inside.

"This is it," she said, pointing the gun in his general direction and handing him the drugs. The gun was heavy and she wondered if she could have hit anything she wasn't actually touching with the muzzle. Not that it mattered. "That's all there is. There's no more where this came from. Once a year, when you deliver fuel oil. That's it."

"Twice a year!" he protested. "You people use up a lot of oil down here. You should try to save on it sometimes. Y'all keep y'all's windows open all winter." He put the Baggies in his pocket and politely tipped his welder's cap.

He was tempted to take the gun, but he was unsure whether it might not be loaded. He recalled that Mrs. Fleming was crazy.

Two hours later, he was dead. He had greatly misjudged the speed of an oncoming dump truck as he made a left turn from a stop sign. The other driver also died. Even the drugs and Baggies burned, leaving no trace.

He was already two counties away, so Meg never heard about the accident.

She was scared of him for months. Visibly scared, as in jumpy. But not rational jumpiness, the kind that makes you pack your stuff and head for the hills. She put the fuel truck driver out of her mind—so far out she couldn't get at him—and worried about things she could talk about with Dee. Temple's love life. Karen's grades.

Gradually her fear faded to the existential angst that incessantly haunts all mankind in modernity.

The existential angst served to mask her fear of Lee. The angst was: That you only live once. That you shouldn't waste your youth. She had no lover, no close friends, no underground theater group to perform her self-censored plays. She had to fake poverty to keep the fuzz off her back. If she wore stylish clothes or drove a reliable car, social services would get suspicious. She didn't spend enough time honing her craft. Et cetera, ad nauseam. It was the worry about not making the most of herself. The thing that troubles nearly all of us, nearly every day.

The fear of Lee was: That he would catch up with her, turn her child against her, wring her heart out like a dishrag, confront her with Byrdie, make her loathe herself, and get her in trouble.

That fear of Lee was useful to her, because it served to mask a deeper fear. One she never feared consciously, because it was unfearable. There was no way to shoehorn it into her emotions, and thus it could not be properly feared—the same way unthinkable things (such as potentially causing an accident by giving an on-duty driver enough drugs to fuck up a twenty-mule team) can't be thought.

The unfearable fear was: Here she was, on her own with a little daughter entirely dependent, surviving in a way that could get her sent up for a near lifetime, or even killed.

And all to protect herself from what? From Lee's emotional manipulation, her powerlessness in a relationship? From being looked down on?

Risking her freedom and her life, the only life she would ever have.

Lee had given her a choice between eviction and therapy. So basically the worst he would have done was throw her out. No way on earth she would have let herself be cornered into getting committed. So the worst-case scenario with Lee was—literally—that she might have to live somewhere other than Stillwater Lake, and miss her kids.

And the worst the state would do with her, if it found that pressure cooker? The worst Lomax might do, if he learned of her mutual blackmail with the driver? He was protective of his supply chain, his income stream, his inventory, his privacy.

Imagine the look on Karen's face, watching Meg be taken away in handcuffs, never to return. Or coming in after school, past the corpse of Cha Cha, to find her tied up in bed with a piece of her head missing.

Or rather, don't imagine it. Meg never did.

When a different driver showed up for the next fuel oil delivery in a different truck, she knew she had been wrong to worry, even unconsciously. She received cosmic reassurance that she would always survive.

Seven

On Byrdie's arrival at the University of Virginia, he was tapped for a secret society, the FHC. Its strict conditions of membership do not permit disclosure of its ritual practice, but suffice it to say that Byrdie had a sheaf of FHC letterhead and used it to write poetry. He liked "Acquainted with the Night" and "Tears, Idle Tears," so his poetry was generally composed of old-fashioned scholar-and-gentleman-type rondos and villanelles on philosophical themes. He showed it to a girl he liked, and she became his lover—a third-year suburban brunette with thigh-high socks and formal training in vocal jazz who swam sixty laps a day. Her praise of the poetry was so effusive that Byrdie showed it to Lee. In the aftermath Lee did not shoot himself, but in silently disavowing his once-perfect son called out one of the great hangovers of our time.

Byrdie got rushed to some degree by every white frat on campus, with bids from all but the one that said the Lost Cause would rise again. He made no effort to join any of them. He would drop by with drinking buddies on Friday or Saturday night for free beer. He did the shag to jangle pop with girls who were suitably prep. That was all. His buddies came from his courses—boys with shared interests who said clever things in class—and collectively they had no shared background or affiliation whatsoever, unless you counted the house where they gathered early in the evening, nearly every day, to smoke pot.

For reasons no one understands, otherwise intelligent young people are often drawn to illicit mind-altering drugs. A cross section of society would probably show comparable interest among the brightest and dullest young people, but at The University it was a matter of public record that the young men not drawn to drugs were less bright: Thetan House had the highest mean, median, and mode GPA on campus, and its students were concentrated in the most challenging majors. Possibly it takes a great deal of intelligence to ace school stoned. Byrdie liked their soundtrack, and if nothing else, he was going to need cheap rent after he'd sat out the first-year campus residency requirement.

So he joined.

The initiation was uncomplicated compared with other frats, since Thetan had lost its charter and was a locus of lackadaisical haphazardness for boys who worked hard in school. No one invested energy or creativity in scaring off potential pledges. There was no hazing involved, unless you counted being forced to do bong hits until you said "No, thanks, I'll pass." For plenty of boys, despite their pride in their intelligence, the challenge was too great. They would do thirty-five and lie there looking unhappy until morning. Prudent Byrdie did four. Then he got talking to some guy about Witness for Peace, maxed and chilled until maybe two, briefly fell asleep in a black-lit attic "meditation room" listening to Bach, and went home to bed. It wasn't far to his dorm. The house was in an excellent location, between campus and the Confederate cemetery, a most awesome place to smoke a joint, as was revealed to him upon his accession to the frat.

Due to his relatively strong interests in arithmetic and cleanliness, Byrdie was named hegemon-elect before his freshman year was out. The drug frat had alternative druggy names for all its officers. Hegemon was more or less the CEO.

To Lee's additional discomfort, Byrdie became strangely noncommittal about his major. He had started off talking of business administration. Then he began suggesting that many community organizing projects needed help with their business models. Then he proposed founding progressive urban communities on a sound financial footing. He wished to use his hereditary power and influence to help others help themselves. He was thinking of designing an inter-disciplinary major that combined architecture, business administration, and social work, and then running for office. He wasn't sure. He spent the next summer working for Habitat for Humanity in Richmond and still didn't know. "I hope you know what you're doing," Lee said to him.

"My task is to discover and respond to community needs," Byrdie replied, seeming to presume that he would never have needs of his own.

Lee met Cary for dinner at the yacht club in Norfolk. They sat opposite each other at a square table decked with several layers of linen and picked at soft-shell crabs. "Two points abaft the port beam," Lee said.

Cary turned to the left and looked over his shoulder. "Swish!" he said. "Those slacks make her look like Quentin Crisp."

The object of their attention was a well-built young man wearing a blue blazer and dove-gray pleated-front gabardine pants. He took no notice of Lee and Cary, but pulled out a chair for his dinner date, a man in a seersucker suit whose forelock had been bleached and cellophaned such a shiny peach shade that it put Cary in mind of daylilies, as he said immediately.

He and Lee were wearing the clone look (white oxford cloth button-downs with distressed jeans and white Reeboks) because they wanted to go dancing later on at one of those new non-underground—as in highly conspicuous, with neon and a line out the door—discotheques where they played sped-up music and featured drag queens so tall and square-jawed they couldn't live as women and had to spend their lives on the run, a.k.a. on tour. Actually Cary was somewhat shy of the mark, with red-soled white bucks on his feet, but his jeans were more distressed than Lee's.

Cary had read and reread the jeans-distressing tutorial in *The Joy of Gay Sex*, struggling to make sense of new tricks' demands on old dogs (Lee's line). His first pair was a total loss (too much bleach). The second pair came out soft and robin's-egg blue, but he ruined them during the "lay them out in the driveway and run them over a couple of times" stage. Maybe the guys in the book had flat driveways made of concrete and not rippled heaps of oyster shells? The guys all looked kind of urban in the drawings. The third pair came out just right.

Cary himself wasn't quite right—soft in the middle, with stubble hiding in folds in his face he was too lazy to shave—but you couldn't really fault him for not trying. Lee had the look down cold, but he, too, was getting old for it. His hair was thinning on top and had to be fluffed with mousse. They stirred their drinks in silence, watching the younger men.

"*Où sont les neiges d'antan?*" Lee asked.

"They should build a monument," Cary said. "All the times I got my ass beat to a pulp so the youth of today could get dolled up like faggots to go out in public."

"They ought to come over here and kiss your hand."

Suddenly, unexpectedly, two women in little black dresses and eye-catching funky accessories entered the room and approached the young men. The men jumped up and kissed them on alternate cheeks, European style. Their collective fluttering wafted odors of Antaeus and Eau Sauvage all the way to Lee and Cary's table. After securing the attention of the entire room, the two couples sat down again. It was unmistakable. They were straight. All four of them.

And the misfits who had shown America the way to flamboyant self-promotion—originally a way of finding comfort in one another's brashness as they cowered in basements, fearing for their lives—sat nipping Scotch in identical shirts and 501s, drilled to conformity and finding scant comfort in other people's flouting it. Lee sighed and lowered his voice. "Cary, are you wearing eyeliner?"

"You are not getting a rise out of me. I cannot abide teasing."

"God, I feel like a Romanov," Lee said. "Deposed monarch of the ancien régime, awaiting execution."

"Welcome to the No South."

"You mean New South."

"I mean No South. You can't have 'New' and 'South.' It's oxymoronic. I'm talking about the No South. The unstoppable force that's putting in central air everywhere until you don't know whether it's day or night. Fat boys used to spend their lives in bed and only come out to fish and hunt. Now they go into politics and make our lives hell. One little thing, all by itself—AC—made the South go away overnight."

"Very astute," Lee said. "Claude Lévi-Strauss, *Sad Subtropics*."

"Freaks everywhere," Cary added, glancing at the two handsome young couples. "Look at those driving moccasins he's got on, with nipples on the soles. Looks like a chew toy. And someone should tell his lady friend black is what a Moldavian fortune teller wears, and pink stilettos is twelve-year-old streetwalkers. Did you know they had to start up valet parking because of all the women who come in here literally unable to walk?"

"All my life, this club's had a no pimp rule."

They watched the two couples for a bit. Cary said, "Well, your life is ended."

They ate. Lee said, "Do you remember how we used to get up at night when it was too hot to sleep, and slip out and swim off the canoe?"

"I remember."

"We never slept in summer."

"We must have slept."

"What for? Did we do anything during the day?"

"*Mais oui, mon frère!* You haven't had a day off since 1954. It's just that your vocation isn't always what you or anybody else would call work."

Lee considered how much socializing he had managed to pass off either as poetry or cultivating Stillwater's endowment and said, "True enough."

"Now, here in climate control, we got a work ethic," Cary said. "We don't tolerate your kind of sinecure. We're upwardly mobile social climbers with unequal unemployment lack of opportunity."

"It pains me greatly that I never noted your poetic gifts. I would have solicited some pieces."

"Let me explain. Say ten years ago, you go to rent a truck. You go into the rental place and how many guys work there?"

"As in work?"

"You know what I mean. There's a guy behind the counter, and his dad in the garage, and four, five boys hanging in the parking lot. And you say 'That's the truck I want,' and the boys get on it and his mom does the paperwork and five minutes later, you got your truck. So what do we got now? You got the white guy. He owns a franchise for three counties, because he's the only one who can get credit. The truck is disgusting, you wouldn't haul a hog in it to slaughter, there's no gas in the tank and it won't shift out of second, and he tells you to call the toll-free number for service. And nobody works there. Not one person. The poor capitalist fucker is there all on his lonesome, raking it in for some chain. That's what I call unequal unemployment lack of opportunity. The South was built on the cheap labor of neighbors. No immigration, no out-migration, no upward mobility, no downward mobility. Land rich, dirt poor, don't matter. Land and dirt are the same damn thing. The rich man charges rent to live on it, the poor man charges wages to work on it. It's the circle of life. Now they're making money off borrowed money from banks that cross state lines. That's squeezing the life out of us."

"So? Do we deserve better?"

"You're the one who's supposed to care that the world is going to hell. You have a son!"

"What's he got to do with it?"

"Dammit, Lee. You bullshitted your way into the last of the bullshit jobs. What's Byrdie going to do? Manage the sawmill?"

"Don't knock my sawmill. He spent last summer working construction." Cary laughed, and Lee added, "He'll be off my hands soon. He's at a big public university, mixing and mingling. That's what they go to school for now. He wants to work. Nobody wants to be a white supremacist anymore."

"Says you. Here." Cary glanced around to indicate their surroundings, and an elderly black waiter stepped up. He shook his head and the waiter moved back to the wall.

"Listen. Byrdie is from the next world, the air-conditioned world to come. He doesn't care where you're from, who your daddy is, or anything about you except how you fit into his master plan. He treats me like a stranger. He engages me in conversation about public policy. I tell him he's my son, not my congressman! But we talk on a level of intimacy I would expect from a casual fuck in an elevator. He worships me from afar. He's just not sure how far is far enough. Did I tell you he wrote me an animal rights protest song?"

"He did what?"

"My son composed in my honor a folk song about a horse's right to run on a banked track. It spares their fetlocks from strain."

"You are shitting me."

"Cross my heart. He wrote a traditional American ballad of mourning for a three-year-old that died of a broken ankle a very short time after it was shot." While Cary wiped his eyes, Lee went on, lowering his voice. "He played it to me on the baritone ukulele, and he dedicates this song to me whenever he sings it in public. My son, Byrd Fleming, expressing his love for me in song. Now tell me chivalry ain't dead."

"Shit, man. What did you do?"

"Does it matter? I want to be like my wild, free young son, a handsome student with my whole life ahead of me, and do however I feel, and not give a shit what anybody thinks, and be high as a kite every damn day."

Cary reached for Lee's drink and said, "You're too skinny to be ordering doubles."

"You know what? It's time I went for a swim." Lee stood up. "I need to cool off."

"With you all wet, they're not going to let us in the club."

"Fuck the club. I don't need to rub shoulders with a bunch of no-name hard-bodies who think I'm death in Venice warmed over. It upsets me every time."

"I can't dance to their music," Cary assented. "It leaves me deaf."

"Jellyfish in the meat market," Lee said. He took off his watch (it was waterproof to thirty meters, but attached to his wrist with orange-and-navy grosgrain ribbon) and laid the contents of his pockets on the table. He walked out the French doors to poolside, leaving them open. Wearing his sneakers, and rather hoping they would be ruined, he climbed the ladder to the low springboard, smoothing his hairdo with a rueful expression as though bidding it good-bye, and bounced into the backlit water.

Cary copied his cannonball, with better success.

After just a few minutes, the pool was full. The couples who had provoked their profound moral crisis sashayed to the pool giggling and pushed each other in. The women shrieked, lost their shoes, swam in their dresses, dye running, lace ripping, feigning modesty wet-sari style as they climbed the stairs with their wrists crossed between their boobs. The tidily shaved men swam a bit in shirts and slacks, then cavorted in patterned synthetic briefs and amulets on leather thongs.

The sun went down and the whole club drifted outside. A waiter served drinks and turned up the music. The younger people played in the pool, or sat on the edge dangling their feet in the water. Cary and Lee had about all the fun they could handle, which wasn't much. Wriggling on a lounger in tight, wet denim will make you miss madras and khakis, and wet boxers: no. Then it was late, and they headed home to sleep while they were both still able to drive to their own satisfaction.

They couldn't go to the Cockpit. It was closed. It had never been an underground club. It had a liquor license and a sprinkler system and clean sanitary facilities. The authorities tolerated it. Hardly anybody knew about it. Then it made the paper in a celebratory article by a well-meaning journalist. He thought hundreds of happy men dancing unmolested to a jukebox in a crowded bar was a sign of gay liberation, which he strongly supported. The name alone: Cockpit. Naval air station or no naval air station, it had to go. Public pressure shuttered it over-night for zoning violations. So many men, so little parking.

*

Karen Brown was a good year and a half older than Mireille Fleming, and she had skipped a grade. At fifteen and eight months, when it came time for her to get her learner's permit and start driving the car, she had in reality just turned fourteen.

But what was Meg going to do? Confess? She recalled hearing somewhere that the legal age to drive in Texas was twelve. Besides, adulthood is never something girls grow into. It is something they have thrust upon them, menstruation being only the first of many two-edged swords subsumed under the rubric "becoming a woman," all of them occasions to stay home from school and weep. Not so long ago, Karen's pregnant schoolmates, who reliably came to Dee for help and were driven to a clinic in DC (it was called Sigma, but Dee called it Stigma or—if they came out crying—Smegma), would have been tied to their assailants for life. Amber Schmidt was already dead of a self-administered abortion (the time-honored handgun method, right on her grandmother's grave at the memorial park). If these girls were "women," with all the responsibility that entailed, why shouldn't Karen drive a car?

Temple volunteered to teach her. It amused Dee to see him in the passenger seat looking perturbed as Karen drew one leg up under her to get a better view of the road. It's not like you need both feet to drive an automatic. Meg ran out with a pillow and made Karen sit on it. She could see the pillow fly over the bench seat into the back as they drove away.

"I have a little shadow who goes in and out with me, and what can be the use of her is more than I can see,"

Dee remarked after Karen backed over a rock, heard the grating sound, and kept going, explaining that once you hit the rock the damage is done and you might as well just go ahead and park the car. Everyone was relieved when Karen finally got her license and gave up driving. The nickname "Shadow" stuck. Even Meg called her Shadow sometimes.

When Karen theorized that Tiffany's, the famous pancake house in New York City, must be fancy enough to have waiters, Meg took her to Pizza Hut. Karen was so impressed. The romantic lighting, the soft music, the groups of happy people enjoying pizzas together. The helpful service personnel! She had never seen anything like it. Meg cried a little after Karen went to bed.

Karen related her wonderful experience to Temple, and he submitted a request to Dee. She explained that pizza is sugared bread strewn with scraps, and that no waiter would survive serving her a pizza, much less a bill for it. Then Temple recalled that Meg had told him about certain excellent ham biscuits served in a restaurant located at Stratford Hall, birthplace of Robert E. Lee. He informed Dee that if having eaten in a restaurant was a necessary qualification for life beyond the sticks, he would start with those biscuits.

It was Dee's one authentic encounter with the supernatural. Temple at Stratford Hall became eerily quiet. He ditched the tour group inside of ten minutes, between the basement and the first floor. She found nothing in the tour to offend her; the black reenactment staff was gone, and even the white staff had lost its awe of Robert E. Lee, pointing to the cradle in a corner of the playroom only to say it had been exposed as a fraud. When she finally found Temple among the outbuildings—she had completed the tour and eaten a stale store-bought gingersnap proffered by a well-groomed black college girl—he was dancing with a billy goat. Standing at the fence, he would raise his hands, and the goat would rear, standing upright. When he lowered them, the goat would crash down, lodging splinters in its horns. He did it over and over and over, making the goat charge straight at him, oblivious to his surroundings and everything else, concentrating on his game. When Dee approached him, he stopped and walked toward her as calmly as if he'd been hired by the foundation to hypnotize goats into killing themselves and just gotten off work. Neither of them said a word about Robert E. Lee, who had still been presented, despite superficial updates, as a reluctant participant in the war and the best of men. They drove to the restaurant. It still had the ham biscuits Meg remembered. Temple ate six.

The spring of his junior year, Temple was nominated by the school district to attend Governor's School for the Gifted. It was a summer program to give Virginia's gifted students hope by exposing them to college-level work. He almost failed the qualifying test, which had been introduced to keep schools from appointing their best-dressed pupils. Arguably it retained a certain bias. One question was "Boat is to sheet as car is to (a) fuel (b) accelerator," and it was pretty easy to think the sheet was the sail if you hadn't grown up reading your father's copy of *Royce's Sailing Illustrated*. Another question asked the gifted to distinguish between golf and bridge foursomes.

Temple was adrift when it came to questions that addressed his environment rather than literature. He had the wrong environment for that. Karen did better on the test, which surprised the school administration briefly and gave them pause. But there was another program they could stick her in, and Temple seemed wasted on it: a three-week enrichment program for minority students at Old Dominion.

Temple knew he was weak in math and science, so he checked on his Governor's School application that those were his main interests. He ended up being assigned for the monthlong session to Virginia Polytechnic Institute, socially isolated and misunderstood, surrounded by people who had never heard of John Barth, who wanted to major in hydraulics or agriculture, and with a crush on a girl who programmed computers in Fortran and—to his profound fascination—was learning to speak Russian from her father, a diplomat. Temple came back from Blacksburg intent on two things in life: to learn Russian and to become a diplomat.

The ODU program they put Karen in was amorphous by comparison. There was little actual instruction, and no budget for college professors—just a few grad students with experience as teaching assistants. Writing was by far the cheapest form of enrichment. You just send them to their rooms and tell them to keep a journal, and the next day you make them read it aloud. You give assignments like "My Most Embarrassing Moment."

The writing workshops felled them all with their hilarity. With no required reading, the children were free to reinvent the wheel and wrote stirring narratives of first sexual encounters and regrettable drug binges. The TAs were awed by their talent and daring, unaware that working-class writing—from biker porn to *True Confessions*—is sparse, economical, and lurid in a way that can only remind grad students of Carver and Bukowski.

Karen couldn't help thinking she had gotten the short end of the stick, especially when she got letters from Temple that started with "Dear Karen" spelled out in Cyrillic. But she had fun reducing the group to hysterics with her tall tales, and she did meet a girl who made her feel almost normal. Angela Mendez was far whiter than Karen, if you score whiteness on a scale from black to pink. Karen in summer was platinum blond with skin like lightly toasted marshmallow. Angela was white as a cotton ball. An hour at the pool gave her a sunburn you could peel off in sheets. "What minority are you?" Karen asked at their first tête-à-tête.

"Hispanic," Angela said. "We've never done the genealogy, but you can tell by my name."

Meg took advantage of Karen's absence to start another play. It was about the commander of a death squad in El Salvador who falls in love with a nun he's supposed to massacre. In the early drafts, they were a man and a woman. They were always in bed by act 1, scene 2, because they didn't have much to say to each other.

She decided to draft them as lesbians to make them more communicative. Afterward she could go back and change the death squad commander character to be male. But it didn't work. The openhearted death squad commander refused to seem male to her.

She rewrote him as a man. Pouty and sarcastic. Instantly the nun became a solicitous bore. He ignored her. And there they were again, back in bed.

She tried again, establishing the female character first, in scenes with other nuns. Now the death squad commander seemed superfluous. She made him win her heart away from the nice nuns by being even nicer, but they were both so unsexy as affectionate chatterboxes, the love story just fell apart. They had to ignore each other to get anything done.

She tried one last time. She rewrote him as a complete jerk. Instead of falling in love with anybody, the commander said he would kill his own death squad to have sex with the nun. Afterward the nun went to bed with him to reward him. It was kind of sexy.

Meg saw a distinct pattern to it: patriarchy.

She had wanted to write about idealized partners. But the impressive men she had known weren't anybody's partner. They were lone wolves and dictatorial heads of families. The idea of partnering with a powerful man— well, it sounds nice enough, but even on paper it won't fly. A novel ends with a wedding for a reason. Partnership is antidramatic. Partners are not adversaries. Partners don't fuck. Yet she dreamed of loving a lesbian partner. Was she stupid?

Lee had been sexy to her at one time. But it wasn't because they had a relationship. It was the opposite. Because they didn't. And then she stupidly became his partner. She wasted her love on a wolf. What an excellent use of her youth and beauty! She glared at the typewriter, blaming it for her existential angst.

She finished the play with the nun sacrificing the other nuns one by one to protect the death squad commander from the revenge of his dead death squad's death squad friends. She tore it into very small pieces and buried it deep in the trash can.

Over milk and cookies after Karen's return, she confessed to Karen that she had no idea what Karen wanted out of life. "You're a cipher," she said. "A mystery. What are your ambitions and desires? When I was your age, I wanted to write plays."

"I want to get good grades and go to college."

"And what are you going to do when you get there?"

"How would I know? I need to get there first and see what it's like. There are all these majors that sound neat, but I don't know what they are. Like 'sociology.' What is it?"

Meg sighed. "Don't play dumb. Come on. If money were no object, where would you want to go to college?"—Meg had something specific in mind involving her now rather large collection of cash. Her native, self-compounding black/WASP/drug dealer aversion to public display—her low profile—need not apply to college tuition. Busybodies who learned that Karen was away at a Seven Sisters school would assume the numbers added up because she was black.

"Wherever Temple gets in." Seeing her mother's expression, she added, "You didn't even go to college! So don't pretend you know what it's like to be away from your friends."

Karen took a few cookies off the plate and went outside to lie in her hammock. Meg could see her from the window. Having developed a sensitivity to poison ivy, Karen seldom went in the woods anymore, but the effects of her early training persisted. She would stare at the sky as if it were a TV—as if clouds were more fun than a barrel of monkeys, as Dee put it.

Karen's mind was racing. She had just finished reading Malaparte's *Kaputt* and was deeply moved. (The library, like the thrift shop, specialized in the leavings of the elderly dead.) She wanted to talk to Temple about it. She seldom confided in Meg. Like many fresh human beings new to the world, Karen assumed people's thoughts resembled the things they said. So she didn't know her mother very well. She had no idea.

Lomax's financial situation had improved to the point where he was considering investing. Not in anything megalomaniac, like his business partner the ex-SEAL who read *Soldier of Fortune* and wanted to buy an Antonov and start flying to Chihuahua, but in something more pleasant, the overture to a well-earned retirement. He had always wanted to retire by age thirty. "Live fast, die young," he would say as he cracked another beer on his grandmother's flowered glider, barely having moved in ten days except to lie down on her sleeping porch. Lassitude was an accepted hallmark of Southern culture even among Indians on disability, perhaps even more so if their non-Indian ("Irish") ancestors were mostly Tajik und Uzbek like Lomax's.

Nonetheless, as it is for many people living more conventional lifestyles, his retirement was supposed to be more exciting than his working life had been. His plan was that in retirement he would fish on the ocean. He had his eye on a deep-V cabin cruiser belonging to a friend who owed him money. He knew it was only a matter of time before it would be his. Then he would lounge on the upholstered bench seat that curved around the back of the boat and watch big marlin come to his lure. He wasn't yet sure how it worked, but he knew that if you played your cards right, you could land dangerous-looking fish that tasted scrumptious (a word that always wormed its way into his vocabulary after three or four days with his grandmother).

Then came the day when the friend handed over the keys to the boat, saying he had no place to park it anymore since he was moving to a hiding place at an unnamed location until it all blew over. Lomax priced the boat at eight grand and accepted thanks for his generosity. Except he had no place to park it either. He visited his more ambitious friend.

"I was thinking to buy a motel in Yorktown and get a boat slip up there," Lomax said. "But shit, it all sounds like work. Even with no guests and no vacancies, you still got to keep the books. What the shit kind of a retirement is that? And Flea and Poodle, when I tell them they got shifts on reception, they're going to lynch my ass."

"Stop right there, my friend," the Seal said, holding up his hand.

The Seal gathered his thoughts in silence, then unexpectedly, lyrically, described a house he'd seen on the Eastern Shore. It sat in meadows spiked with volunteer pines and surrounded by serious forest, a big old wooden mansion with porches on every side and a widow's walk around the roof lantern. From the widow's walk there was a view across the barrier island to the ocean. There was a boat ramp and a dock on the creek. An earthly paradise. And it belonged to the state for back taxes. Nobody wanted it because you couldn't develop it. It had an endangered species.

"Won't that get hairy?" Lomax asked. "Walking into the state and telling them I want to buy a wildlife refuge for cash?"

"Delmarva fox squirrel, dude."

"Oh, shit," Lomax said. "Oh, shit!" In retirement they both were consistently kind of wasted and their dialogues were often as cryptic as their thoughts, but Lomax knew exactly what the Seal was trying to say.

When he brought the subject up to his father, he was initially met with raised eyebrows. However, Lomax's gift was an undeniable godsend for the Virginia Squirrel

Conservation Association, established many years before and, by dint of his father's hard work and dedication, now boasting twenty members, only nine of whom were over seventy-five. The association was happy to accept a substantial windfall in the form of a dedicated capital gift from an anonymous donor. It was a tax-exempt charity, and donations to date had totaled $148. Purchase of a rodent reserve of international importance would catapult it from irrelevance to significant standing in the conservation world. Lomax's father shook his hand with real appreciation, pumping it up and down. It seemed to Lomax a benevolent fate had intervened to launder his income in a way he never anticipated. As he left his parents' house he dropped to his knees, crossed himself, and thanked the Great Spirit.

The house on the Eastern Shore had originally been named Kenilworth, but the new sign said KEEP OUT. Lomax called it Satori. It was posted NO HUNTING NO TRESPASSING all the way around its vast perimeter. Except for the big clearing and some areas of open water, it was second-growth wilderness, full of old trees. Lomax and the Seal took up running around. Literally: running around. They would drop acid and race around the clearing in circles like dogs rocketing, and then top it off by diving from the little sandbank at the edge of the old bowling green and rolling over the soft turf like pill bugs, tumbling blissful and invulnerable. With time the Seal became softer and rounder from rolling, Lomax leaner and harder from running. Huge skies of seaborne cloud turned pink in the light of sunset, and swallows and seagulls met and turned away from each other in the air. Thunderstorms brought rains like an Indian monsoon, wet and fast as invisible buckets slicing through the air and sand on their way straight down to China. Twice a week they rubbed filet mignon with garlic and barbecued it. Fridays they alternated crab feast, lobster, and scallops.

Flea took up gardening, hoping to add vegetables to their diet. She didn't get very far. On her knees in the sand, she planted radishes she thought would sprout in three days and be ready to eat in two weeks. A typical country girl, raised between the TV and the car. Agriculture to her was clouds of pesticide raining down on corn. She knew traditional uses for many wild plants—as toys. Which seeds would fly farthest, how best to step on puffballs, how to make a daisy chain.

Meg's first visit, she refused to bring Karen, not yet having the lay of the land. She left her in the care of Dee and Cha Cha. It was a smart choice. For whatever reason, the first floor of the house was filled with hay to a depth of six inches. Flea wanted her to stay through the full moon to raise the Wiccan cone of power (she was getting an education of sorts through courses in Virginia Beach), and the Seal wanted her to try his cocaine, which she did. "What is this shit?" she said, looking up with burning eyes. "This is crank."

"It's the finest coke on the East Coast," the Seal insisted.

"Listen to me," she said. "I know you're experienced and all, but I used to run behind international faggotry, and I know cocaine when I taste it. This doesn't even feel like cocaine. Yecch!" She clenched her teeth and shuddered.

"It's the stuff we been selling," Lomax said. "Are you telling me they been shitting me?"

"I'm not a chemist," she said. "But seriously, if you were picking somebody to trust, at random, would you pick a drug dealer?"

"We're all drug dealers here," the Seal said.

"Are you wearing a really weird-looking shirt?" Meg asked him.

"It's my sweatshirt I always wear."

"Oh shit. I think it's PCP. Honest to God. Fucking angel dust, man. I can't believe it. You guys are the worst drug dealers in the whole godforsaken world!" She stood up and sat quickly back down. "Fuck!" she added.

"And we had them all paying cocaine prices," Lomax said. "Aw, man. We were dicking people over right and left. Is that the kind of person I want to be?"

"Those assholes played us like a violin," the Seal said. "You can bet if we'd lost one gram, they would have charged us for cocaine. And it was hard work! I mean, it was fun running up the bay in my boat, but it was all night, like swing shifts. For a white trash drug I'm embarrassed to have anything to do with. Shit!"

"I'm worse than you are," Lomax said. "I went into retail on that shit. But nobody said a word! Doesn't anybody know what cocaine is anymore? Not me, apparently."

"People don't fuck with drug dealers," the Seal said. "But we should have made friends with a chemist."

"So what's in that acid Flea says you take all the time?" Meg asked. "Agent Orange?"

"Something jittery for sure. It gets us running around like rabbits."

"That's it," Meg said. "I'm going back to drinking wine."

"I wasn't going to retire yet, but I'm losing all my ideals right here, right now," the Seal said. "I mean it. I'm going to give up narcotics and go to work as a mercenary in Sri Lanka."

"Sure you are," Lomax said. "And what about my squirrels? Who's going to defend my squirrels when you're out there blowing away Tamil tigers?"

"The squirrels need you, man," Meg said. "You got to stay. Give me a hit of that wine." She glugged it and passed the bottle back to Lomax.

"Why don't we deal booze?" Lomax said. "Like in Prohibition."

"Are you nuts?" the Seal said. "Going up against a state monopoly! You want the ATF coming down on us? If you're going to do a crime, you got to do something illegal, so you're not competing directly with the government. That would be like if I started my own army instead of hiring on in Sri Lanka. Or smuggling cigarettes. That's not little piss-ant drug dealer shit. For that, you need the Mafia."

There was a brief silence, broken by the sound of Flea struggling with a thick brownie batter in the kitchen.

"You know what's fun?" Meg said, leaning forward suddenly. "Tennis. You have any idea what a high that is, when you stroke the ball hard right into a corner? It's total power and control."

They turned to face her. "Tennis," the Seal said. "I mean, popping gooks is a high, too, but I wouldn't want to do it every day."

"Tennis never gets boring," Meg said. "It puts you in a trance. That's what we should do! Play tennis!"

Lomax blushed, warming to her vision and spontaneously admitting its profound truth. He said, "You know, a tennis court would fit perfect on the old bowling green, and it wouldn't bug the squirrels none. I like sports. I went duckpin bowling once. Sports would be a nice change from falling down. Flea!"

She padded through the swinging doors, anklets jingling, licking the spatula. "Break out the champagne!" Lomax called out. "We got a new action plan. We're giving up drugs for tennis!"

"Why would you do that?"

"Don't ask me. I am higher than a mountain."

Shortly after that, there was a huge cocaine bust with hundreds of arrests all over the papers, but it didn't seem to affect anybody they knew. It struck Lomax how funny it would be if he had been transporting angel dust from some lab in Floyd County the whole time, "laundering" it, so to speak, in the Atlantic. Then he realized that he'd never seen it in inner tubes on the shore. Just being unpacked from a flimsy bass boat in Poquoson. And he realized there was a lot he didn't know. He shook his head and returned to his belated reading of *Eastern Chipmunks: Secrets of Their Solitary Lives*.

Contractors experienced in the building of tennis courts were rare on the Eastern Shore in those days. But the Seal had built entire landing strips. Meg declared the bowling green off-limits, so he repurposed a parking lot that had been the kitchen garden. From then on, Meg regularly brought along Karen and Temple. (Cha Cha boarded with the Moodys, as dogs were not allowed in the squirrel sanctuary.)

The tennis-playing Temple acquired a retro look that became his uniform: a white cable-knit tennis sweater with a red-and-blue V-neck. When Karen stood next to him, leaning against the sweater with her arms around his torso, she didn't look white at all. Compared to that sweater, nothing was white. Dee was a master of laundry chemistry. On sunny days, the sweater would hurt your eyes.

Meg began the day's tennis lesson. The two children took their positions at opposite corners of the court. Temple's windup was dramatic. What happened next made them all groan. The ball didn't rise very high, and in a midswing attempt to avoid bonking his racket into his left knee, Temple threw his weight to the right, disregarding his right foot, which turned over. He sat down on the court, holding his ankle in disbelief.

"Smooth move, Arthur Ashe," Meg said.

"I think I sprained my ankle," Temple said.

"You need an ice pack," Meg said. She headed for the house.

"Flea learned a shamanistic technique that would heal that ankle immediately," Lomax remarked from his Adirondack chair. "She's used it on me many times."

"I want to see her do it," Karen said.

"You know what? I feel all right," Temple said. "I might try to hop on over to the house."

"No, stay here so Flea can do shamanistic healing!" Karen said.

"Then at least be my pillow," Temple said. Karen complied, sitting down cross-legged on the concrete. He arranged his head on her lap and said, "That's better." Meg returned with Flea and a dish towel full of ice cubes.

Temple was a little afraid of Flea. It was not difficult for him to let Meg palpate his ankle through his shoe. But when Flea took her place, squatting barefoot before him in her long skirt, and told him to relax so she could summon his totem animal, his thoughts were distilled to one rhythmic litany: No, not now, do *not* get an erection. She untied his shoelace. "No, please no," he begged her and himself. He wiggled his foot in self-defense, trying not to kick her. "Please no, Flea. Please."

"Trust him," Karen said. "You don't want to smell his feet." Flea lowered her hands and backed away, and Temple exhaled.

He felt his body lighten and withdraw from the dangers that surrounded it. He stretched out his arms and felt stillness and birdsong. Beyond the edge of the tennis court was the lawn, and beyond the lawn was the meadow, and beyond the meadow stretched the forest where you could hear the huge crested woodpeckers hard at work building nests for the squirrels. Beyond them lay the back bay, the cities, the oceans, the continents. The earth, endless and replete. The sun, straight up, a blinding hole leading to an immense void.

Temple stared at it unflinching and had an insight that stuck in his mind forever after. Behold the Sheltering Sky, he thought. I was understanding it wrong. It's not a shelter because it protects you. It's a way out. A sanctuary, a place you can go when things get out of control. Say for example you cripple yourself hitting a tennis ball and there's one girl's sweaty crotch cradling your head and another girl's perfumed hair tickling your legs and nothing in between them but your dick and nobody watching but the one girl's mom and the other girl's boyfriend: There's no need to run away. You can ascend to the region of blue sky and great wandering shadows. The shelter that received the risen Christ and Port in *The Sheltering Sky*, that comforted the mortally wounded Prince Andrei and the young W. E. B. Du Bois. Now I know.

Temple closed his eyes and his vision took on a very definite shape. He saw his winged soul appear risen to Karen. She would never doubt his innocence. Even his crucifixion wouldn't worry her in the least. She was an angel, one of the birds of the air of the Sheltering Sky, born to lead him there. He would fly through space and time with his Shadow at his side, in front of him, behind him—it didn't matter where she was, she would always be linked to him, always respond to him.

He woke up (teenage boys fall asleep with astonishing suddenness in the most unlikely situations) and saw her face above his, upside down. She was not thinking of herself, but of him, like Mary in a pietà. He felt a need to increase the distance, a sudden conviction that if there were more space between them, something worth having might grow.

That night he crept to her bedside and said, "Shadow. Shadow!"

"What?"

"I'm in love with you!"

"Go to sleep!"

Eight

His third year at UVA, Byrdie declared as his major an exotic conglomerate unknown in the history of The University or any other. He asked for an extra year to finish because he needed engineering credits. He saw his decision as the right and proper thing to do. It was planning that would save the world, not commerce. Economic growth driven by investment would exhaust Earth's resources in a matter of years.

His theories were strongly influenced by the Kipling novel *Captains Courageous*, which he had found on a shelf at Lee's parents' house. A spoiled boy, heir to a railroad empire, learns the value of technological progress on a sailboat pursuing shoals of cod around the North Atlantic. Byrdie got to thinking: With today's technology, the fishermen in the book could have hunted the cod to extinction. Cod now would be fabled creatures like the great auk. It was going to take clear-eyed young visionaries such as himself, powered by hereditary fortunes and thus immune to the forces of greed and speed, to pioneer the new antitechnology technologies that would restore helplessness and ineptitude to their rightful place as Tools for Conviviality (the Ivan Illich book had been Meg's). For instance, a return to narrow, bumpy city streets with trolley tracks and bike lanes instead of parking would send quality of life through the roof. The elderly and handicapped could ride in the bike lanes on golf carts. Byrdie called his imaginary planning bureau "R&D," for Regression and Deceleration or maybe Density. He had already drafted a scheme to eliminate the west end of Richmond entirely, integrating it with the desolate north side of downtown and doubling the density to achieve quality of life squared, and gotten an A-plus.

Lee's fantasies of feudal power had always been confined to strict geographical limits. On further analysis he found them even more appealingly modest and humble. Had any Fleming ever aspired to anything more than to create a pleasing environment for himself and his friends? Had Flemings interfered in the lives of others since being knocked off their high horse at the close of the 1860s and/or 1960s? He thought Byrdie might be a clinical case. After all, the mother had been insane.

He informed Byrdie that his social engineering ambitions betrayed all the delusions of grandeur that you might expect from the son of a poet. Then, pretending to hesitate to break the bad news, he pointed out that the hereditary fortune was a bit of a question mark. Lee was, he said, broke. His salary was a drop in the bucket. He didn't own the house he lived in. His parents were spending his inheritance right and left on increasingly expensive vacations, tootling around Norwegian fjords on first-class ferryboats and dabbling in the Himalayas. Exclusive inside knowledge of the world financial system, acquired from Lyndon LaRouche for $5,000 a year, had not stopped them from buying a town house in Georgetown right before the stock market crash. He was starting to wonder whether they hadn't mortgaged everything they owned. Byrdie might be well advised to pursue a career that involved such niceties as an employer.

The irony was not lost on Byrdie. He listened to Lee's complaints and said he would take them under advisement.

Dee had feared the best she could afford for Temple was community college, but when he began getting letters from historically white colleges all over the South, soliciting his application and offering scholarships on the basis of his PSATs, her mind was made up. She said, "Temple is going to The University. If it was good enough for Thomas Jefferson, it's good enough for my son."

Self-confident Temple dashed off his essay in an afternoon. Karen's application caused her weeks of grief. After abandoning several memoir-like drafts about various aspects of her life, which seemed more incoherent the deeper she got into it, she wrote about her ambitions. When the past is hard to explain, it's best to concentrate on the future. She wrote that she wanted to work hard and get good grades and pick an interesting major.

Charlottesville being far away, the admissions office had a local alumnus interview the applicants. He wasn't a professional, just a public-spirited businessman prepared to meet the children of country-club acquaintances and recommend their admission. He volunteered a Saturday afternoon and borrowed the librarian's office adjoining the high school media center.

Karen felt insecure, but it had little to do with her qualifications to attend college. It was puberty. Just turned fifteen, she had attained maximum unfamiliarity with her own body. She always expected to grow up boyish like Meg, but she took after Lee's mother instead: an eye-popping hourglass in miniature, but nervous about it, with skinny legs and bitten nails.

For the interview, she wore a blue double-knit suit, bought at a thrift shop in an ancient gas station, that had been hand-sewn before her birth for an even smaller woman. She mumbled, feeling shy, and left with tears in her eyes. The interviewer looked down at his form and tried to formulate a way of calling her childlike, yet trashy. He regarded the box checked "black" as evidence of functional illiteracy. Her grades did not impress him. This, he said to himself, is a corn-fed heifer who lets teachers feel her up.

Through the glass window of the librarian's office he watched her shuffle away in her short, tight suit and strappy sandals with three-inch heels (hand-me-downs from Janice), unwittingly waggling her ass—the only black thing about her, in his opinion. He would have compared her to the one secretary in *How to Succeed in*

Business Without Really Trying, but given her size, mood, and clothing, he kept thinking of *Taxi Driver*. He watched her collapse sobbing into the arms of a gangly black boy in a blindingly white old-fashioned tennis sweater. He said something that made her smile. She responded with something that made him nod. Their brief conversation gave the strange but distinct appearance, to someone who couldn't hear it, of being charming, witty, and enticingly mysterious. The girl uttered a long sentence, tears on her eyelashes, and the boy looked at the ceiling for a moment before replying with another long sentence that made the girl cock her head quizzically, and so on. The two seemed oblivious to the prep school boys and girls slumped nervously in upholstered chairs. Then the boy looked at his watch. The next interview slot was his.

The interviewer forgot to make any notes about Karen at all. Because Temple blew him away. After he met Temple, he called the dean of admissions and gave him a heads-up. Modest, handsome, well-spoken, sharp as a tack. Temple in his essay had done his best to be funny, sprinkling it with quotations from Montaigne since French was the subject he enjoyed most. As a Joyce and Beckett maniac, he didn't see himself as having a choice. The interviewer spoke a bit of French to see what would happen and Temple replied, his grammar convoluted and his accent proving beyond a doubt that he could also spell, that whether his ultimate posting was in Francophone Africa, which of course fascinated him, or the Soviet Union, as he dared to hope, a command of the French language would be indispensable to his activities as a diplomat, a career he felt The University could help him work toward. The interviewer felt a pang of envy.

The admissions office made Dee drive him to Charlottesville to interview for a merit scholarship. Temple left them bewildered and excited. What egg did he hatch from? Since when do things like that crawl out of the woods? They called the high school to make the principal nominate him, and handed him a four-year free ride. And not because he was underprivileged, but because they considered him one of their best applicants that year. The chief admissions officer described him to the committee as a high-potential whom they could not afford to lose. Financial aid, he could get anywhere. They would lose a bidding war with the Ivies. They needed a prestigious scholarship as bait.

As for his classmate, well, they'd be fools to admit a kid black as the ace of spades without admitting his girl-friend. There were maybe two hundred black girls enrolled at The University. One was absurdly fat and in a wheelchair, and another was a hair-trigger feminist with a habit of standing up in lectures and yelling, not to mention the two girls from prominent families in DC, both majoring in prelaw—whatever that was—who were so extremely attractive that it hurt the dean of admissions to look at them. These were the black girls one noticed. It was safe to assume they would be of no assistance to Temple. The dean recalled the one Black Student Alliance party he had attended as a bleak affair. It was hard to say what had depressed him more: the stud-ied footwork of the couples on the dance floor, or the heartrending petty bourgeois piteousness of cucumber sandwiches passed around by accounting majors whose overly colorful bow ties had been expressly chosen to keep them from looking like waiters. Lonely, Temple might become a danger to himself and white women. The light-skinned girlfriend was a ready-made shock absorber and, after all, a legitimate applicant in her own right.

They let her in and gave her a grant. As the dean said, she could have qualified for food aid in Biafra. She was about the poorest applicant they'd ever seen.

To say Temple was ecstatic would be an understatement. He was lit from within. He had always suspected he had potential. Now he had official confirmation. The State Department beckoned. All he had to do was ace a triple major in international relations, Slavic languages, and government while slaking his thirst for math, science, literature, history, various upscale PE offerings such as rock climbing and squash, etc.

Meg, too, was overjoyed. Karen was fifteen and three-quarters, awfully young to go to college, but she had a commonsensical, matter-of-fact way of approaching things. You couldn't call it maturity. It was passivity, that was all. Who knew what she really wanted from life. She seemed to regard Temple as her hereditary betrothed, which somehow got her off the hook for getting sexually involved with him. Meg and Dee agreed on that score: Temple and Karen were like Hansel and Gretel. They worried that Karen, surrounded by college boys who thought she was white, would ditch Temple and break his heart.

With UVA in the bag, Temple felt he had time to catch up on his black studies. He enjoyed *Soul on Ice* and *The Autobiography of Malcolm X*. Then Meg bought him *Coming of Age in Mississippi*. It was like giving a Jewish kid a coffee-table book about Auschwitz. Before then nothing had occurred to shake Temple's belief in universal ethical values. Black men overcame (an intransitive verb), and that was that. Now he wondered if black people might not be owed a hearty collective thank-you, perhaps in the form of trillions of dollars.

His cogitations culminated, late in his senior year, in an ill-advised one-man show adapted from Ellison's *Invisible Man*, to be performed onstage at the shuttered black high school where he had attended first through seventh grades. (The new high school's auditorium was also the gym, so it was a bit cavernous for the arts.) The set was not ready until dress rehearsal. The many lightbulbs onstage in the final scene blew an irreplaceable antique fuse, necessitating the postponement and ultimately the cancellation of a one-act festival that had cost the senior English teacher an awful lot of work.

Ike Moody grumbled silently that if Temple were a little smarter he would notice not only that his people were victims of prejudice, but that his family had been run off their property and was living in a housing project. But of course a future diplomat thinks in world-historical terms, unfamiliar with basic post-Marxian concepts ... debt peonage, land reform, grumble, novels that leave him innocent as a newborn baby, grumble, grumble ... Not being a big reader or a particularly determined steward of pieces of paper, Ike didn't know his creek bank had its origins in Reconstruction land grants that totaled nearly four hundred acres. Nor did he know he had held on for an unusually long time.

After World War II—in the years of the "Great Migration," when black people came out en masse as cold-loving proletarians—many Virginia counties had become dotted with vast and beautiful army, navy, air force, and CIA bases. That is, certain people's land was taken in great swathes by eminent domain for national security, and where black people once hunted, fished, and farmed, servicemen now dwelt in high-ceilinged brick mansions on the water, watching pleasure boats come and go. Whenever the US Congress leaned on the services to stop being dogs in the manger about such valuable real estate, they would—just an example here!—sell part to developers for a golf resort and the rest to retired officers. If you have to be bad, be so bad sympathetic hearers just shake their heads and give up.

Nobody suggested to Temple that his family had been cheated. Nobody wanted him growing up thinking people are bad or that the world is a bad place. That would have been Christianity or the Gnostic heresy, though they didn't put it in those terms. They portrayed the world as in need of repair, not as populated by people you'd be insane not to hate. Resentment of collective ill-treatment of the race was fine, if it helped him fine-tune his sense of justice.

*

High school graduation was a triumph. Temple gave an earnest valedictory speech on independence cribbed from Thoreau. Whenever he raised his voice, he reminded the white parents of black activists they'd seen on TV, and they shrank back in their seats. It wasn't what he was saying, which involved hopes for a more just world if people would sit down and do the math like Thoreau, but his wearing a suit and not being a preacher, yet speaking in public.

Karen as salutatorian reminisced about the years their class had spent together in a scholarly way. The parents were used to hearing more comprehensible things at commencement speeches such as "We sold out of Brunswick stew and our class spirit was psyched," but many were pleased to find their children had been exposed to learning. They regarded Karen as an honorary white person and applauded extra loud.

Hearing the term "Jefferson scholar" as he took the scroll and shook the principal's hand, Temple was hard put not to jump up and down and squeak. He looked out and saw his mother gazing up with her hands pressed against her chest. His grandparents appeared transfigured by joy, blissful, liberated, expansive. His siblings were standing and whooping. His father's place was empty, since he'd gone to the back of the gym to face the wall and dab at his eyes with a hankie. After Temple came the quarterback of the football team, with an athletic scholarship to George Mason, who got a lot more applause. But it was still the proudest moment of all their lives up until then. Dee was out of control all summer, high-fiving everyone. Trotskyite or not, Ike seemed to float around on invisible roller skates.

Given residency requirements that put them far apart—Temple was in a special dorm for Jefferson scholars—and their differing class schedules and busy orientation programs, Karen and Temple weren't able to spend a lot of time together in their first few weeks at school. Karen had been warned by her mother not to spy on him and by Dee not to follow him around like a puppy, so she figured it might be a good thing.

He was busy anyway, disoriented and discombobu-lated, having typical adolescent experiences without knowing they were typical. Making long speeches to distracted eighteen-year-olds who were thoroughly occupied washing down fish sticks with Pepsi, feeling that they, despite their inattention, were understanding every word. Watching them stand up and wander off as though he did not exist. The invisible man. He was not used to seeing the faintest trace of comprehension dawn on the face of anyone other than his mother, Karen, Meg, the occasional teacher, and others predisposed to be nice to him—mostly Meg—so he had naturally assumed that anyone smart enough to understand him would find him fascinating. It was a shock to discover that suburban kids could follow his argumentation and find it hopelessly dull. "*Pale Fire* is so overwritten," they would say, yawning. He began to talk less, shortening his speeches to make them more efficient and effective.

It never crossed his mind to be tender, charming, or witty. Those were his ways of interacting with Dee and Karen. He didn't know you could fake affection and manipulate people into loving you that way. Temple never pretended. He merely watched himself with eagle eyes. He saw that he was a nerd, possibly even a geek or a pedant if not a boor, definitely a name-dropper, and certainly not as well informed on certain topics as he would have liked to think.

Lectures, where he could be anonymous, were what he enjoyed most. At tutorials he felt he was wobbling over thin ice, keeping in motion to avoid plummeting into the sucking hole of his own ignorance, reliant on generous teaching assistants to bridge gaps in his knowledge, hyperaware that his problem was not stupidity but a basic approach that was all wrong in every way. Because he wanted to work hard, concentrate on things, dig in, move more slowly. But that was too slow. If you did all the reading, you wouldn't have time to eat, sleep, go to class, or anything else. He needed to pick and choose, but he was not the type to question the potential relevance of material prescribed by professors. If they said read Thucydides, he read Thucydides. Maybe not every statesman had read him, but they ought to. He assumed no one would knowingly place obstacles in his way.

He threw himself into learning Russian with intense fervor, hanging around the Russian House at all hours. There he got into a game of Risk—a game at which he had thought he was the ruling expert master, since he always beat Karen and the neighbor kids—and got slaughtered by a pimply fat girl whose laugh was like the rhythmic call of a monkey. *Heenh, heenh, heenh*, alternating with a pseudo-Mayfair screech of "Boring, Sidney!" borrowed from a movie about the Sex Pistols. She seemed thick as a brick in every way, horribly repellent, yet successful. The next time he saw her, she took him apart at chess and informed him that they made first-semester Russian easy as falling off a log to attract more majors. They don't spring the six noun cases on you until the spring. It was even easier than introductory ancient Greek. Then she recited a poem in Greek, and Temple, who had been proud of getting an eighty-eight on the first pop quiz in Russian class, began to feel that as a Jefferson scholar his goose was cooked. Or maybe not cooked, but getting warm on the bottom and in need of a change of location.

He kept moving. He took up drinking coffee. He did his reading in the library, staying there until late at night. He realized with a shock that he might have to withdraw from Physics 101. He had neglected to sign up for a lab because he didn't know you were supposed to. Now he was weeks behind. They had entire particles that hadn't been in the textbooks in Centerville. When he saw Karen, he would shake his head and smile wanly.

What he didn't know: He was tall and broad-shouldered like a boy on an athletic scholarship. He wore white V-neck undershirts instead of dark crew-neck pocket tees. He didn't wear glasses. No one could place him. Generally, faculty members were in favor of giving him a chance, or a tutor—it's not like you could put a star scholar in a remedial course. What would you have been trying to remedy, anyway? His grammar and spelling, his diction and syntax, his study skills, it was all fine. It was his dated frame of reference that needed hoeing to let some sun through to the post-1960s vegetation. Temple needed someone to sit by him in lectures and say "Ignore this. Ignore this. Ignore this. This matters, because it's new. Ignore this." To him, everything was new and mattered.

Karen took a more pragmatic approach and was having more fun. She planned, tentatively, to major in English. As she explained to her mother in a letter, she knew English already, so she could probably get okay grades. There was no point majoring in something she didn't know already, as she would just get into trouble or, more likely, major in the wrong thing. Whereas with English you can't go wrong. Employers always need English. Besides, she had to take all sorts of electives to graduate anyway. She took cosmology, architecture, and economics, saving philosophy, chemistry, and military science (a special subject for ROTC members, but Karen had heard it was an easy A) for her second semester. They all sounded entertaining to her. Kicking back and listening to a lecture in a survey course was her idea of a good time. It was so much more interesting than high school or TV or anything else she'd done up to then. She loved college.

Reading statements like that made Meg get all choked up inside. After all, she had gone to Stillwater to meet women, and rather than a program of high-quality info-tainment, it had turned out to be the low-budget, audi-ence-participation version of college where professors leave content generation up to the students. She regret-ted that part of her life in its entirety, with the exception of its having produced Karen. Now she envied Karen so much it hurt. She wanted to be young again.

She wondered if it was too late to start over. She placed herself squarely in front of the full-length mirror on Karen's closet door and took stock.

Her face hadn't changed much. Her hair was al-most the same. Her feet weren't any different. Her hands had aged. And that was all she could see of herself. The rest was covered by a rugby shirt and carpenter's pants.

Grimacing, she took off the shirt and looked at the mirror again. The baggy pants looked ridiculous with her upper body, like a jug holding a calla lily, so she took them off, too. Her dingy bra and underwear were also unflattering and she took them off. Clad only in her own soft hair, she remembered the day she had danced with her beautiful debutante gown. All her naive joy about showing the world her long neck, straight shoulders, and weensy waistline.

The body parts were still there, but she wanted the dress back.

You idiot, Meg thought. You're a femme!

She rifled through Karen's things and found a dispos-able razor to shave her legs. Her own smooth legs drove her wild with lust.

The next morning she drove to Broad Street in Richmond and spent three hundred dollars at Thalheimers. She didn't care who saw her. After she put on the first outfit and shoes she bought, she couldn't even recognize herself.

She let a salesgirl do her face, but she didn't buy any makeup. One step at a time.

The Saturday after that, buying milk at the bait shop while wearing a close-fitting knit dress with tights, almost as an experiment, she saw a slightly younger woman climb out of a black Fiero. The woman had low-slung jeans on, with a big silver belt buckle, and her hair was cut to expose her ears. To Meg she seemed a pretty person done up tough, like a puppy with a spiked collar. Her hair and eyes were black and her skin was tan, with red lipstick like Malibu Snow White.

Meg lingered at the cash register and said, "You're not from around here."

"I'm looking for a house," the woman said as she paid for a six of Molson.

"I know one for sale that I could show you." It was true. Karen's ten-dollar pediatrician and his wife were liberals who had despaired of meeting like-minded couples and were looking to move away. The only thing still tying them to their five-acre farmette was the hundreds of yards of antenna wire strung from the trees. The pediatrician was a ham radio operator.

"I only need a year lease."

"They would do that. If they rent and hold, they'll get a better price. Property values around here go up and up."

"Are you a Realtor?"

"No!" Meg looked down. "I'm a ..." She paused, unable to think of a job title that would justify her nice outfit. "Housewife!" she said finally. She could be one of those Ladies Who Lunch.

She got in the strange woman's car and after a twenty-minute ride zigzagging on numbered country roads, naming the unmarked crossings, showed her the sign, FOR SALE BY OWNER.

"Let's drive up and see it," the woman said.

"But don't get out of the car," Meg said. "They have dogs."

The woman rolled the car slowly up the last bit of driveway and said, "Wow, this place is really country." The pediatrician's house was new. It stood on a high concrete foundation and had blue vinyl siding and small windows. It looked like a plastic toy. The wires connecting bare treetop to bare treetop were hard to miss. The trees were black walnuts that had grown in the woods and been left standing, scarred by the bulldozer they'd used to grade the clearing. The pediatrician's wife's chickens had scratched half the yard bare.

"And you were expecting?"

"Well, Realtors are always showing me places that are beautiful and historic and, I don't know, kind of totally gay. You know what I'm saying?"

"You mean those Victorian gingerbread houses you can turn into a bed and breakfast, and old general stores with porch swings."

"You got it. This house is reality."

"Humankind cannot bear much reality," Meg said.

"T. S. Eliot," the woman said. "This house might be a little too much reality." She swung the car around and drove back to the road.

"You into poetry?"

"Not exactly. I teach women's studies at CUNY, but I'm on sabbatical next year with a gig at Hampton U because Howard was booked solid, but maybe it's better to get south of DC. You know DC is a world all its own. I'm trying to write a book about this black lesbian playwright nobody ever heard of, and the thing is, maybe I know her work up and down and inside and out, but I cannot tell you what's drawn from life. Empiricism is a huge big deal right now. Authenticity. Reality. So I decided to do a sabbatical abroad. Spend some time at a historically black school, learn the words, the rhythms. Know what I mean? You hear poets read, but if that's all you hear, you're not hearing them. You have to hear them talk. At Hampton I'm in the theater department."

As she shifted into fourth the woman turned her head and smiled. She added a trace of condescension and sympathy, softening her smile around the edges, when she saw that Meg had not understood a word she said. Meg was staring blankly as a veal calf tied out in a field.

"I don't get this state at all," the woman said, changing the subject. "It's a strange world down here, economically. All that stuff you read about sharecroppers and tenant farmers doesn't seem to fit. It's rent-to-own shops, and people selling the same real estate over and over for a balloon payment due in two years. Poverty, poverty, everywhere you look, but no check-cashing places. You can't throw a rock without hitting a bank! I just don't get Virginia. I wish somebody would just explain it to me—"

"Enough," Meg said, shaking her head. She looked at her knees and wriggled in the bucket seat so she could straighten her skirt. "Just stop. I can't take it. If you don't let me out of this car, I'm going to go crazy, and I don't even know your name."

The light dawned. The woman downshifted and pulled over to the side of the road. Meg jumped out and across the ditch into a soybean field. There was nowhere for her to hide. She just stood there cowering while the woman bore down on her with purposeful strides. "I'm going to fuck you now," she informed Meg, simultaneously kissing her and pushing her to the ground between two rows of soybeans in a sort of combination tango step and wrestling move.

"Aaanh!" Meg wailed in response.

"What was that?" The woman drew back.

"Please don't mind me. That was just my life flashing before my eyes."

"One more time. I need to fuck you." Meg dissolved in a flash of white light. It was like the sex scenes in *Cosmopolitan*. "That's better," the woman said.

*

She introduced herself as Luke, short for Loredana De Luca. She was able to free Meg from her writer's block with one well-placed observation. "You're such a separatist when you write," she said. "If you would just put your lesbians out in society, you'd have your dramatic conflicts. You'd even have roles for men!" Audiences, she added, love watching women, but actors hate being sidelined. That's why all the great female roles predate actresses. Antigone was a guy in a mask. Portia was a guy in a dress. So don't sideline your actors.

Meg's next draft was about lesbians in Iran. It had only two female roles, but very good ones, with a stoning and a suicide. Luke sent copies to friends in New York. The scene in which they take off their chadors to reveal rugby shirts was compared with the nude scene in *Equus*. People wanted to produce it and give Meg money. Her life had finally begun.

The lovebirds spent a lot of time at the squirrel sanctuary, as their lifestyle was incompatible with family values in Centerville. The horizontal light making the maples glow flame orange, the deep blue water dappled with the shadows of fish. Lying entwined in a rowboat, letting the wind push them into reeds, hearing the call of migrating curlews. Because she had to teach, Luke couldn't be on the Eastern Shore all the time. But she was a fast driver.

Meg wrote to Karen saying she would be staying on the Eastern Shore as much as she could, but would be back to pick them up at Thanksgiving. Dee was handling fall break.

Karen wrote to her mother at least once a week, usually on Sunday mornings, but more often if something interesting happened. The squirrel sanctuary's address was general delivery, so her letters went to the little post office in the nearest town and waited there to be picked up. Meg always sat down at the lunch counter at the five-and-dime across the street and wrote a reply right away, to save extra trips.

That was the sum total of their communication. It was not very communicative. Karen did not write that Temple was struggling to keep up with his course work, and Meg did not write that she was in love.

Nine

Parties at The University were considered a chance to blow off steam. To be three sheets to the wind and not show it: That was the ideal, attainable only by the most accomplished teen alcoholics. Visibly drunk: undesirable. Sober: geekdom (undesirable). Enter Temple and Karen.

It was Halloween, their first away from home. They had never seen middle-class trick-or-treaters in a town with houses. Charlottesville featured elaborate jack-o'-lanterns with real candles inside and wreaths of autumn leaves on doors. Halloween was aromatic and beautiful, and obviously as big a deal as Christmas. They were excited.

They surmised that in wild, uninhibited C'ville anything goes. Yet the costumes they chose were in doubtful taste by any standards. Temple wore a three-dollar thrift-shop suit of beige polyester gabardine from the seventies with wide lapels and no shirt. On his bare, hairless chest, Karen painted a large swastika in Wite-Out.

Her costume was more or less the same, except that she wore her blue interview suit, while her swastika was in black Magic Marker on a T-shirt. On her feet were ratty gray Keds, her only shoes. There was a hole in the toe, but only on one side. Thus clad, they tasted a variety of miniaturized sweet cocktails at a progressive drinking party in Karen's freshman dorm, telling anyone who asked that they were dressed as crypto-fascism.

It was Temple's idea. It didn't particularly make sense. But after eight weeks of self-imposed boot camp, he wasn't expecting anyone ever again to notice anything he did. It was theater of the absurd, and its target audience was Karen. She was excessively amused. They collected stares and no comments of any kind, trawling the town and then the grounds for candy. At Temple's request, they switched from saying "Trick or treat!" to singing "Here We Go a Wassailing."

Eventually they reached a brick mansion with a wraparound porch where there was clearly a party going on. They rang the doorbell. They swung their candy sacks from side to side in rhythm and started singing the song. A boy answered the door dressed as a wizard in a pointed hat and a long cape covered with stars. He gave them each a Reese's Peanut Butter Cup and said, "So what are you? I mean, you're obviously assimilationist self-hatred, like W. E. B. Du Bois, but what's she?"

"She's my shadow," Temple said. It didn't quite make sense, but Temple was not accustomed to having logical rigor enforced by anyone other than his conscience, and it had dozed off from exhaustion.

"Say, you guys want to come inside before somebody shoots you?"

The wizard opened the door on a room that was relatively quiet, relatively bright, and not the least bit smoky. There were many boys, and a few girls, sitting in costumes on sofas arranged in squares. Three boys were playing a complicated board game while others looked on and commented. A handsome boy stood in a corner of the huge room by the fireplace, one foot up on the hearth, playing a Violent Femmes song on a baritone ukulele.

"We'll come inside for a little while," Karen said.

She and Temple set their candy bags down in an armchair to reserve it and went looking for the bathroom. They worked their way toward the back of the house all the way to the kitchen but didn't find it. They climbed the stairs to the second floor and found only bedrooms. They stood in the hallway looking confused, which is easy to do alone at a big party wearing swastikas, and were discovered there by the musician, who had come upstairs to put his ukulele away. It was Byrdie Fleming.

"What are you looking for?"

"The bathroom," Karen said.

"You can go in my suite," Byrdie said. "The bathrooms are all between bedrooms. You can't get to them from the hallway." He led them down the hall and opened a door. There were about ten people in the room, an odd smell Temple and Karen didn't recognize, and on the coffee table a black brick of compressed Afghan hashish that had seen better days. A girl was prying shavings off it with a cake knife.

While Karen went to the bathroom, Temple sat down. The discussion in the room revolved around Friedrich Nietzsche. "He was a radical feminist," a girl said. "That's proof positive that something is wrong with radical feminism. He's just like them. He thought women need to be radically different from the way they are."

"He thought everybody needed to change radically," Byrdie said. "Except him. So calling him a feminist because he hates women is like calling him a leftist because he hates the working class." He turned to Temple and said, "You're obviously a fascist. You explain it to them!"

"I just want everything to stay the way it is and then repeat itself," Temple said. "I call it eternal recurrence. Then there's no way out for any of us."

"That's exactly right," Byrdie said. "You can't claim you have some kind of critical outsider perspective just because you hate the situation you're in."

"There's a way out if you call Cthulhu," another boy said. "Cthulhu destroys your world, and then you can start over."

"Which parts of this are my world?" Temple asked. "I'd hate to have Cthulhu destroy my world and then it turns out nothing's changed except the parts that were mine. So I'm still sitting here talking to you, but, like, where's my pants?" He looked down.

"What about your friend? She must be from your world. We never saw her before."

"Me and Shadow don't live in the same world," Temple said. Then he looked embarrassed. "I mean, nobody shares a world. We all have our own worlds."

"World*views*," Byrdie said. "I mean, it's one world, but people have different perspectives on it. Otherwise I couldn't change your world, and you couldn't change mine. There's advantages and disadvantages."

Karen came out of the bathroom, occasioning a brief hush because you don't see an outfit like that every day. Byrdie said, "Would you like a drink?"

"Maybe a beer," Karen said. "I don't really drink."

"But by the way, I've been wanting to ask you," Temple said. "Is that opium, or hashish?"

"It's hash," the Lovecraftian boy volunteered. "We burned through all our reefer this morning at the ounce blitz."

"I've been fascinated by the topic of hashish ever since I read a certain masterpiece of black literature, *The Count of Monte Cristo*. And that was before I got turned on to Baudelaire."

"My mom's heavy into Baudelaire," Karen explained, seeming embarrassed by Temple but not by her own mention of her mom.

"So I was just wondering, is it the kind you can eat?" Temple asked. "Because I don't smoke. I mean, I tried smoking once, but I ended up coughing like crazy."

"We were going to make brownies," the girl with the cake knife said. "But we're not getting very far. It's hard as a rock."

"Let me try," Temple said. He accepted the knife and proved to be much stronger than the girl, able to cut slices from the block of hashish as though it were a fruitcake.

"Slow down!" the girl said. "You're going to get us all fucked up. That is a lot of hash."

"Is it? I didn't know. I'm sorry."

"This is plenty for brownies," she said. "You want to hang out and help eat them?"

"Oh, Temple!" Karen cried. "Don't you dare!"

"Just one little taste?" he asked her. "For Baudelaire's sake?"

The whole room laughed.

"We don't do illegal drugs," Karen said. "Don't you have, like, alcohol or anything normal?"

"This is the drug frat," a boy explained. "Didn't you see the sign?"

"There's no sign," the girl said, in an aside to Karen. "They lost their charter."

"I didn't want to join a fraternity anyway," Temple said. "I was going to join a liberty first, and then an equality."

"There's punch downstairs," Byrdie said to Karen.

"I'll get you some punch," Karen said to Temple.

Byrdie accompanied her down the stairs, admiring the deft way her sneakers skidded down the slick carpet below her short skirt. He thought: I know this girl. But how? He put the question out of his mind and led her to the back porch, where a plastic garbage can stood filled to the brim with rum punch nearly invisible under rafts of floating strawberries that had been soaked overnight in grain alcohol. He dipped out two generous servings and watched her walk back upstairs.

About seven hours later, Byrdie thought to reascend the steps to his room. Temple was on his sofa. Something smelled bad, like bathroom. He looked closer. Temple had puked and soiled his pants. He tried to rouse him and got only groans. The others were gone.

But where? That motherly little girl wouldn't have left Temple alone. The lowborn damsel who unleashed all the protective urges in Byrdie. He walked the length of his hall and then the length of the halls upstairs, and heard nothing. Then he walked the halls again, opening every door.

Finally he found people awake and switched on the light. Karen lay on her back on a bed that had been shoved into the middle of the room, at the center of a group of boys wearing only boxer shorts. They had swastikas drawn on their chests in Magic Marker. There was a smell of incense and sweat.

"What the *fuck* are you doing," Byrdie said. "I mean, what the *fuck* are you doing?"

"We convened a fraternity council to assess her eligibility to become our fertility goddess," a boy named Mike said.

"We're casting lots for her garments," another added. Karen didn't move or make a sound.

"Get the *fuck* out, *all* of you," Byrdie said.

"This is my room," Mike protested.

Byrdie repeated himself yet again. Then he picked up a broadsword that was leaning behind the door because Mike was in the Society for Creative Anachronism. All the boys retreated to the hall. He closed the door, locked it, and turned to Karen.

She was fully clothed, which was a relief. He peeked up her skirt to make sure. On her T-shirt, below the swastika, someone had written "Sex Receptacle." His eyes burned with shame. She was breathing evenly, with a slight gurgling sound. He turned her head and body to the side and a thread of drool trickled from her mouth. She made a humming sound and never opened her eyes. One arm reached out and touched his leg.

Byrdie hoisted her into the air easily, cradling her in his arms, and carried her down to his room. Her boyfriend hadn't moved. He positioned her on his bed and poked Temple a couple of times in the side. "Yo, bleed, wake up," he said.

"I can't. I'm dead," Temple said. "Where am I? Oh shit." He choked out a strange sob and buried his face in the couch. Then he suddenly sat upright and said, "Where are those guys? Where's Shadow?" He lurched into the bathroom and vomited, moaning. As he ran, Byrdie saw that his pants were stained brown in the rear. It was not Temple's best moment.

"Your friend's okay," Byrdie called to him through the door. "Where does she live? I'm going to take her home if you don't mind."

"Get her out of here," Temple said. "This place is cursed. It's literally hell. I deserve to be here." Another catastrophic heave took him by surprise, and there was a sound like a long, damp fart.

"Take your suit off and throw it away. Throw away all your clothes, man. Put them in the trash bag and tie it up real tight, and take a shower. I'm serious. Take some of my clothes. They'll fit you."

"Oh, God," Temple said. "This is the worst day of my life."

"Where does your girlfriend live?"

"Dabney three-oh-two," Temple said.

Byrdie was surprised. He had figured she was a townie.

"Tomorrow I'm going to a revival and surrendering to Jesus," Temple added, burping loudly and returning to the toilet.

"Stand in the bathtub when you take your clothes off," Byrdie suggested.

"I'm so sorry," Temple groaned. "I can never make this up to anybody, ever. This is rock bottom."

Mike, the boy who had hosted the fertility ritual with Karen, spent most of the following day in a police station downtown. He was interviewed by two local police detectives, playing good cop and better cop. With him were two young criminal defense lawyers hired by his father. They occasionally resorted to holding their heads and gasping in horror. One of them eventually said, "Please can it and leave the talking to us. One more word and I'll pop you this time for real."

The reason was this: The Thetan House Halloween party had been the occasion of a very straightforward entrapment sting.

The political background of the police's actions was unimpeachable. There were murmurings of dissatisfaction in the local black community that had spread to the Democratic Party, endangering the mayor's reelection campaign. So many black people had been busted for crack cocaine while college students went on snorting the expensive stuff unimpeded. All sorts of hard drugs drifted around the college, nearly always ignored. A cloud of pot smoke at a concert on-grounds was a chance for campus cops to roll their eyes. The same cloud in front of a black nightclub in town led to convictions and ruined lives. It was high time, the liberals and the fuzz agreed, that some lives be ruined on the other side of the fence.

But it's hard to catch someone in possession of a drug he takes once a month or so, bought in the quantity he'll need for a single evening. The dealers were impossible to pin down, because they seemed to overlap with the users. When one had drugs, they all had drugs, in uninteresting small quantities, and when the town was dry it was dry. Once you bust them, they get careful. They didn't get into UVA for nothing. They're smart.

Thus it was decided to run a sting. Armed with little more than longish hair and a superficial knowledge of Tolkien, a grown man moved in with the Thetans. It wasn't a dorm, after all, or even officially a frat house anymore—just a big rented house, and he demonstrated his superiority to competing student applicants by laying claim to a reliable source of excellent LSD. To no one's surprise on the official, organizing end of the sting, the students didn't bat an eyelash. Why exactly it would be legal for him to do that—poison college students in their home—no one could say.

Mike had accepted three tabs of four-way blotter from the paid informant. The police knew that twelve hits of acid cut with methamphetamine is much too much for one person. It would make him feel desperately ill for a good long while. Thus if the next day he can't produce it, yet walks and talks, he is—with near certainty—a dealer of LSD.

But instead of claiming to have lost the LSD, or even to have consumed it, Mike reasoned that if possessing a substance is illegal, the best thing to have done with it would be to have gotten rid of it ASAP. So he said, "I didn't have that acid for more than five minutes. I gave it to somebody else."

His lawyers groaned. "What's the big deal? There was this girl at the party, too young to be drinking, so we—"

One of his lawyers reached over and slapped him, gently.

"What's wrong?" he demanded to know. "What am I saying wrong?"

"You didn't give acid to an underage girl," the lawyer hissed. "Try to remember what really happened."

"Giving drugs away is dealing," a detective said. "You may not be aware of this, but if there's a marijuana cigarette going around the room and you touch it, you're guilty of possession. If you pass it on, you're guilty of distribution. That's the law of the land. And that makes you a dealer."

"I didn't sell it! I gave it away!"

"Did you have any more contact with the girl? Did you try to get it back?"

"She was in my room passed out the whole time."

That's when the lawyers begged him to shut up.

"I don't get it!" Mike wailed. "All I did was take drugs, I mean accept them as a gift, from somebody I don't even know, and only because he was driving me crazy, begging me to take this acid off his hands. And he was working for you the whole time, and now you're acting like I'm the drug dealer here! It's not fair!"

"You gave that girl enough LSD to poison the water supply of the entire campus."

"What are you talking about? Twelve hits is twelve hits!"

"LSD is an extremely potent substance. According to our records, a typical square of four-way blotter weighs at least a gram."

"Of paper! That's the weight of the paper!" He appealed to his lawyers for help. They shook their heads. "This is way fucked," he said. "I have no chance. They're insane."

Conferring with him privately, his lawyers explained that he would be well advised to identify witnesses who might contradict his story—particularly the girl. But he could barely remember Karen. His memories of the evening were all rather hazy. He knew she had blond hair. He couldn't say how tall she was. "She was lying down when I met her," he explained. The part he remembered best was being herded out of his room with a claymore.

Byrdie Fleming: That's who ended up with the girl and the drugs. But rat out a brother? His own beloved hegemon?

The police typed up a summary of his inadvertent remarks, and he signed it so he could go home.

When Karen woke up, it was midafternoon. She was on her bedspread, still wearing her suit, but her T-shirt and her shoes and socks were gone.

She checked her jacket pockets and found a handwritten note. "Dear Shadow——," it read. "If you're missing any stuff, it's probably at Thetan House, or I know where to find it. Your friend Temple stayed over there last night. He was not feeling too well. Thanks for a very interesting evening. Very truly yours, Thetan Hegemon."

She remembered the hegemon well. He had been smart without being nerdy. That was something new to her. Intelligence paired with dignity, a stark contrast to Temple, especially as his behavior became more embarrassing over the course of the evening. She hadn't dared leave him alone. It shamed her to think that the hegemon had found them "interesting." What a condescending term. Yet there had been something pleasant and dreamlike about her night—but she couldn't say what. She recalled the hegemon's face opposite her own in dim shades of gray, like a face in a dream.

With the note were three squares of thick paper that resembled markers from a board game, each printed with four tiny yellow kangaroos. Other than that her pockets wcre empty. She stood up and looked around her room. There was no sign of her coin purse or Halloween candy, but her keys were in the door.

She thought hard. What had gone on? Why did she have no shirt? How did she get home with such clean feet, if she'd lost her shoes?

She went looking for Temple. He was in his dorm room, suffering. His roommate was watching a movie on video, and every word of dialogue seemed like a dull knife sawing at Temple's brain. He willingly followed Karen outside. They walked to a little planting of trees with a bench.

"We are not telling anybody about this," Temple said.

"Damn straight," Karen said. "That was the top secret night from beyond. Never again."

"It's top secret even to me," he said. "I remember going to their party, and I remember coming home."

"I found this in my pocket." She showed Temple the squares of paper with the kangaroos.

"Blotter acid?" Temple said. "Get it away from me. Like, hide it, right now."

Karen was intrigued. She had overheard Lomax and Meg talking about LSD once. Meg had said there were few more delightful things in life. Meg had been treated to some real Owsley acid from San Francisco by a famous poet, dribbled by the poet himself on a sugar cube, and had never forgotten how the swallows looked swooping over the yard at dusk. Billions of them. Karen remembered the sugar cube part vividly—nothing about paper. "How could I have bought LSD?" she objected. "I only had two dollars! What makes you so sure?"

"Blotter is cheap. I read about it in a book on Jimi Hendrix."

"What should I do with it?"

"Throw it over your left shoulder. Shake the dust of it from your sandals. Except you don't have shoes on. Put it down." Karen placed the acid on the damp sand in front of them. Still sitting, Temple slammed his shoe heel down on it and twisted around. "Get thee behind me, kangaroo Satan!" he said. The soft paper sank in shreds into the dirt. Temple smoothed the surface of its grave with his hand.

"Mom always said acid is the greatest thing since sliced bread. It's supposed to be valuable."

"Your mom! Acid was really great in 1968. I bet she took pure pharmaceutical-grade acid dropped on sugar cubes by Allen Ginsberg."

"God, how did you guess?"

"Maybe she told me. Now it's just this dirty crap cut with crystal meth. Cheeta"—that was Janice's boyfriend—"told me whatever you do, never shoot up anything, and never take anything that's not available by prescription and been tested for safety. If you can't find it in the *Physician's Desk Reference*, leave it alone."

"But I could have traded it back to them for my sneakers!"

"Trading that much acid for your sneakers would evidence a lack of business sense. Plus it would be a felony, sort of like even *owning* that much acid."

"There was a note with it from their hegemon saying 'thanks for an interesting night.' Maybe it was, like, payment for an interesting night?"

Temple's eyes narrowed.

"Not that interesting. I mean, I was missing my shirt and my shoes and socks, but nothing happened."

"How can you tell nothing happened?"

"Do you really want to know?"

"Yeah."

"Well, I'm on my period, and my tampon string was still—"

Temple grimaced and said, "Ugh! Stop it!"

"You asked."

"What about your shirt?"

Karen frowned.

Up to that point Temple had been thinking grateful and admiring thoughts about Byrdie. Now he declared to Karen that instead of laundering Byrdie's clothes and returning them to Thetan House, he would keep them in trade for her sneakers, his undershirt, and the mortal affront of saddling her with illegal drugs.

The police told Mike to go back to the house and relax. For him it had been a confusing day. The law was so friendly, and his own lawyers were so hostile. The police made him feel important, caring about what he said. But his supposed allies kept calling him stupid and saying he should shut up.

Back among his brothers, he saw an opportunity to be a hero after all. They all knew Byrdie had humiliated him by driving him from his room and refusing to hear him out, but he could still take the moral high ground. He bragged that he could have saved himself by naming names, but instead he protected Byrdie. He had *not* told the police it was Byrdie who ended up with both the teenage whore and the large quantity of drugs she had accepted in payment. He, Mike, had taken *full* responsibility for the events of the night. The buck stops *here*.

"That was right Christian of you," Byrdie said. A short time later he sidled out of the kitchen as though to take a leak, crept up to his room, and called Lee.

Lee praised his presence of mind, set his alarm, and went back to sleep.

Byrdie regarded his large block of hash and several lesser items. He wished they were somewhere else. They had to vanish. But not by leaving the house on his person. It might be staked out. And not on his girlfriend's person. That was too much to ask. Thinking of Grandma Fleming, he went to the refrigerator.

His solution was loosely based on her trademark dumplings. Ground beef, hashish, raw egg, and a little pancake syrup, rolled in cornflakes for a better grip. At the center of each ball, a peyote button and a cannabis flower, finely crushed. Five of them, baseball-sized, on a plate, looked to Byrdie like something raccoons would eat.

He carried them up to the meditation room on the top floor and softly opened the half-moon window. He could hear the ruckus from the kitchen below. His waited until his eyes adjusted to the dark. He positioned himself away from the window to make sure his movements didn't attract attention and threw sidearm, hard. The first ball vanished invisibly into the night. He didn't hear it land, but he felt sure it had crossed the garage roof next door and landed at least two hedges away. He heard a dog bark. He launched four more.

After meditating briefly, he returned downstairs to call his girlfriend. He asked her to come over, saying he needed "sexual healing." That was in case his phone was tapped. When she arrived, they began cleaning his room.

Lee drove to Charlottesville at first light. He picked Byrdie up from a nearby gas station in silence. No one in the house had been awake to see him leave. Even the cops in the stakeout van missed his tiptoed exit through the bike room. Lee drove out to the bypass and checked them both into a nice motel.

Around nine a.m., the police cordoned off the house and began a comprehensive search. They interviewed every boy individually, except Byrdie, who was nowhere to be found.

The informant had lived in the house for months, so the boys naturally assumed he had witnessed every drug transaction during that time, along with a majority of instances of drug use. To preempt his accusations, they came clean. They were chatty as sparrows, convinced cooperation buys leniency. They detailed others' narcotics-related activities and even their own as though they'd never heard of jail. You had to bark "Shut up already!" to get a chance to read them their rights. They would get bored waiting for their lawyers to show up and tell the investigators funny anecdotes about the time they dropped acid and swam in a fountain and campus cops took their clothes. They would get in this angry mood like they wanted their clothes back and could the FBI get on the case.

The Commonwealth's attorney was getting frustrated. Their crimes were so petty and selfish. Buying a joint to smoke alone in your room! A single hit of ecstasy! He was almost ashamed for them. Had no one taught them to share?

He was the democratically elected head prosecutor of the city of Charlottesville. Since victims outnumber criminals, he favored victims. He knew there is no such thing as a victimless crime, whatever casual drug users might say. A person whose harmless actions are criminalized becomes a victim of the law. That paradox helped him out every day by showing him the unreality of his job.

Mike had confessed in writing to serious crimes. He had given a young girl twelve hits of acid. He had even conspired, he admitted somewhat bashfully, to bestow on her the honors due a fertility goddess, though nothing had come of it. Absolutely no one else had been at fault in any way. His confession was typed and signed, if only because he didn't believe he had done anything illegal.

Mike was unknowingly committed to civil disobedience. He sincerely believed his persecutors would be exposed as criminals.

But then his parents showed up—nice, working-class folks from Long Island who had sacrificed much to send Mike to a Public Ivy to major in accounting. They alternated standing outside the house in tears and calling the Commonwealth's Attorney's Office from a pay phone to beg for mercy.

Mike asked if he could make another statement. He said he was very sorry for providing false information, but in fact it was Byrdie who had done all those things.

Mike's fingering Byrdie was the first good news the Commonwealth's attorney had heard all day. At last a credible suspect: the frat president who had waltzed off at the end of the night with the girl and the drugs, who was incommunicado and well known to the informant as a connoisseur of organic psychedelics.

He had the cops tell the other boys that Mike had accused Byrdie. Now several agreed that the girl's name was Shadow. Probably an underage townie. No identifying marks. An indistinct person. Not a high school kid, at least eighteen. An anthro major if anything. Came with that freaky African guy who completely lost it at the party. Who on earth let them in? The wizard boy who had let them in remembered that Temple was a Jefferson scholar. A few remembered Byrdie's barging in on a social event upstairs and spending time alone with the girl. Some remembered him, surely drunk and drugged out of his mind, attacking Mike with a sword, which might explain why Mike was afraid of him. Some remembered Byrdie sneaking the girl away unconscious.

Duly noted, their accounts began slow transmutations into misdemeanor plea bargains, suspended sentences, hours of community service, etc.

The prosecutor relaxed. He thought he could lean back and enjoy playing the big fish on his hook. But a search of Byrdie's room produced nothing. Not a trace. His Jewish girlfriend had seen to that. Years of pre-Passover training, taking books off shelves to hunt for crumbs. The entire room appeared to have been wiped down. It smelled faintly of bleach.

As the day went on, the prosecutor began to feel a creeping sense of nascent professional embarrassment. He was staging a high-profile drug bust with no drugs. Thinking of the spotless room, he began working up a catchphrase for the press, something about "arrogant shit's ass on a stick."

He felt certain the dramaturgy of going to trial against Byrdie would benefit his career and justify his expensive sting operation. There was similar excitement among the rank and file. They might be looking at undreamed-of success: Not penny-ante possession cases, but heavy-duty hard drug dealing. Not just any white kid, but the crème de la crème. Not just drugs, but statutory sexual assault on a minor on drugs! But they needed corroborative evidence. For his own peace of mind, the prosecutor felt he should not lay himself open to charges of failing to question statements by loosely wound kids who may or may not have been tripping when they witnessed various events and/or confessed and/or retracted their confessions. With some it was hard to tell. Mike in particular was such a sweaty-palmed, incoherent little guy anyway. The hard evidence adequate to indict Byrdie was in the pockets and/or bodily cavities of a petite junior female named Shadow, whom it was incumbent on the police to find before she had a chance to excrete certain metabolites or douche her organs. It was still less than forty-eight hours since the party.

To find her, all they had to do was find Temple. Luckily he was one of the more conspicuous people in Charlottesville.

A number of officers were assigned to track him down. It took them a while. He was still too headachy to endure his roommate or go to class. He slept for a good long while with his head down on a study carrel in the library and then moved to a sofa. Instead of his tennis sweater he was wearing an elegant blazer that had once belonged to the poet Mark Strand. A couple of times a security guard approached to rouse him, noticed the clothes, and let him lie.

"Run this by me again, Bird Dog," Lee said to his son. "Why does it make any difference what underage slut gets gang-raped in your frat house? Where's the novelty?"

"I'm saying, she was not a slut. She was a good kid. And Mike says I carried her home with an amount of drugs in her pocket that could get us all sent to prison."

"So?"

"What if the police had stopped me? I don't even know if it's legal to carry girls around."

"They didn't stop you. They didn't catch you. What are you so worried about?"

"You're the one who checked me into a motel! What are you so worried about?"

Lee said, "I'm not worried. But we don't talk to cops in our family. You're too young to know that. We have a different level of access to the law."

"What about the girl?"

"What about her?"

Byrdie remembered the note. "When I dropped her off, I left her a note."

"You didn't sign it, I assume."

"I signed it as 'Thetan Hegemon.' 'Byrd Fleming' looks, I don't know, kind of freighted. She was black. But so, so cute."

Lee went to the refrigerator and got them each a beer. "Go on," he said.

"I wanted her to be able to find me if she wanted. I thanked her for an interesting evening," he said.

"Jesus, Byrd," Lee said. He pulled out his address book and added, "I'm going to put you on the phone with your uncle Trip, because this is way over my head."

BTF III, Esq., had been in politics only very briefly when a scandal in the 1970s earned him an unelected appointment, but he still had some pull, and Byrdie told him the story: Mike, his housemate and brother, had returned from a police interrogation telling all and sundry that he had nobly covered up Byrdie's crimes.

Those crimes were possession of an amount of acid large enough to suggest dealing and a black woman small enough to suggest an age of around fifteen. Both were Mike's crimes, but that didn't seem to penetrate Mike's awareness. In his own mind, he had handed off his crimes in a lateral pass when Byrdie relieved him of the victim and—unwittingly—the drugs. Byrdie feared that transporting a drugged girl laden with drugs might be construed as smuggling. In related news, he had assaulted his accusers with a long, heavy sword.

Trip said, "You're fucked. Bend over like you mean it."

"How do I do that?"

"Go down to the station and say hello. Then don't say another word. That's the hard part. You're going to think you can manipulate them, because they're going to be such obligate jackasses, but pride goeth before a fall. Never, ever give in to the temptation to tell them what really happened. If it conflicts with their theories, they'll take it out on you. Make them think, and they'll want revenge. Your job is to sit tight while I play my hand. It'll be interesting, making a neat tidy felony case out of this, fit for circuit court."

"Could you repeat all that to Dad?" He handed the receiver to Lee.

"I wish you could see what Byrdie has on," Lee told Trip. "A rainbow shirt and a black girdle. He looks ready to sell his tail end on Ninth Avenue."

Byrdie looked down and said, "These are bike shorts!"

"I can see his fundament," Lee continued.

"This shirt is Deadhead, not gay pride," Byrdie said pointedly. "It's batik!"

"Go out now and buy him some trousers," Trip advised, cackling.

"But why? They might not even take him into custody."

Byrdie had already peeled off the shorts. He handed them to Lee and requested his pants and shirt.

Lee drove him to the police station in town and announced his presence. Byrdie stood contritely, looking at the floor, a guilty schoolboy. A routine book-and-release on his own recognizance, with an appointment to come back the next week to be arraigned on felony hard-drug-dealing charges to be determined in circuit court by a grand jury. They guessed bail wouldn't be set too high, and that his lawyer should bring his checkbook.

"See?" Lee said, cradling his genitals for safety as he sat down in the car. "That wasn't so bad. Trip will pull some strings and get the charges expunged. No need to fuss and fret. I really do love these pants. Comfiest I ever had on."

"Keep them, Dad. My gift to you."

"And if you can't move out of that house full of pizza-face losers, at least exclude me from your future shenanigans. Let Trip handle this shit from now on. It depresses me no end."

Byrdie settled in at the motel for a few days. Criminality was the kind of novel experience he felt he would be best able to handle with salty snacks and daytime television.

He was glad to be away from the house. He imagined an obsequious uproar. All the brothers excited by official attention, flattered by interrogations, reenacting hard-boiled noir movies. Jabbering hoarsely about the need to protect themselves, about what should be done with stool pigeons, about who had known what when. Presenting a united front, looking to their fugitive hegemon for leadership. He realized how wrong he might be. Suddenly he found them all immensely irritating.

He would have liked to send for his girlfriend, but his stress levels made him hesitate. Her presence would have necessitated talking to her. So much for burritos and *Night Court*. She was such a good girlfriend. But he felt no longing. He wondered instead how he could warn Shadow.

He wrote her a postcard from the lobby, in care of her dorm room. "The police were there. Be careful!" he wrote. He couldn't think of anything else to say that wouldn't be incriminating to one or the other or both of them. He didn't sign it at all. He assumed she would remember his handwriting from the earlier note and draw her own conclusions.

It was too succinct. Karen had been nursing a crush on him, but that two-sentence letter killed it. She didn't think she had been warned by a friend. She thought, This is a threat from an asshole drug dealer in trouble who thinks I might fink!

*

So far the prosecutor knew one thing for certain about Shadow: she had twelve hits of acid. She might have been a sexual assault victim, too, in theory, but time to prove that was running out. So she was trading sex for drugs. Not in reality—reality wasn't directly relevant—but in the case he might make against Byrdie. Shadow could be Byrdie's acid whore. Like a crack whore, only with acid.

He turned the thought over in his mind and realized his equation didn't quite hold, because acid isn't addictive. Her motive would have to be money. Money is as addictive as air. "Shadow" could be a prostitute's nom de guerre ...

The prosecutor wasn't asking for much—just guilt beyond a reasonable doubt and a courtroom free of conflicting information. He wasn't anybody's nemesis! He had nothing against Byrdie or Shadow, either one! He just needed to put away some criminals for his résumé.

"Acid whore," he said aloud, rehearsing for the newspapers. "A so-called fraternity house where a drug lord lured a penniless local girl ..." Decency forbids further reproduction of his shameful imaginings.

"Karen Brown," Temple said, readily. "We grew up together."

The cops traded looks. "Can you give us a description of Miss Brown?"

"Black, short, built, long blond hair, light blue eyes, ivory skin."

The cop was confused. "Did you say black? What's black?"

"Karen."

"She's a black girl."

"Yes. She's my girlfriend."

"And she's light-skinned."

"Yes."

"But black."

"She's on a minority scholarship."

"And she has what you call a passing complexion."

"Anybody can tell looking at her that she's black. She has full lips and a little flat nose, kind of like Barbie."

"Barbie is Swedish."

Temple was silent, thinking maybe they weren't believing him.

When Temple called home to say the police had questioned him in connection with drugs, Dee uttered a scream she was sure could be heard in Charlottesville. She sat down hard, pounding the table with her fists. Meg was far away, incommunicado, at a squirrel sanctuary without a phone, and for several minutes Dee hoped somehow to conceal the revelation from Ike forever. She felt very alone.

"Take it easy, Mom," Temple said. "It was a coincidence. We went to this party where there was a bust going on. How were we to know?" He described the conversation, adding that Barbie could be black and Swedish, the way Pushkin was black and Russian. Dee told him to keep his mouth shut and not to talk to anybody until she conferred with Ike. Understandably, she kept putting it off.

They didn't ask him anything else, and they never questioned him again. There had been a request from the university administration to keep the scandal within limits. They were not about to sacrifice a black Jefferson scholar. And of course he was exempt from the prosecutor's project of railroading white students. There was even a danger that if the public became aware of his presence at the party, all the white boys would be off the hook. Temple was not a welcome addition to the case.

The news that Karen was also black greatly disappointed the prosecutor. He wouldn't be able to charge her with anything, or even throw around his new catchphrase "acid whore." It would alienate the very constituency he was trying to reach. With a sigh of resignation, he set his sights on Byrdie alone.

The authorities didn't catch up with Karen until the next day. She had been so busy with meals and classes and buying new sneakers. Most of her classes were well-attended lectures, and Temple's description applied to half the women at UVA. You couldn't tell by looking who was a natural blonde, and certainly not which blondes were black. Any short girl might wear heels. They were waiting outside her dorm room when she got back from breakfast.

They asked whether she had been given blotter acid at the party, and what she had done with it. She said she had thrown the acid away, because drugs are bad. She gave them the first note from Byrdie, explaining that she had found it in her pocket with the unwanted blotter, and the unsigned postcard.

"Did he do anything to you? Any evidence of a sexual encounter?" She shook her head, looking offended. "Would you be willing to submit to examination by a physician?"

"There's nothing to examine!" Karen said. "I'm not that kind of girl!"

She led them to where she and Temple had disposed of the acid. And there it was—in tatters, laden with sand, but extant. Two nights underground including an episode of light rain had boosted its weight to a respectable five grams. They put the acid and Byrdie's correspondence in Baggies and thanked her for her cooperation.

Not twenty minutes later, the prosecutor finally had his case. The poor, innocent black coed, the substantial amount of acid miraculously saved from the college dump, the note in Byrdie's hand written with Byrdie's Cartier fountain pen (it had been in the prosecutor's possession since the search of Byrdie's room), the revelatory postcard from the safe house, a.k.a. Holiday Inn.

The prosecutor put it all together, imagining himself a newspaper reporter, and experienced a moment of unexpected heavenly bliss.

Karen ran to Temple's room and threw herself in his arms, wide-eyed with fear. Drugs. Sex. The police. This was not how she had imagined college.

She was scared straight. Instead of sitting still on his lap as she was used to doing, she squirmed. Temple leaned down and kissed the top of her head. Then he kissed her mouth. But instead of enveloping her in a bear hug as usual, he put one hand on the nape of her neck and the other on her breast. Then he got up and locked his roommate out. "Shit, why didn't we think of this before?" he asked.

"Because we're retarded," Karen said.

Hours went by before a loud knock and a stern, stage-whispered "Temple!" alerted them that Dee had arrived. He let her in almost immediately, and her dismay over his metamorphosis reached a peak. The bedspread was smooth, their clothes were on, but their underwear was in a corner of the floor, and their hair ... Dee trembled. The shape of Temple's coiffure, which wanted cutting, was that of a topographic model of West Virginia, and Karen's hair was ratted all up the back like dog hair in a brush. Her lips had that bitten red look, and she was reading *The Myth of Sisyphus* as if she didn't have a care in the world.

Dee slid past the bed and opened the window. Looking at Karen, she said, "Don't be afraid to say hi. I'm not going to hit you."

"Don't rag on her, Mama," Temple said. "She's my best friend in the world." He hugged and kissed his mother on the cheek.

"You smell like a bear," Dee said. "And let me set something straight. *I'm* your best friend. But right now I feel like sending you out to cut a switch."

"The situation is not good. We went to the wrong party."

"You went to a party on Halloween? You're not nine years old!"

"This is a party school. Everybody says, 'Work hard, play hard.' It's not entirely clear to me how you can learn physics chronically hungover. But they all do it. I'm serious, Mama." He took her hands. "They don't work eight hours and go down to the pond with a fishing pole. I could go to community college and have better odds of working at the State Department than here. The way it's going, I'll be lucky to have a C average."

"Don't change the subject."

"What subject?"

Dee turned. "Miss Karen, would you please explain yourself? How long has this been going on?"

Karen put the book down and stood up to borrow Temple's comb. "You think I'm the reason he's getting bad grades? You know when's the first time we had sex? About twelve thirty. Today!"

Dee looked at her son and back at Karen, who was busy struggling with her hair, leaning forward with her head upside down.

"Was she experienced?"

"Drawing on the vast sophistication about women I've amassed in my long life, I would say no," Temple said.

Dee reached down and threw back the bedspread. A conspicuous spot of blood appeared. She covered it up again quickly and said, "You know, I'm starting to think I might be angry at the wrong person."

"You could say that."

"Now I feel mad at myself, but that's still the wrong person."

"Keep on, Mama. You're getting there."

Dee sat down on a chair. "Why don't you go and bathe yourself, and let me fix your hair, and we'll go out and get some pie and you can tell me the whole story from the beginning."

The hair project lasted fifteen pages of Camus. Pick pick pick, pat pat pat, coaxing it to maximum fluffiness and then trying to get it more or less spherical with the scarf from around her neck. As she worked she pondered how brilliantly she had raised a tall, handsome, noble boy who was the smartest child in the state of Virginia. She kept sneaking looks at the puny Shadow on the bed. Black my ass, she thought. You could tell by the food. White people were always eating things you couldn't identify. Chicken nuggets, fish sticks, hamburgers from some in-between place beyond meat. Her food, you could tell what it was. If you left white people alone, they would put crawfish in a blender. It was no wonder Karen was undersized. Eventually she gave up. "After pie, the barbershop," she said.

Ten

That evening Karen wrote a long letter to Meg.

Meg read the letter three days later, sitting on the porch swing at the post office on the Eastern Shore. She didn't get back on the road and drive like a bullet straight to Charlottesville. She didn't even write a reply. She just shuffled to the car, sat in the driver's seat, and looked in the rearview mirror, thinking of Luke.

I was happy, she thought. I was finally happy.

She put the car in gear and drove slowly back to the squirrel sanctuary. The sun pierced the charcoal-gray clouds with golden light that made even scraggly pines lining the roadside seem to burn like torches, and the water on the back bay was jiggling like mercury. But she felt like shit. More than anything, she was afraid. Joining Flea and Lomax in the living room, she started with the chief locus of her fear: "My baby's a narc."

"What?" Lomax said, jerking upright.

"Not about me, or us. But listen to this." She unfolded the letter. "'Dear Mom,' bla bla bla, 'the police showed up and somebody took me home, but I only know that because when I woke up I found a note thanking me for a good time and, believe it or not, all these hits of acid in my pocket. Temple told me what it was. I guess I dodged a bullet there.'" Meg rolled her eyes. "'But don't worry, nothing happened. I was just wasted because they soaked all these strawberries in 151. I felt like crap the day after, but now I'm fine. So this morning the police came to my dorm asking do I know anything about any acid, because somebody said he gave it all to me. Ratting me out to save his own ass! But it was okay, because we knew where we basically buried it, so me and the cops dug out what was left and I could prove that I didn't want his stupid acid in the first place. What an asshole. They said next time if I find drugs to bring them to the lost and found. I still had a note from that asshole, so I gave it to them as well. I cooperated and was very polite like you say. It will all blow over, but of course Temple's scared shitless,' bla bla bla."

"How is she a narc?" Flea asked. "I don't get it."

"The acid was gone. She could have denied all knowledge of it. But she remembered it for them, dug it out of the ground for them, and handed them written proof that it was intended for her personal use. It's not going to blow over. She's going to be testifying at some asshole's trial."

"Oh."

"*Ça veut dire*, my baby the narc."

"You scared me bad," Flea said. "Karen is so cute, and I thought you wanted to sell her out."

"You have no idea," Meg said. "You don't know the half of it."

"What do you mean?"

"I've been living a lie."

Flea looked at Lomax for a moment and said, "We know you're a lesbian. I think of it as possession by the moon goddess."

Meg rolled her eyes. "And what if ..." She hesitated.

"What if what?"

"What if I told you my name was Margaret Randolph Vaillaincourt Fleming and I'm probably wanted for kidnapping?"

"Kidnapping who?" Flea asked.

"Karen."

"For sexual purposes?" Lomax asked.

Meg's facial expression was indescribable. "She's my daughter!"

Lomax thought it over. "Adopted, or real? She looks so white."

Meg sighed.

"Does she know anything about our business dealings?"

"Offhand I would say, nothing whatsoever, if she thinks acid in her pocket is a reason to sell somebody down the river."

"Well, shit," Lomax said. He lit a bong and passed it around.

Flea said, "You know what you should do. You should go home right now and give your place a really good exorcism. Like, get some of that Haitian floor wash against bad vibes and make sure you get it into every corner, and lay down a new coat of paint. You do not want them finding one single molecule if it comes to them searching your apartment."

"Thank God this place isn't my property," Lomax said. "They can't divest the squirrel huggers for ill-gotten gains, I don't think."

"That's true," Flea said. "Nobody can civil forfeit a squirrel. But now tell me about this kidnapping."

"It was a marital spat," Meg said. "We split the kids down the middle."

"You have another kid? That's so sad! Is it a boy or a girl? Older or younger?"

"Boy, older," Meg said. "Five years older than Karen. Only three and a half now, though, because Karen's actually this dead baby whose birth certificate I stole."

"So what's her real name?"

"Mickey. Mireille."

"Maray?" She rolled the word around her mouth with her tongue and needed several lessons to say it with the proper Languedoc growl. "Is the father French?"

"The father is Lee Fleming."

Lomax's eyes widened and he said, "*The* Lee Fleming? *La Fanciulla del West?*"

"What?" Meg said. "Fanciulla del West? I know he has some nicknames, but Fanciulla del West?"

"People don't tell wives everything." Lomax paused for a moment to fake a discretion he did not possess and said, "Lee Fleming pulled a train in a club in Staunton that was a hundred and fifty guys. I kid you not."

"That's bullshit," Meg said. "Just the kind of pathetic crap straight guys with nothing to their names say to comfort themselves over the fact that a stud like Lee can give it to anything or anybody he wants."

"Look who's still in love," Flea said.

"Oh, man," Lomax said, pouring himself a glass of Jägermeister. "Back to your daughter the moray eel. What are we going to do about her?"

"Is that a threat? She knows nothing. I raised her right. She's a good girl. Too good if you ask me."

At that very moment, Karen was saying to Temple, "If I stick my tongue in your mouth while your dick's inside me, we're a human yin-yang symbol." She demonstrated.

He got to his feet on the bed with her clinging to him like a limpet and said, "Au contraire! I alone am Abraxas! All forces are combined in me! Male, female, good, evil!" He shoved her against the wall and fucked her until she turned her face away and came with a series of minor screams, then turned around to lean his butt on the wainscoting and let her push off with her feet, caressing him with her cunt in a way that was truly obscene and continuing to have occasional orgasms. Temple was reordering his priorities in life at an alarming rate. Schoolwork, what's that? Physics, who cares? He was considering taking a year off, maybe make the Grand Tour of historic European capitals with Shadow, working on his French.

*

Meg took Flea's advice and spent early November in Centerville, scrubbing and wallpapering. She burned nearly everything she owned—anything that might have a trace of white powder on it anywhere—in a clearing in the woods. She made a New Year's resolution to change her life.

Not her clothing this time, but her life. She would tell Luke and Karen the truth ... or not. If her life changed enough, maybe she could skip the explanations. That recurring thought generally inspired her to pour herself a glass of wine for courage.

In Centerville, Thanksgiving and Christmas came and went uneventfully. Luke was off with her clan in Brooklyn. Nobody was interested in admitting that anything had happened.

And in a sense, nothing had happened. Karen and Temple were not charged with any crime. Like Temple, Karen was not the kind of student the police in Charlottesville were after. She was black.

They were after her brother, but without drama. To the prosecutor's mind, Byrdie had by surrendering agreed to help his career, in a way, and might even be owed a certain amount of gratitude. Submitting to be tried was a deeper genuflection before the law than any guilty plea. The prosecutor wanted the case to stay in Charlottesville where his voters lived, so he held off going to the papers. All in good time.

Of course no one in the family told Meg's parents. Byrdie visited them over the holidays as he always did. In conversation he stayed with the topic that had become his standard with them: his vocation for public service. They never mentioned his mother or sister, hadn't seen them in a long time, and didn't know how to get in touch with them. The Vaillaincourts were great respecters of privacy.

Karen and Temple didn't come out of Karen's room much. She said she had homework, and Temple had to catch up on his reading. Dee put her ear to the door and heard Karen say, "I think your mom is eavesdropping."

They talked a lot about Meg. They agreed that she was living vicariously through Karen. "We should make her read some Jane Austen," Karen said. "If she knew how happy men make a person, I know she'd relax and meet somebody. When I was at home, I figured she was just holding back because of me, but now I think she might be shy around guys. I mean, didn't you ever notice Lomax's way cute friend the Seal?"

"Not really."

"He likes Mom a *lot*. We ought to send them out in the boat together when there's a storm coming. They'd get trapped, and the Seal would save her. It would be so romantic."

"But you wouldn't actually try to kill your mom to get her laid, right?"

"I just wish she had a life, so she wouldn't pay attention to me."

*

Christmas at Lee's parents' place was less relaxed than usual. Lee boycotted Byrdie's legal situation. If the subject came up, he would leave the room. That helped him stay calm, but it made the conversation revolve around Byrdie for several minutes every time.

Byrdie's grandfather always took the same line: Go straight to the top, highest court you can. Don't get a judge who reads case law, get a judge who makes it. Trip said it would never come to that—a trial—because the judge he had chosen had the case well in hand. Byrdie agreed that a trial would not be necessary. They were all a little drunk, nearly all the time. It was Christmas!

The facts of that long-ago October were mentioned only once. Byrdie remarked, "I don't see how they can convict me. The plant gave the drugs to the dweeb, and the dweeb gave them to the blondette. We subpoena the informant and the dweeb and make them give sworn testimony. Case closed."

"You're thinking again," Trip said, shaking his head. "Think harder. Prosecutorial misconduct as a defense! So far it's nothing personal. You're a martyr for the cause of freedom. Keep it that way."

Byrdie's grandfather said, "It would break my heart if they went after Lee."

"He's safe," Byrdie said. "I've been over the house with a fine-tooth comb. And the yard, too. You know how visitors hide stuff and forget it. But it's been years since I found anything good."

"You should have known him when he was younger," Trip said. "People always left something on the nightstand, and your mother was such a good hostess, whatever it was, she'd bring it downstairs and dump it on the coffee table. And the doors of perception were opened."

"Do *not* tell me," Byrdie said.

Lomax became antsy. He would get hunches that a raid was coming, and send Flea out at odd moments—in the middle of a meal or the middle of the night—to inspect the driveway and report back with a walkie-talkie. They had their first disagreement.

Meg and Luke had gone to bed, and Flea sat down next to Lomax and played with the little wreath of hair over his ears. "Stop that," he said.

"I need tenderness," she said. "Maybe if you didn't smoke so much pot you could get it up?"

He said, "Maybe if you weren't so big and heavy?"

She looked down. She was as slender as ever, but there was no denying that she was five foot eight, with breasts. "I can't help it. I'm not a little girl anymore."

"Are you accusing me of something?"

"I'm just saying I've been with you for ten years. My body's changed."

"Well said. You're free, white, and twenty-one. Maybe Luke likes her ladies voluptuous."

"Why are you hurting my feelings? You know I never look at anybody twice, especially not a woman."

"When's the last time you met a man? Being my prisoner and all. I could sell you to the Seal for a night. Would you like that?"

"You are seriously shitting all over my love for you!"

Seeing her tears, Lomax felt a pang of remorse. "Come here, Flea. Don't pout. You're still cute as the first day I saw you. We can be an old married couple forever and ever! I promise!"

"I'm sorry, sweet pea," she said, nestling into his lap.

"And you got one other thing wrong. I am habituated to the chronic. That means it is physically impossible for me to smoke too much pot."

By January the Commonwealth's Attorney's Office and the police force were unanimous: Prosecuting the case was an exercise in frustration. Mike had gone overboard as state's evidence, taking responsibility for things that contradicted all their best theories. He said he put twelve hits of acid in the girl's pocket. But it didn't wash. He had never been alone with her. No one had seen him do it. It was obviously a false confession, intended to protect someone he was afraid of. Whom the girl had incriminated directly—a big fish, a much more desirable catch. But the big fish was stonewalling.

They had indicted Byrdie on felony charges of distribution of a hard drug. And he seemed to find the indictment something approximately as troubling as ... as nothing at all. He showed up to his arraignment unshaven, in boat shoes and ostentatiously wrinkled natural fibers. He asked his taxi driver to wait for his lawyer since he was fresh out of cash. He said not one word. He just marked time until they finished, like someone waiting to get the check in a restaurant with service issues.

The prosecutor was pleased to be frustrated. A garrulous penitent is useless in a trial situation.

The legal process known as "discovery" entitled the defense to see Byrdie's previous criminal record, copies of his statements to the police, and the physical evidence.

Since there was no criminal record and no statement, there wasn't much to discover. His lawyer looked at the damp, dirty blotter paper (the actual LSD had washed away in the rain), the friendly note from "Thetan Hegemon," the cryptic postcard, and Karen's lost coin purse containing twenty-one cents. De jure, that was all Byrdie's attorney could uncover about the prosecution's case.

De facto, the pretrial hearings were exclusive affairs, conducted over afternoon cocktails at the country club. As an experienced criminal defense attorney with a high caseload, Byrdie's lawyer led with a motion to dismiss. "I don't have time for a trial, but I can't negotiate with a mandatory minimum sentence," he said.

"Well, I can't dismiss out of hand," the judge replied. "It's bad enough that I'm trying it. Calling it off would be blatant nepotism. The press would have my ass in a sling."

"I don't want to go to trial. It's too big a risk."

"But you said it yourself. I got zero latitude."

"A year and a day suspended and he retains his civil rights?"

"Who are you working for, anyway?" the judge asked. "Do I have to explain myself?"

"You see a chance?"

"Look. You're forgetting that a different boy confessed. Now, you can't talk about that in court, but you and me know it. And on the other side, what's the prosecution got? Some pieces of paper and a little high yellow girl. That's what indicted Byrdie. How hard would it be to stop her from testifying? And if she does get on the stand, who's saying she didn't steal that LSD from the other boy, or sleep with him for it? Go to trial! Ask her about it. There won't be a trial to speak of, not one worthy of mention."

"To me, that sounds too much like a sensational case all over the papers."

"So I'll put a gag order on it. I'll venue this in a little courtroom with, I don't know, maybe six spots for the public? We'll get a few friends in there early on, and there won't be room for any gentlemen of the press. The only question mark is can we trust Lee and Trip to get up that early in the morning." He drained his third martini.

Soon after that, the prosecutor called a press conference to present the results of the Thetan House sting to the waiting world.

He worked hard to prepare his talk. It was a tour de force of dialectics in which hundreds of task force members contributed details to a picture that assembled itself in his mind alone, so that all the credit was his. The villain: R. Byrd Fleming, wealthy degenerate. The prosecutor knew Byrdie didn't have money. Byrdie *was* money. He was "old money," and the prosecutor was the kind of suburbanite whose wife blows his salary hunting a quarter horse sidesaddle in a blue veil and chirps (Lee's term for a fake riding habit, chaps plus skirt—he was not a famous poet for nothing!). Byrdie was money incarnate, and the prosecutor looked up to him as slightly glamorous and decadent in spite of himself. That's what he thought the First Families of Virginia were: aristocrats. Not a passel of redneck landlords who think their serfs have cooties. He expected the reporters covering the case to feel as he did, since at that time it was still mostly rich people who owned newspapers.

But the press conference was canceled at the last minute. The gag order came through, and he had to stand up in front of the reporters and say the case had been affected by unanticipated developments. He looked helpless and unhappy and refused further comment.

During the winter, Karen saw Byrdie a couple of times on campus. She glanced at him and thought, Asshole! It made her feel brave.

Byrdie saw Karen only once. She was kicking a vending machine that refused to turn loose the bottommost soda she'd just paid for. He thought, I should go give her thirty-five cents now. Then he thought, No contact with the witness. Could be construed as pressuring. Plenty of time for that later.

Byrdie saw Temple several times—Temple was always conspicuous—and thought, When this all blows over, I will try to get that jacket back.

Temple saw Karen every day and Byrdie not at all. He had other worries. While pretending to study in the library, he had struck up an acquaintanceship with a zaftig junior girl who clearly thought he was very sweet. She was majoring in international relations and learning Chinese, a language she claimed had no verb tenses. She seemed sincerely perturbed that he would waste his time on Russian. "Russia is doomed to irrelevance. The Soviet Union is breaking up. God, Temple, why are you doing this to yourself?" He went to see his adviser and came back unhappy. Jefferson scholars were not supposed to struggle this way. Indecision, okay, but existential crises? Where was the accomplished kid they'd recruited? Did he need a semester off?

Karen remarked that he had started learning Russian because of a girl, and now he wanted to switch to Chinese because of a girl. "You're like in Plato's symposium," she said. "You fall in love with any fat, ugly person who knows more than you do."

"Plato was justifying pederasty," Temple said. "You should read Xenophon's symposium. That'll open your eyes."

"Give me a break, Mister Know-It-All," Karen said.

"I'm the opposite of Plato," Temple insisted. "If Plato was right, I'd be craving sex with my Russian professor. Maybe it's not the worst idea. I need an A."

Karen lay back on the bed, wriggling and caressing her body, and moaned, "Comrade Moody, *nyet! Nyet! Pravda!* Take A! I must give you A!"

He lay down on top of her. "My blond feeble goosefat whore," he sighed.

"Don't you James Joyce me!" she said. But it was too late.

The trial was set to start on the eighth of March. The weather was pretty and sunny, with soft carpets of crocus blooming everywhere.

Jury selection was brisk and efficient. Finding jurors sympathetic to handsome white students is not rocket science. Almost no one but middle-class retirees came to jury duty anyway. The defense felt safe on that score.

For the CA it was six of one, half a dozen of the other. White jurors might favor Byrdie, but they were also more likely to disapprove of drugs. His case hinged on how Karen presented herself. The jurors would regard drug use by an upper-class boy as sowing wild oats. Seeing that the wild oats had been sown on a black girl who looked white and too young would shake their faith in Byrdie's probity. He felt they would believe Karen's testimony no matter what. All the physical evidence was on her side: the notes, the drugs. So the more pathetic she came across, the better for the prosecution. Her unfitness would rub off on Byrdie. The jurors would send him to jail to teach him to pick on someone his own size.

The defense was pursuing the same strategy, while expecting a different outcome. If Karen was not credible, the prosecution had no case. So the strategy of the defense team, including the judge, was to make her nervous.

The venue was a tiny courtroom where the judge and jury took up nearly half the space. It was usually used for things like traffic infractions and divorce decrees. It was not the judge's usual circuit court, but he had insisted on a small room to reduce threats to security. The courthouse had no guards at the outside doors. Reporters and hostile frat boys were wandering around at random. Byrdie's brothers were out in force to support him, and other frats had joined the cause in solidarity. Hip flasks were making the rounds. The bailiff told Karen gently that the judge would rather violate protocol than have her get "lynched," so he brought her in after the courtroom filled and sat her down by the door. She hunched there looking miserable.

Opposite the judge sat the lawyers, the court reporter, Byrdie, Lee, Trip, a few of Byrdie's frat brothers to pack the house, the bailiff, and Karen. The room was wider than it was deep. Everyone in it was wearing a suit, except Karen in a gray rayon dress with a white lace collar. It was brand new and too large. It made her look like a thirteen-year-old Mennonite.

Outside in the hallway, the press, fraternity brothers, and assorted curious spectators were lurking with Meg, Dee, and Temple, who had arrived much too late to get inside.

"Why's the docket say *Virginia v. Fleming?*" Meg asked.

"I guess the frat boy's last name is Fleming," Temple said.

"Tell me what he looks like," she said, rather unsteadily.

"Like imagine Paul Newman in a Cheech and Chong movie. He's almost as tall as I am"—a fact Temple could readily verify, since he was wearing Byrdie's clothes. Meg pulled her watch cap low over her brow. Raising her sunglasses, she stepped up to the double doors and applied her eye to the very narrow gap between them. She could see the back of Karen's head. She maneuvered and contorted until a security guard asked her to step back. She felt a little ill. But she couldn't run away from Karen. She clutched Temple's sleeve.

Inside, the frat brothers glared at Karen evilly. Mike whispered "Bitch."

Irritated by the noise, Lee turned to get a look at the star witness. And that was that. He stood up and said, "Your Honor, I request a recess."

The judge said, "Mr. Fleming, let me remind you that you can fake being an attorney in a letter to the IRS, but here in a court of law you need to have passed the bar. So sit down, before I cite you in contempt."

Lee sat down and whispered urgently, "Byrdie."

Byrdie leaned toward him, and Lee pulled out his wallet. Hidden deep inside it under the tattered business cards of plumbers through the ages was a family portrait snapshot from 1975. He pointed at the little girl.

"Holy shit," Byrdie said. He stood up and said, "Your Honor, we have a holy shit situation."

"Sit down! You're on trial!"

Byrdie sat down. The formalities began. The charges were read. They were very serious. Byrdie didn't seem to be listening. He swayed and seemed on the verge of leaping up, like he was having an out-of-body experience and fixing to levitate.

Lee sat next to him, looking at the picture, still as a statue. And then, because the room was so small he could almost reach out and touch her anyway, he turned around and handed it to Karen.

Karen looked at it for a second, drew it close to her face, and said "Oh." She let it fall to her lap and her mouth remained a little round O. She pressed her hands against her cheeks. Then she turned around and yelled "Mom!"

The CA paused in his opening statement and the door to the hallway began to rattle.

"This is a little much," the judge said. "Don't make me use my gavel."

Karen leaped to her feet and grabbed the door handle. She was about to run out, but the bailiff held both her arms.

"Don't you restrain her," Byrdie's lawyer said. "She's not on trial here." The bailiff let her go and she opened the door.

"She's my witness!" the CA said. The bailiff grabbed her arm and shoved the door shut.

"Miss Brown, please, could you tell us what you want?" the judge asked.

Karen was blotchy, with tears on the tip of her nose. She pointed at Lee and screamed "Mom!"

"Is Mom here?" Byrdie said excitedly, leaning toward her.

"Are you feeling ill, Miss Brown?" the judge asked.

"I need to leave, right now!" Karen said.

The door rattled.

"You need your mother to come in here?"

A flash of intellection hit Karen. She realized that whatever was going on, it might be the sort of thing policemen and courthouses only complicate. She said, "No, thanks."

At this point Meg had done the math. *Virginia v. Fleming*, her self-sufficient child screaming for her. She slipped away from the door and down the hall. She needed time to think.

"Have her mother come in," the judge said. The door opened and Dee squeezed into the room. The bailiff struggled to force the door shut behind her. "You're her mother?" he asked.

"I'm her aunt," Dee said. "It's hot in here! Karen, baby, you all right?"

"I'm just fine," Karen said, sitting down. "Come sit with me." She patted her own chair.

"If I could have a minute alone with you," Lee said to the judge, "that would be really helpful."

"That would be entirely out of order," the judge said, glancing at the CA.

"Then fuck it. This girl is my daughter and I've been looking for her for thirteen years. Her mother ran off with her, and there's a warrant for her arrest, and she's out there in your hallway."

The judge was silent, then said, "How do you know that's your daughter? She was six."

"She was three. But, Mickey, sweetheart, you know that's your mom in the picture."

Karen nodded and cried.

Byrdie stepped over the back of his chair and squeezed in between her and Dee, which was not easy. He hugged her and patted her head. Karen looked up at him, sobbing, and Byrdie began to cry tears of joy. Lee wept silently. Trip's eyes were moist. The jury was rapt. They had expected nothing like this.

Even the judge was moved and said, "Well, is this any way to reunite a family?" He shooed the jurors toward their door and glared at the frat boys and the prosecution. "Can we get these people some privacy?"

"Hey," Byrdie called out, looking up. "Before we get rid of them, can we go back to my trial for a second? Because now I know why I carried her all the way to Dabney and left her that note. I didn't even go through her pockets! If I had, I would have found the drugs that dweeb put in there and none of this would have happened!" He paused to digest his own statement, forced to admit its incompatibility with the Fifth Amendment of the US Constitution. "So now I'm glad—so glad—" Byrdie was succumbing to the sentimentality that permeated the room like a fog. "You know, I didn't tell you guys, but I saved her from being, you know …" He looked at his frat brothers meaningfully. "I can prove it. I still have her T-shirt where you dickwads wrote 'Sex Receptacle.' "

He didn't mention the swastika, not thinking it germane to the case, or that the T-shirt fit him, being an old undershirt of Temple's, and that he'd worn it several times since to masturbate.

Through her tears, Karen said to Lee, "Could you please forgive my mom? If you don't, she'll run away to Chihuahua."

He said, "I hereby drop the charges."

Karen punched Dee's arm and said, "Go make Temple catch Mom before she gets in the car!"

Dee tried to do as Karen suggested, but when the bailiff cracked the door, the population of the hallway surged in, with Temple in the lead. He saw Karen cuddling with the Thetan hegemon, and Lee and Trip hovering over them. He pulled his mother out into the hallway to hear what he felt must be an interesting explanation.

Trip was pointing out that abducting Karen had been a crime, the kind where the state presses charges, so it wouldn't be much help for Lee to lose interest, unless he was planning to bring back Old Testament law.

"Sober up," Lee said, addressing himself to the judge. "*L'état, c'est nous.*"

"Ahem," the judge said. The jurors hadn't budged. "That's it, we're calling it a day. Case dismissed. Trip, Lee, Byrdie, Miss Fleming, I'll see you in my chambers. Leave those things you call attorneys here to talk to the press."

Temple was a lot faster on his feet than Meg. He caught up to her next to the Dumpster behind a drugstore, not far away, counting her money. "Lee Fleming's not mad," he insisted. "He was really happy to see Karen, once he got over the shock. Come on back with us! We'll all go out to dinner!"

"My kids are grown up," she said, staring at the money in her hand. "I'm free. I can start over. I can get on the next bus to New York."

It wasn't even self-pity. It was blank denial via panic. Meg looked back at her own life and thought, Did any of that have anything to do with me? She felt strongly that her life had begun the day she met Luke. Luke didn't know she had a son. Meg didn't want to disappoint Luke by opening this particular can of worms. She really was a very romantic person.

"No, you're not. Come on, this is great! The Thetan hegemon is your son! I knew that guy was all right. My trouble times are done. I'm going to marry the King of Elfland's daughter!" He sang several lines of "God Has Smiled on Me" and did a little heel-and-toe dance.

At that, Meg's heart softened slightly. She asked, laughing, whether Karen was aware of his plans.

"I don't know, something about that name 'Fleming' has a certain 'ring' to it. Get it?"

"You're counting chickens big time," Meg said. "You know she's only sixteen. You think I would let her get engaged to a bratty kid who puns?"

"She's crazy about me."

"Everybody's crazy about you. I'm crazy about you! Half the time Karen makes me feel like I'm raising an iguana. She looks at me all walleyed and I have no earthly idea what's going through her head. None. *You* make me feel like a mom, because you're transparent and you have *no* common sense. You seriously believe when she figures out she's rich, her first step is going to be to marry *you*?

And what makes you think it's so smart, marrying a kissing cousin of Harry Byrd? They call it a white machine, but it's people! Individuals. My family, her family, all the other charming people who if they had their way, you'd be picking cotton. That's who we are. There are nicer people you could get involved with, trust me!"

"Well, I love Karen very much."

"I know it. There's never a reason to take a word you say on faith, because you couldn't tell a lie to save your life."

"Also, she loves me," Temple said.

"Maybe so. I don't know what goes through her pea brain. Except that right now she's figuring out I screwed her to the wall, and she's wanting to trust Lee Fleming. And now you think I should trust him, too! But I'm not going back there. You don't know him. He's about five hundred times smarter than you are. He can dominate people and make them do things they never thought they would do."

"But he can't fuck with you now, because Karen would never speak to him again."

"You wish. My problem is whether anybody will ever speak to *me* again."

"Are you kidding? You're Mom. And you should have seen his face when he looked at her. It was love." Temple lowered his voice like a soul crooner on the word "love." "Not I—love—you love. This was unconditional love, Christian agape, like his top priority in life is how he can fatten her up. If we don't hurry up, he's going to buy her a pony." Almost whispering, he added in an undertone, "I am rushing so hard on pure euphoria, it makes me frightened."

He leaned down and Meg stood on tiptoe so they could hug. A deep male voice boomed through the alley. "Get your hands off her, boy!"

Temple raised his arms and stepped away from Meg. It was a uniformed cop, sidling down the alley with his hand on his revolver. "Ma'am, are you all right?" he called out.

"I'm fine," Meg said, stepping between Temple and the cop. "We're friends."

"We had a report you were under pursuit," the cop explained.

"We were having a footrace," Meg said. "I won, and now he has to buy me lunch. But thank you for your concern."

"Why don't you take two steps toward me and turn out your pockets?" the cop suggested to Temple. He obeyed, starting with his jacket. A battered paperback of *The Confessions of St. Augustine* flopped to the asphalt, and a prerecorded Herbie Hancock cassette landed next to it with a sharp click. "Open it," the cop said, pushing the cassette case into a puddle with a leather-clad steel toe.

Temple crouched to retrieve the cassette from under the policeman's boot. "Oh, no! The tape's all wet!" he said, shaking it. "My sister is going to kill me!"

Out on the sidewalk, a pedestrian paused to watch. Suddenly bored and somehow also disappointed, even disgusted, the cop wished Meg a nice day and returned to the street.

Temple stood poised in front of the Dumpster, mourning the ruined cassette and weighing whether to put the damp, dirty book back in his jacket pocket or in the trash. "I've read it an awful lot. I could leave it for someone else," he concluded, propping it against the wall.

"I'm going to walk you back to the courthouse now," Meg said.

Eleven

Meg and Temple arrived at the judge's office. Karen was clinging to Dee, and Byrdie and Lee were gone, to Meg's profound relief. But they had left a forwarding address. Trip handed Meg a note torn from Lee's black book—an invitation to dinner at a restaurant. She stared at it in silence.

Karen took the note and folded it and said they would be there.

It was hard work dissuading Temple from coming along uninvited, but Dee finally extricated him and drove him home. She felt Meg and Karen needed time to talk. Which was true, though they spent most of the afternoon playing pool in Karen's dorm. At suppertime they were late.

The restaurant was hidden down a back alley, up a narrow staircase, with nothing to mark its presence but an old Pepsi sign. Inside, the high-ceilinged loft space was painted white, there were huge crimson roses in white vases, and the prix fixe was a hundred bucks. Lee and

Byrdie were waiting in a private back room with oyster shooters and two bottles of champagne on ice. The atmosphere conveyed was that of a 1960s-themed surprise party.

When Meg was led into their presence and made to sit down, everyone could sense the hurt. Lee felt more hurt than he expected—he was used to feeling angry—and Meg felt so guilty she could have gutted herself with a teaspoon. "I'm so sorry," she said to Byrdie over and over as Lee opened the champagne.

"It's okay," Byrdie said. "You did the best you could. I just wish you would have written to me, or called me or something."

Meg writhed and covered her face.

"Why are you picking on Mom?" Karen finally asked Byrdie. "We should be celebrating! I feel so happy and lucky. I always had the best mom and the best boyfriend in the whole world, and now I have the best brother and the best father, and maybe even the best grandparents!"

"You were a baby the last time we saw you," Lee said. "Don't be one now."

"Whoa," Karen said.

"When you're older, you'll see there's more to life than the future," he added. "Byrdie has pent-up negative emotions. If he can't let them out, they'll spoil his dinner. Drink up your champagne and let us talk."

"What about my pent-up joy and happiness?" Karen protested. "I mean it! You could all just be happy for me. If everybody would stop blaming each other and just think about me for a second, we'd all be fine!"

Lee laughed. "Sorry," he said. "You're just like a woman. It's something your mother never mastered."

"It's not fair! I'm the one who got the biggest shock today. Everybody here knew what was going on but me."

"Knowing just made it worse," Byrdie said. At that Meg exploded in helpless sobbing.

"Stop torturing us!" Karen said. "You think it was any fun? You think she wanted to go on the lam? We didn't even have heat or running water! We had possums coming in the house!" She looked at Lee accusingly, and her eyes narrowed to a squint.

"And whose fault was that," he said. "Possums in the house."

"Is this what family dinners are like?" Karen wailed to no one in particular.

"You're asking me?" Byrdie said. "How am I supposed to know?"

"It's awful! It's perverted! Mom, help me!" she begged, but Meg was too busy crying. When she touched her mother's arm, Meg pushed her away, covering her face.

Karen eyed the door, longing to escape. She wanted Temple. But she also wanted the truth, not in manageable portions but now, and not as information but as experience. The situation was unbearably formal and tense and she was alone, but the formality and the tension, and even her being alone: They all might be integral parts of the truth. There was no way to find out but pay attention and wait. She let Lee refill her glass.

He leaned back, folding his arms, and said, "Now listen, Peg, it's true that most of the time I was ready to shoot you on sight. I wanted Mireille back more than anything in the world. Mickey, darling. I love you. I wanted you back so bad. I paid every spare dime I had to private eyes to look for you. They told me you were *dead*. Because it never crossed anybody's mind that your mother would be so fucking afraid of me she'd go underground, refuse to cross state lines, live under an assumed name in a shack, never go to college or get a job, and let you turn into this undereducated, underfed—you know what I mean—physical and intellectual pygmy. Like I was the Manson family!"

Karen stared. She had never imagined a father like this. A large, strong creature with an emotional hold over them all and no gears except overdrive. It went way beyond Anne Sexton, deep into Sylvia Plath territory. Yet her mother's alliance with this animal had been long and voluntary. She looked at Meg.

"You did say you'd have me committed," Meg said, straightening up in her seat. "And you're still an asshole."

"She killed my car," Lee explained to his children.

"I remember," Byrdie said. "She drove it right into the lake. And then she stole her own car, and we got to borrow Grandma's Lincoln."

"But why on earth are you still in Virginia?" Lee asked. "You could have gone to the Frankfurt School of dramatic arts, like you were always saying."

"The swamp fox," Meg sniffled. "There's no better place to go to ground than in a swamp. It was a foxhunting thing, in your honor."

"It's a Revolutionary War thing."

"In New York I couldn't have thrown a rock without hitting some friend of yours. You would have found me in three days." Meg hung her head, thinking it might have been proper to commit her after all. What had been crazier—marrying Lee, or leaving him? "I don't remember why I did any of it," she added. "But I must have been very unhappy."

"Well, you did marry a founding member of NAMBLA," Byrdie said.

"I beg to differ!" Lee said.

"Who seduces baby dykes for kicks," Meg added.

Lee's protests were drowned out by Karen's sudden squealing. "Get out of here! You're gay?" She threw herself on her mother and hugged her with vehemence. "Poor Mom! That explains so much! It explains everything!"

"Don't feel sorry for me." Meg laughed, sitting up straight and patting Karen's hair. "It's not a sickness."

"Nor does it explain a goddamn thing," Lee remarked.

Meg glared at him. "So I've wasted half my life," she told her daughter. "So what? I still have you, and my son back. I even have a way hap girlfriend. Before, I went around feeling angry, like I was the victim. Now I feel ecstatic, but so guilty I could kill myself." She wiped her eyes and grinned, and Byrdie shook his head.

"Girlfriend? Where'd you meet her?" Karen asked eagerly.

"At the bait shop. I'll introduce you. She's spending next semester in Hampton on sabbatical, and then I'll probably move with her to New York."

"Dykes, always with the moving van," Lee remarked.

"Dad, you are such a *fucking* bitch," Byrdie said.

"Are you really a pederast?" Karen asked.

"I don't go out loaded for bear. Your mother is a case in point. I'd say there's a difference between her and pederasty."

"Well, that's something," Karen said.

Meg tried her champagne and said, "Aw, shit. I forgot about this stuff."

To everyone's surprise, Karen stood up at her place at the table. "So I'm just wondering," she said. "Is anybody here truly unhappy?"

"What are you doing?" Lee said.

"I mean, this isn't easy, but none of us is sad to be here. Right?"

"Sorry to disappoint you, but me," Byrdie said, raising his hand. "I think I have whiplash of the brain. I want to spend the next month in Florida playing golf with Grandpa and pretend I never saw you. But first I want to talk to you and Mom for a week without Dad around."

"There's no rush," Meg said to Lee. "We can hang out with Byrdie first, and then you can get to know Karen."

Karen said, "See, Mr. Fleming and Mom? Everything's going to be fine."

"Why are you trying to be cool with them?" Byrdie asked Karen. "They're both insane."

"It's because I raised my insight to a higher power."

Lee said to Meg in a low voice, "Where'd she get that? You want to come out as an alcoholic while you're at it?"

Meg turned to Karen and said, "Higher power does sound awful twelve-step."

"I mean the Sheltering Sky. It's something Temple told me about. He's my boyfriend."

"It's a novel by Paul Bowles," Lee said.

"Really? He told me it's that when life gets too hard, you can go up to the next level."

"Like Pac-Man," Byrdie said.

"No, Pac-Man is the exact opposite. In Pac-Man the higher levels are harder, so it's like the Peter Principle in college, where if you pass a course they make you take a harder course until you flunk out. In the Sheltering Sky you go up to where things are easier. Temple says"—her voice, now grave but filled with faith and conviction, rang clearly through the room in a way that betrayed her exposure to dissenting rural churches—"that in the ancient world they believed the earth is a turtle resting on an elephant on another elephant, and then it's elephants all the way down. So if you don't understand things, it means you didn't dig deep enough. That's how science works. But society is a legal system. It goes in the other direction. If you don't like what you're getting, you appeal to a higher power. And the higher you go, the better off you are, like Thurgood Marshall. So that's why I believe in my heart that it's right that we're back together, even if on the level of grunginess it's a tale of sound and fury told by an idiot. When Mom said she was gay, and Dad said he married her because he got her mixed up with boys, and everybody's white, that was *way* too complex. And there it is! You take it to the next phase."

There was an awkward silence during which everyone drank, as though Karen had proposed a toast. "Your Temple is clearly an autodidact, but he's not stupid," Lee said at last.

"He's a genius," Meg said. "Within five minutes of finding out she's your daughter, he asked me for her hand in marriage."

At this announcement, Karen turned to Meg, squirming in such an ultra-excited and happy way that even Byrdie began to laugh. "Don't laugh at me!" she cried.

"I have to admit, you know each other pretty well," Meg said. "But you're way too young, Karen. Did you know you're sixteen? Your birth certificate is a fake."

"I'm sixteen and I'm at UVA? I am *so cool!*"

"The age of consent is seventeen," Lee said. "Temple could go to jail."

"On paper I'm eighteen, and you won't rat me out."

"Far be it from me. Pederasts in glass houses. But I will prevent you from marrying Temple until he's had at least four years of school. That theory of his sounds to me like Kafka in a blender with Hegel and Manichaeism." A waiter entered the room as Byrdie began to giggle. "Appetizers, thank God." Lee sighed. "You all are really going to like this quail."

*

Later, when Karen went to the bathroom, Byrdie remarked, "You're scoping out Temple already, you sick fuck."

Lee replied blandly, "Mireille thinks she's fated to marry Temple, because otherwise she's going to have a hard time explaining to herself the advantages of growing up in a housing project."

"I know exactly what you mean," Meg said to Lee. "Going up a level resolves the cognitive dissonance. But if you say it to her, I literally *will* kill you."

"And I'll hold him down while you do it," Byrdie said. "Temple is the one constant in her life." His parents gazed at him in surprise as he pressed on. "Letting her think she has no father! Not knowing when she was born, or where she's from, or even her name, thinking history starts and ends with Temple! Look at how you dress her! What is that thing, a nun's habit from the dump? She calls herself his shadow!"

"That was something his mother said," Meg said. "We thought it was funny because he's, you know, dark."

"You're her mom and you make racist jokes about her?"

"I said it was his own mother! She's black!"

"How does that make it not racist?"

Meg gulped and looked around for help.

Lee came to her aid by saying gallantly, "You just reminded me of a terrific racist joke. So Jean-Paul Sartre decides to tour the back roads of the South, and he runs out of gas at the bottom of a long hill. He takes the gas can out of the trunk and starts walking up the hill. He can see there's a black guy at the pumps, so he yells, 'Y'all got any gas?' and the black guy yells, 'Yeah!' So Sartre keeps walking and he gets up to the top and he says, 'I'll take three gallons, please.' And the black guy says, 'Sorry, man, can't sell you no gas today. *Huis clos.*'"

Byrdie wailed, "Mom! Why are you laughing?"

"Because I haven't heard that joke in a long time."

"You should relax, Bird Dog," Lee said. "You're just jealous of Temple because he got to be big brother and you didn't."

"That's it," Byrdie said. He picked up his napkin off his lap and dropped it on his plate. "I hate the both of you. I'm out of here."

"Don't go. Karen will be back in a second," Meg said.

"Mom, I'm glad you weren't around when I was growing up. I just wish Dad hadn't been there either."

When Karen returned, Meg was dissolved in tears with her head thrown back, and Lee was finishing Byrdie's entrée.

"What's wrong, Mom?"

"I'm a horrible person. I stole you away from a happy life."

"Am I missing something? I thought Dad threatened to have you committed, so that if you stayed, we would have both grown up without you."

Meg wiped her nose and sat up. "Good point!" she said.

"Did Byrdie leave? Why is Mr. Fleming eating his food?"

Lee said, "He got upset. He'll be back. He's very emotional."

"I like him a lot," Karen said.

"So do I," Lee said. "He's feeling bad because he chose to grow up with me. He's thinking what his life could have been like if he'd gone with his mother."

Lee expected to be called a bitch as usual. But Karen proclaimed resolutely, "It wouldn't have made any difference. Everything that happens is predetermined. We just don't know how until afterward."

"What, you don't think he had a choice?"

"He was nine years old. You and Mom had a shotgun wedding. How was any of you going to make a choice? It's silly to think you have choices. That's what we learned in philosophy class. It's very liberating."

Byrdie came back after half an hour, never having gotten farther than the bar. He had drunk two cups of coffee and calmed down a lot. "You ready to grant a general amnesty?" Lee asked him. "Mireille has us convinced we need not postpone joy."

"You and Mom need to cop a plea," he said.

"Guilty as charged!" Meg said. "I should have written to you."

"That's a start," Byrdie said.

"I should not have terrified her into going underground," Lee said.

"I should have told Karen the truth and let her make her own decision."

"I should have been faithful to your mother, not that I had any choice in the matter."

Karen and Byrdie cast bewildered looks on Lee, and Byrdie said, "What's that got to do with anything?"

"It's true! I screwed around on her because I couldn't help myself. The first time, it was with a girl she was in love with. I can't believe I was such a crumb."

"You're hardly displaying remorse," Meg observed. "You're trying to distract them and show off. What about the time you broke all my portraits of you and your pinhead friends?"

"I should have filed for divorce and paid you to stay far, far away," Lee said. "You would have done it, too."

"You don't make that kind of money," Meg said.

Byrdie said, "You know, on second thought, forget the plea bargain. Go back to pretending you're innocent until proven guilty. I like you better that way."

"But to find out what happened, we need a guilty plea under conditions of amnesty," Karen said. "And then tabula rasa!"

"That's only if you want to love me," Meg pointed out. "Love's optional. I wrote my parents off a long time ago. I know next to nothing about them, and I could care less. I don't deserve any better."

"But I want to love you," Karen said. "You're weirdly fascinating, plus you're my mom."

"If you think she's weirdly fascinating, wait till you get to know Dad," Byrdie said.

"They're ganging up on us," Lee said. "Time for another distraction." He rang for the wine steward.

"Here's the deal," Karen said. "We forgive you if you promise to tell us the truth, the whole truth, and nothing but the truth. Okay, Byrdie?"

"I don't think Dad ever lied to me once," Byrdie objected. "He never cared enough about how I feel to lie."

"We could make him promise to be nice from now on," Karen ventured.

"I'm in," Lee said. "Love means never having to say you're sorry."

"I would take that deal," Meg said.

"And what do we get?" Byrdie pleaded. "Nothing?"

"Parents!" Karen said.

It was weeks before Byrdie would let his guard down with Meg. But they were reconciled only a short time after he first glimpsed the beautiful squirrel sanctuary.

His hosts were aware that he had invoked his right to remain silent and refused a plea bargain. This raised him numerous notches in their estimation above a certain immature and dangerous little sister. After all the others went to bed, Flea took Byrdie under her wing. She read his palm and told his fortune with playing cards. She led him through meadows and down to the dock. She started the boat and steered it quietly toward the center of the water where the shadows were palest. She bade him take the wheel and do full-throttle doughnuts. The stars whirled above his head and the lights of the inlet twinkled red and green. He bounced over his own wake until the cabin swayed and shuddered like the howdah on an inebriated elephant. Flea stood straight as a reed in the light of the Milky Way, hair blowing across her face, watching him. Suddenly she reached down to cut the engine. In the noise of water lapping against the agitated hull she whispered, "Save me, please, Byrdie."

She was sweet and fragile, lithe and delicate, innocent and ignorant, with the face of an angel and primroses in her hair. In short, a person Byrdie had thought existed only in Grateful Dead lyrics and the photography of David Hamilton. Yet here she was, swaying atop her boyfriend's cabin cruiser, demanding sex as an urgent moral imperative.

Byrdie understood. He would drop-kick Lomax into the shitcan of history. Erase the memory of Lomax from her body. It would be ignoble to refuse a service so necessary and overdue.

When he hugged her his elbows met behind her rib cage. Her waist almost fit in his hands, if he squeezed. Her teeth, her ears, everything was perfect. Her hair was dense and liquid as a child's. Her long, tiered skirt was nearly as soft as her skin, and instead of a bra, she wore a slippery, patchouli-scented camisole. She was trembling with joy, crying on his shirt, mystified by his belt buckle. When he entered her, he noted that it was epoch-making. He had never been a matter of life or death before, or anybody's savior. He liked it.

He liked the motion of the creaking boat, like a house trailer standing in the living waters of the lagoon. It was loud with splashing creatures, nothing like a river, so unlike Stillwater Lake. The moon began its metallic rise above the ocean. Satellites chased each other across the sky, and something in the boat beeped because the depth was less than two fathoms. Flea lay exhausted on his cashmere coat, her soft body powdered with fluids drying in the breeze. In his mind he was on the edge of dark water, preparing to dive. She was the last of her kind, endangered, like the squirrels. Of course he would save her. He would fight to win her, and work to preserve her habitat.

When they brought the boat back in, Meg was waiting for them on the dock. "You kids were in trouble for a while there," she said. "He wanted to tie you to the boat and burn it. But we talked it out. He's cool now."

After that, no power on earth could have induced Byrdie to be on poor terms with Meg.

As for the rapprochement between Karen and Lee, it took several minutes. "I underestimated you," he said, as soon as they were alone together at a gay (the owner, not the patrons; it's important to realize that progress isn't when minorities come out of the closet—generally speaking, black people have been out of the closet since time immemorial—but when they can make money selling vital necessities, not cream soda and carrot cake) bakery on Cary Street in Richmond. Byrdie's sojourn with Meg, Luke, Lomax, et al. had gone on for nearly a month, but Lee was still wearing his bike shorts. Karen had invested in a nine-gore hip-hugger suede wrap miniskirt, red cable-knit sweater, khaki trench coat, orange tights, and saddle shoes. It was a thrift-shop look that combined punk, golf, and Antonioni in a way Lee could not help but admire. "Compared to you," he declared, "we all have frontal lobe damage. You're the one who noticed the ground rules had changed."

"Thanks!" Karen said.

"Yes, our brains are like Swiss cheese," he added, sort of undermining his compliment after the fact. "So what do you plan to do with your newfound freedom, besides follow Temple around?"

"Just be myself. I like having a new identity. It's like being in witness protection. I can drop everything and start a new life like Mom."

"Ooh, and what does Temple say to being dropped?"

"He doesn't care about my identity. He's been calling me Blondi, like Hitler's dog."

"You should make him stop that."

"No, it's just since this morning. I think it might be his art. Nicknames are a major art form in the black community. Mom's girlfriend is a scholar of black culture. She's been collecting them. It's so aggravating. Temple's meeting her halfway, and then some. He started calling Mom Hal, like the insane computer in *2001*."

Lee said, "Priceless. So back to my question. Is there anything else you might want or need, as part of your new life? I'm here to help!"

"I think a new life is plenty enough on its own. It's confusing but exciting. I mean, I'm glad I grew up black, because it's cooler, but it's white people who run the place, obviously."

"Not all white people."

"Well, *some* of them. Like Byrdie at his trial, telling the judge what to do. That was cool. I want to be white like that."

"So your goal in life is to be white? Isn't that a tad, uh, minimal?"

"What do I need a life goal for?"

"You refuse to be pinned down."

"What do you mean? With a pin like a bug, or somebody holding my arms?"

"You're your mother's child."

"Well, if you really want to know, I was thinking I could go to law school like Uncle Trip. I could help Byrdie. His housing projects are a really horrible idea, because what's cool is when poor people get to move into rich-people neighborhoods. The houses they build for poor people are not nice. Houses should be for rich people only, but shouldn't discriminate by income. Let people live in them even after they lose all their money."

Lee sighed. "Listen, kiddo. That's cute, and insightful, but there's something imperialist—something third world—something profoundly *Southern* and just *wrong* about the way you and your brother both approach thinking on this issue. Neither of you has ever seen money being invested, just harvested, and you think it grows in the ground. It's what the structuralists call a homology, like people believing in the trickle-down effect after they spend their lives waiting for their inheritance to trickle down. Byrdie's my son, I raised him, but more than that he's a child of his generation. And his generation can kiss my ass. Freelance city planner. My God. He's going to wake up fifty years old in a squat on Church Hill. And Temple is worse. Temple ought to be at West Point, learning discipline, with a job when he gets out and a place to stay. But no, it's got to be comp fucking lit. Those pretty-boy parasites are going to bankrupt both of us. I won't be around to see it, but I can see you already. Picking up the pieces, paying their bills. The levelheaded little woman, keeping things in line. Darling, take my advice and major in accounting. Get your CPA."

To this outburst, Karen replied evenly, "That's why I'm glad we might move to New York. Mom says the wife needs to keep control over the purse strings and be the chatelaine. In New York they have an aboveground economy, so I can practice. This cake is so great. Mmm. It's the first real buttercream I ever ate."

As he finished his Death by Chocolate, Lee pondered how he might steer the conversation around to a survivable second date. He wanted to get to know his daughter, he really did. Yet drawing her out was possibly not the most rewarding exercise, while doing the talking himself was evidently also a piss-poor idea.

Ever quick on his feet, he concocted a fallback strategy: See her in action, preferably doing something that would endear him to her if not vice versa. That is, get her to have fun at his expense while looking pretty and not getting sticky or irritable. She might not inspire his love, but he could command hers.

"Mireille," he began, "the truth is, when I said goals, I meant stuff you might need or want, like fall clothes for school. I'm well aware you're a teenage girl. I'm lucky you didn't ask for world peace and a cure for cancer." He paused, made a mental note that errant and rueful was not the aesthetic to go for, and continued. "You need a winter coat and some clothes that fit you a little better. How about a shopping trip to New York? You need everything, and I think it would be nice to go on a father-daughter excursion before school starts up again. You should let me spoil you a little. See the world. Your experience thus far has been rather circumscribed."

"A shopping trip?" Karen said.

"We can hit the highlights," Lee said. "Stay at the Plaza. Go to shows. Art museums. Get you a haircut. Eat some sushi."

"But I'm going to New York anyway," Karen said. "That's where Luke lives."

"If you don't want to go there, we can go anywhere. London, Paris, you name it. All you need is a passport. We could have lots of fun."

"Anywhere at all?"

"Anywhere."

She hesitated. "Anywhere?"

Lee rolled his eyes and said firmly, "Yes."

"Well, there is one place I always wanted to go."

"If it's Disney and Epcot, summer is out of the question."

"Dad. I can call you Dad, right?"

"Of course."

"Did you ever read *Kaputt*?"

Lee did not answer, so she went on. "It's my favorite book. It's a memoir of World War II by a guy named Curzio Malaparte. He starts out by visiting his friend Axel Munthe on the Isle of Capri, and he thinks his friend Axel is, like, *dumb*, for caring a lot about birds. But before that, he visits his other friend, King Bernadotte, whose hobby is embroidery." She pronounced the names "Mallaparty," "Monthy," and "Burnadotty," but Lee did not smile. "He's the king of Sweden, but what he does all day is embroider, like, napkins! And then Malaparte goes to the war. And he realizes that people really are exactly like birds. They're innocent bystanders only an asshole would kill"—here Karen developed fierce-looking tears in her eyes—"and embroidery is symbolic of the very best part about them. He goes all around the war, seeing beautiful people and animals suffer and die for no reason, but he never looks away. He writes it all down. And in the end he goes back to Capri to build himself this house …"

Her voice slowed as she saw his eyes, which had turned glassy, being squeezed shut. "Dad, why are you crying? Do you think he's a fascist? Temple says he's a fascist."

She lowered her eyes to her empty plate. She saw that to a sophisticate like Lee, reading Malaparte was equal in puerility to eating scabs, and that she would soon be in New York, acquiring modish things to make herself less of a rube.

Lee said, "Don't mind me. It's just my life flashing before my eyes. You were raised under a rock, yet your life's dream is to see the Villa Malaparte. And now I realize I must have passed something down to you in my semen after all. The divine spark. It's the first time in my life I ever felt like a man."

The hush in the room was punctuated by a creaking of chair legs as interested parties leaned closer. The hush deepened, and a quiet stillness fell. A girl begging for something to do with fascism, a man in spandex moved to tears by semen: Everyone present felt that something significant was happening. Awed silence is the universe's clutch. Which it now released, propelling Karen and Lee from lives of neutral idling into a world of irreversible events and irreplaceable objects. She had a parent. He had a child. A busybody approached their table and whispered, "Sir—"

As one, they rose and walked together out of the café to take possession of their new abode, the sky over Capri, which just then was glowing dark blue over Cary Street.

The press had wheedled the gist of the story out of various onlookers, so it wasn't long before Karen got a letter from The University saying her minority scholarship and financial aid package were in jeopardy.

"Quand même," she said, tucking it under a placemat. She and Temple were transferring together to NYU on the best scholarship of all: Daddy's Money. It turned out Lee's parents had not spent everything. There was still plenty left over, plus the land, and he had forgotten all about his one great-grandfather who was alive somewhere in a home. Until suddenly he wasn't. He left a huge estate in Albemarle County to so many people it had to be sold for cash. A great deal of trickling occurred. Lee could even get the Corps of Engineers to come in and stabilize the level of Stillwater Lake. He was landscaping the banks with poet habitat-clematis arbors, espaliered fruit. Slowly, the poets were coming back.

Conveniently, certain people who taught at CUNY owned a studio apartment in the Village and were planning to pool their money with Meg's to buy a loft in Chinatown. Karen and Temple didn't even have to apartment hunt.

Meg had confessed to all manner of wrongdoing. Luke's response had been to become sexually aroused and steer the conversation around to Meg's body, which she compared to a Stradivarius. Meg knew then that she was in the presence of something inconceivably precious: a woman literally crazy about her. She began to subscribe to Luke's belief that she had never made a mistake in her life. Luke was her destiny, and her life was the road leading to Luke.

Absolved of her guilt, she got up the courage to visit her parents. They were unchanged. She was floored. Here she was, a woman with grown children and a story to tell, and her mother was still putting peonies and irises in exactly the same places. Her hair had gone gray, but it was still in the same symmetrical little perm. Her dad had no new hobbies or opinions. Between them lay an unbridgeable emotional gulf. It had been there ever since the day she told them she would grow up to be a man. Her mother had stopped expecting any joy from her that day. Her father had never started. As far as she could tell, her role in their plan for producing descendants had been to bear Byrdie.

Karen was collateral damage. They refused to let her visit. They said they would see her if and when she left Temple, but not before. "That will put a crimp in Thanksgiving," Meg said. "You're alienating your only granddaughter, and I don't think your grandson really goes for this kind of thing either."

"You'll all face facts soon and come to your senses," her father said. "Until then, we can look after ourselves."

"We're retiring to Vermont," her mother added.

Meg drove out past the Browns' house, where she saw Leon out in the yard, trimming a hedge. Her borrowing of his dead daughter seemed to have caused no ill effects. A little son or grandson was helping him out by squashing a nest of gypsy moth caterpillars one by one with a brick-bat. A contented child.

That is not to say that Lee immediately kept his promise to be nice all the time. But his redeemer Karen disapproved of meanness, so he had to stop making fun of people, even sitting ducks like Temple and Meg, and then he got out of the habit. He had never meant to be cold. All his life he had been out of his depth. Sexual abuse, domestic violence, a transparently evil social order, poets, academia, etc., had taught him to respect people's boundaries. In a world where people have fixed limits, it's safest to be an arrogant bastard and push yourself and others to come out on top. But Karen was larger on the inside than on the outside. She had no boundaries. Anything might affect her. She was significant everywhere, like one of those atom bombs that fits in a suitcase. He began to speak and listen and care about the world, and it made him a different person.

He did not mention life goals again. Life has a goal, he noted, and harping on it is counterproductive.

Given Lee's love, Karen started paying somewhat less attention to Temple—which was not a bad thing! She was sixteen! Does a sixteen-year-old really need nonstop trysts with a wild-eyed fiancé? Wouldn't she be better off benefiting from the sophistication and knowledge of a supportive, attentive parent? What if it was your daughter, assuming you were that kind of parent?

Still, she insisted on living with Temple, explaining to Lee that with him around she could always be assured of finding leftover pizza in the refrigerator. She would never have to cook. Lee admitted it was a strong argument.